Other mysteries by Mignon G. Eberhart
available in Bison Books editions

The Mystery of Hunting's End

MIGNON G. EBERHART

INTRODUCTION TO THE BISON BOOKS EDITION BY

Jay Fultz

University of Nebraska Press
Lincoln and London

♾ The paper in this book meets the minimum requirements of American
National Standard for Information Sciences—Permanence of Paper for
Printed Library Materials, ANSI Z39.48-1984.

First Bison Books printing: 1998
Most recent printing indicated by the last digit below:
10   9   8   7   6   5   4   3   2   1

Library of Congress Cataloging-in-Publication Data
Eberhart, Mignon Good, 1899–
The mystery of Hunting's End / Mignon G. Eberhart; introduction to the
Bison Books edition by Jay Fultz.
p.   cm.
ISBN 0-8032-6737-1 (pbk.: alk. paper)
I. Title.
PS3509.B453M97   1998
813'.52—dc21
98-9956   CIP

Reprinted from the original 1930 edition by Doubleday, Doran & Co.,
Inc.

FOR LOU
WHO KNOWS ABOUT
THE PAPER DOLLS

INTRODUCTION

Jay Fultz

Mignon G. Eberhart was always horrified by the thought of murder occurring anywhere near her. She never visited morgues or crime scenes and never rode in police cars down mean streets. Repelled by newspaper accounts of actual murder, she refused to make fiction of them, not wishing to exploit the tragedies of real people. So, who knows from what dark crannies of her disciplined mind issued the mystery novels that have attracted readers for almost seventy years. They all carry the Eberhart signature: an atmosphere of all-encompassing dread, a polished style that barely puts the lid on the underlying barbarism of some social sophisticates.

In 1930 Eberhart was already mastering the most artificial of genres, the whodunit that satisfied the reader's need to participate imaginatively in dark doings while expecting a safe outcome, with guilt pinpointed and order brought out of disorder. That year she published her third detective novel, *The Mystery of Hunting's End*. Though a construct of literary convention, it comes closer to home than anything else she wrote. The setting is clearly the Sand Hills of her native Nebraska. As a bride she lived in the town of Valentine, surrounded by those rounded barren hills reminiscent of beehives or primitive outdoor ovens. That's where she finished *The Mystery of Hunting's End*, before going off to more cosmopolitan places that would provide book settings more exotic than, but never so strange as, the Nebraska Sand Hills.

Born 1899 in Lincoln, a long-winded crow's flight from Valentine, Mignon was the daughter of William and Margaret Good, an enterprising iceman and a genteel homemaker. Her sister Lou, to whom this novel is dedicated, used to dress paper dolls while Mignon made up stories about them. The creative Mignon had an ordinary upbringing insulated from the kind of violence she would write about later. She attended Nebraska Wesleyan University and in 1923 married Alanson Eberhart, an engineering graduate of the University of Nebraska. While he built bridges and dams, she waited in various remote places, finally turning to writing to save her sanity. Before long, the Eberharts settled in Valentine, where he engineered for the state highway department and she worked at the kitchen table to produce *The Patient in Room 18* in 1929 and *While the Patient Slept* the following year.

Those first two mysteries introduced Nurse Sarah Keate. Tart-tongued, gimlet-eyed, proud-nosed, and crowned with abundant red hair, Sarah was immediately popular with the reading public. She reappears in *The Mystery of Hunting's End*, on special assignment to care for a social dragoness who devours everything in sight. Almost to the detriment of duty, Sarah snoops around and reports her findings to a dashing young detective named Lance O'Leary, who is present at Hunting's End in the guise of a guest. They make an unlikely team, with amused respect on his side and fond-auntish forbearance on hers. Nurse Sarah Keate would figure in several more mysteries, but Eberhart was about to dump her for younger heroines who could become romantically (and dangerously) involved with handsome men of ugly character. Sarah would have seen right through them: handsome is as handsome does, she always said.

Mignon Eberhart would build her reputation on mysteries compounded equally of romance and suspense—on titles like *The White Cockatoo, Fair Warning, The Chiffon Scarf, Speak No Evil, Escape the Night, Wings of Fear, House of Storm, The Crimson Paw*. But the Nurse Keate books first made her a name, and they owe as much to the classical detective story as to romance. *The Mystery of Hunting's End* plays out in a miniature closed universe, an isolated hunting lodge from which invited guests cannot escape because of a great snowstorm. The weather abets the trap set by the hostess, who wants to know which one of them murdered her father in the same lodge five years earlier. The controlled and limited arena serves to highlight the presence of every colorful character. Everyone is under a microscope, so to speak, and things as they normally are and ought to go on being are suspended.

This closed setting used so effectively by Eberhart is familiar to the devotee of detective fiction; variations of it are the English country house, the snowbound hotel, the men's club, the moving train or ship. Other classic aspects are not hard to find in *The Mystery of Hunting's End*: the floor plan (probably drawn by Alan Eberhart); the sinister-seeming servants; the collection of privileged suspects more likely to dress up than down for dinner, more used to fine wine and fresh-cut flowers on the table than hunter's stout and dead animal decorations; the sifting of clues and testing of hunches and the final cornering of the killer. And, for one of the few times in her career, Eberhart has arranged a locked room, wherein crime cannot possibly occur but evidently does. Introduced to American readers by Edgar Allan Poe in "The Murders in the Rue Morgue," the sealed-off murder room became a feature of detective fiction between the two world wars, most notably in the works of John Dickson Carr and Ellery Queen.

But, as suggested above, Mignon Eberhart's talent was developing in the direction of Gothic romance and not Sherlockian ratiocination. Nurse Sarah Keate boasts of a strong stomach but has the good sense to be scared much of the time. She belongs to the Had-I-But-Known school pioneered by Mary Roberts Rinehart in mysteries like *The Circular Staircase*. Had I but known the horror in store, thinks the heroine, I never would have opened that door. Then there's Eberhart's skilled use of shadow and light. The lodge in *The Mystery of Hunting's End* was modeled on a real one in the Sand Hills that depended on pewter lanterns for illumination. The spookiness came naturally.

The most personal element in this novel, and perhaps the nicest living thing, is the sensitive collie named Jericho. Alan and Mignon Eberhart loved big dogs and always kept one around. Jericho is the literary incarnation of Jerry, their pet collie during those days in Valentine. When *The Mystery of Hunting's End* was dramatized in 1933 by students at Nebraska Wesleyan University, the collie's role was taken over by a German shepherd owned by Enid Miller, the longtime head of the speech department who adapted the novel for the stage. By this time the Eberharts had left Nebraska for Chicago. The Depression brought a dearth of engineering jobs for Alan and, for Mignon, the necessary determination to succeed as an escape artist.

Mignon often came home to Lincoln while her parents

were still alive, but now she belonged to a larger world populated by readers avid for the stylish shudders she could provide. By 1940 she was arguably the leading woman mystery writer in America and, after Rinehart and Agatha Christie, the highest paid anywhere. Her corpus, some sixty novels, earned her the Grand Master Award from the Mystery Writers of America in 1971. Amazingly, her career spanned six decades, from 1929 to 1989, when Random House published her last, *Three Days for Emeralds*. After Alan's death in 1978, Mignon lived in a condominium in Greenwich, Connecticut, her only companion a devoted dog. She died in October 1996 at the age of ninety-seven.

Though a lifetime has passed since the first publication of *The Mystery of Hunting's End*, it remains vivid. Nurse Sarah Keate still has more life than many of her contemporary crime solvers, among them the cultured and sometimes irritatin' Philo Vance, the famous creation of S. S. Van Dine. If Vance had been present during those endless terrible days at Hunting's End, Nurse Keate might have acted on Ogden Nash's urge to kick him in the pants. And sometimes even Lance . . . But read on.

CONTENTS

THE MYSTERY OF HUNTING'S END

CHAPTER I

ONE OF THOSE DOORS

IT WAS, I am sure, the most extraordinarily desolate place I had ever seen in all my life. It did not seem possible that twelve hours from Barrington, from midnight until noon of the next day exactly, could bring me so far, apparently, from the haunts of man; from a crowded, pavemented, humming city into a region so wild, so strange, so morose in its barren reaches of sand and pine-dotted buttes and somber emptiness.

Two notes had brought me there, one in a strange handwriting which signed itself "Matil Kingery," a name which I recognized at once, for, like most nurses, I got a vicarious kind of thrill out of reading the society columns of Barrington's newspapers and the Kingery name figured therein frequently and with a certain dignity and importance that was denied lesser names. The note was written in extremely black and vigorous ink on plain notepaper, very heavy and lovely, and said this:

DEAR MISS KEATE:
My aunt, Miss Lucy Kingery, needs a nurse, and at the recommendation of Mr. Lance O'Leary I am writing to ask if you will take the case. My aunt has been unable to walk for some years but is in fairly good physical condition otherwise

and a nurse's task is mostly a matter of massages and general care. Her former nurse left unexpectedly this morning. We are taking the six o'clock train this evening to Hunting's End with a party; if you decide to take the case, and I hope you will, you might meet us at the Union Station at that time. However, if this does not give you time to make your own arrangements, you might follow us on the midnight train. Take a ticket to Nettleson, which is the nearest point to Hunting's End; a car will meet you there and bring you to the lodge. Please send a messenger with your reply.

Thank you.

Sincerely,
MATIL KINGERY.

On first reading the note my eyes had leaped at once to the name of Lance O'Leary and lingered there speculatively, so the underline she had given the name, as if to call it to my attention, was entirely unnecessary. If Lance O'Leary, that enterprising young detective whom I knew rather well, had told her of me then there was that about the case which demanded something more than ordinary nursing care. I decided at once to accept, and was just despatching a messenger with a note to that effect when another note arrived for me. It began "Sarah, my own," and was, of course, from Lance O'Leary, himself, who is always much warmer and more friendly on paper than he is by word of mouth—a trait which might lead him into difficulties were I other than I am, plain Sarah Keate, a spinster of uncertain age, unromantic tendencies, sharp eyesight, and an excellent stomach. I mention the last because it is really quite important: a good digestive apparatus and common sense walk hand in hand through life.

SARAH, my own [said the note]:
This is to urge you to accept Miss Kingery's request.
Frankly, I need you. Also, unless you have changed considerably in the last year or so, the business will be something
after your own adventurous heart. Meet me simply as a
former patient, which, indeed, I am. No one of the party
save Miss Matil Kingery knows that I am there profession-
ally, or, in fact, what my profession is.

Yours in crime,
LANCE O'LEARY.

Since then I have often thought of the somewhat
flippant tone of those words of O'Leary's; afterward
I knew that, in the first place, he did not quite credit,
as who would, Matil Kingery's story, thinking that,
while she was quite sincere, the affair, as she told it,
simply could not have occurred. And in the second
place, he had not the faintest idea of what was in store
for us during those grim days at Hunting's End.

I had not been able to take the six o'clock train so I
followed the others (who and how many other than my
prospective patient, Matil Kingery, and O'Leary, himself, I had not the least idea) on the midnight train.
As I have indicated, the trip took exactly twelve hours
and I never knew any twelve-hour journey to make
such a difference in one's physical surroundings, unless
it is the first twelve hours of an ocean voyage, when
you go to sleep in harbor with the lights and surging
motion of a city at hand and awake in the middle of a
trackless waste of water with boundless horizons. In
fact, that portion of our country which I believe is
called the sandhill country and abounds in duck hunting is not unlike the ocean in its loneliness, its immeas-

urable horizons, its effect of existence bare of everything save still, swelling reaches of water and sky. But
the waves were sandhills rolling so boundlessly and silently that they gave an impression of incalculable
power and strength in whose grip I and the driver beside me and the little car which had met me at Nettleson were like paper toys, unreal and flat and entirely
without meaning or value. And the sky was not blue,
being instead a heavy, leaden gray which blended imperceptibly into the dun color of the far reaches of
sand. And there was a track through the sand. Only
a track, however, along which the automobile pitched
and lurched and struggled.

For a distance that the driver informed me nonchalantly was only twenty-some miles but which seemed to
me at least a hundred and twenty, and which would
have been quite that, I am convinced, if the up-and-
down motion and that from side to side could be calcu-
lated, I had clung to my side of the car, kept my hat
on my head and my head on my shoulders (which was
no mean feat), hoped my bag was still in the back of
the car but dared not turn my head to see for fear of
breaking my neck which had already endured more
than seemed anatomically possible, thought of the two
notes, which I had destroyed, and speculated concerning the rather curious name of the hunting lodge.

Hunting's End. Possibly some person by the name of
Hunting had lived thereabouts. Had his end been suicide or murder? I did not consider a natural death;
the extreme desolation of the place and a curious hint
of threat that was in the very air itself induced me to

surmise that end had been a sinister one. I was to find that the late Huber Kingery had named his hunting lodge "Hunting's End" merely because the hunters returned to it at the close of a day's sport, which was a very obvious reason, and my own dark speculation regarding the name only goes to show that the brooding atmosphere was already working a little on my nerves.

Snow began to fly half an hour or so before we reached our destination; it was a very fine, powdery snow which felt cool and soft on my face and to my mind did not warrant the anxious way in which the man beside me kept glancing at the leaden sky and up toward the dark line of buttes along the west. Nor did it seem to me to warrant the determination with which he urged the little car more and more furiously through the sand until its very bones seemed to vibrate and rattle so that it was a marvel the thing stayed together at all. And as to that, my own bones were in a like condition.

"Isn't this—early for snow?" I shouted presently, my voice jerking out above the roar and rattle of the engine.

"Always have snow—in November." He negotiated a sharp twist, climbed a steep slant, and added cryptically and very spasmodically, owing to the plunging car: "All I hope is—it ain't what—I think—it's going to be." He applied his brake and we stopped so suddenly that I pitched violently forward and only escaped being brained against the wind-shield by the car's giving another unexpected leap ahead which plunged me with equal violence backward.

"There's the lodge up that path," he shouted. "Can you carry your bag up there?" He was out of the car, my bag was out, I was out, standing on a sandy, rock-bordered path. "I got to hurry back." With one long step he was behind the wheel again and I fumbled in my pocketbook. "Miss Kingery will pay me when I come back with supplies from Nettleson to-morrow." He added something indistinguishable which sounded very much like "If I can get here," and was gone.

Owing to the snow, which was increasing in volume until it hung like innumerable soft folds of gray white chiffon shrouding everything, I could distinguish only a dark bulk sprawling against the butte above me and up the steep path. There were lights here and there shining through windows and making yellowish blotches of radiance, and as I neared it I saw with faint surprise that it was rather magnificently proportioned to be only a hunting lodge. Rich man's plaything though I knew it had been, still I was in no way prepared for the lavish elaborateness with which it had been built and equipped.

The snow had begun to sting against my eyes and the air was sharp in my lungs when I reached steps that led upward to a rustic porch—a very rustic porch, I might add, with criss-crossed saplings for a railing and rustic chairs and benches turned upside down along its length. Suddenly the door, which was heavy and very solid, being built of small but unsplit logs, swung backward, letting out a sudden flood of light and warmth and voices and the sound of a piano, and a girl stood on the threshold for a moment before she advanced to meet me.

Beyond her I had a glimpse of open fires leaping and people here and there, with rugs and cushioned divans for a background. But I had my first view of Matil Kingery there on the porch, with the snow enfolding the rest of the world in thick white chiffon and a black blotch of scrub pines by the railing reaching out stiff needles toward us and the cold, still air touching her hot cheeks and finding its own unfathomable stillness in the blue-black depths of her steady eyes. I knew that she was considered beautiful but I was not prepared for her proud poise, her slim straightness, and the hint of arrogance and wilfulness in her lovely face. For her face was lovely; I think it was the straight severity of her rather heavy black eyebrows and lashes, the remarkable steadiness of her eyes, the tilt of her small head with its soft black hair, that made one think first of character, then of beauty. Her brilliant color was due, I think, not to gayety, but to the heat of the fires in the room beyond, for she actually had a grim, rather bleak look; her mouth was set a bit too firmly and there was a hint of the stubborn Kingery jaw beneath the finely rounded chin. Even so, she possessed, I suspected, more charm in her feminine beauty than her father, Huber Kingery, had possessed in the heyday of his career and he had been accounted a man of extraordinary charm. Toward the last, years of good living had pouched his eyes and drawn downward lines on his face.

"You are Miss Keate?" she asked, interrupting my train of thought. I was oddly pleased to find that her voice was lovely, too: low and grave with a curious little break in it that was rather fascinating. As I made a motion of assent she continued: "I am Matil Kingery. I'm glad you decided to come. My aunt is partially paralyzed and quite helpless. She has been anxious for your arrival." She spoke very clearly—so distinctly, in fact, that I had a momentary impression that she wanted those in the room beyond to hear every word she said to me.

There was a movement behind her and a big gold and white collie dog walked slowly around her, glanced at me without much interest, and pushed his head against the skirt of the crimson wool sport dress she wore. She looked downward, smiled a little, and let her hand lie on his long forehead. The white silk frill around her slim wrist was not whiter than the dog's magnificent ruff.

"Poor Jericho," she said. "He dislikes trains and has been unhappy ever since we started last night."

The dog walked out from her hand and went slowly, his tail drooping, to the railing, looked sadly out into the snow for a moment, whined a little, and returned to press closer against Matil. If it hadn't been for his gloriously heavy coat I would have said he shivered; as it was, it struck me that, while the train ride might have made him unhappy, the present surroundings did not appear to improve his spirits.

The girl looked at me and smiled again. It was not a gay smile; it was a little sad and wistful, and at the same time there was something paradoxically courageous about it. And I may as well admit here and now that I liked Matil Kingery from that moment on.

"You are cold," she said. "We must go in. "May I help you with your bag?"

As she reached for it a manservant who was tall and bulky and awkward-looking appeared beside us. He had a flat pink face, light hair, and neither eyebrows nor eyelashes, which gave him a singularly unfinished look and which emphasized the wide black pupils in his light eyes. He took my bag and followed us into the lodge. The lights and warmth and voices surrounded us, and through the confusion I saw the servant depositing my own bag upon a heap of luggage beside the door. For a fleeting second I wondered why he did not immediately take it to the room that was to be mine. Then O'Leary's face emerged from a group of people near at hand. He was looking at me casually, then, returning his gaze with more interest, as if identifying me as an old acquaintance, he permitted recognition to enter his face, rose and advanced toward me.

"Isn't it Miss Keate?" he said pleasantly.

"How do you do, Mr. O'Leary?"

"Oh, you are acquainted?" said Matil clearly.

The little hum of voices had ceased, and I was conscious that other faces in the room were watching us rather more closely than was quite natural. A man had lounged forward, following O'Leary, and he stopped at Matil's side; he was about her height or a little taller, with heavy, very well-developed shoulders and chest and a dark, swarthy face from which greenish-gray eyes twinkled in a boyish and disingenious way. He was smiling, disclosing very white teeth between red lips.

"The nurse?" he inquired of Matil, quite as if he had a right to know, and as she nodded he looked at O'Leary. "You two know each other?" He said.

Matil murmured something by way of introduction, in which I only caught the words "Signor Paggi," and O'Leary said:

"Indeed we are acquainted. Miss Keate was my nurse during a very trying period of my life."

"Ah?" said Signor Paggi, eyeing me curiously. "A very trying period?"

"Have you ever suffered the prevalent American malady known as appendicitis?" asked O'Leary dryly, and as Paggi shook his head in a knowing fashion O'Leary added: "Miss Keate took care of me while I was in the hospital."

"Jo," a woman's voice called possessively from the opposite length of the room. "Terice says she will try that duo. Will you sing with her?"

Paggi's dark face became a little darker and something that was not boyish looked out of his eyes for a second. Then he whirled very lightly and started across the room with a buoyant step.

"A pleasure," he said gayly.

"Wait, please, Jo," said Matil. "I must make out the room chart. We have been here since morning and have not found our rooms yet." She added the last sentence as if speaking to me, laughing a little, but her voice was so very clear and distinct that I am sure it carried to the ears of the eight or ten people in the enormously long room. At least there was a renewed silence and a young man seated at the piano let his hands drop. "The room chart, please, Brunker," went on Matil, her lips still smiling. "I shall take my old room there in the corner." She motioned over her shoulder toward a door on the same end of the room and quite near the outside door.

All along the west wall were log doors, seven of them, with panels of rather well-done hunting scenes on the wall spaces between. At each end of the long room was a great, deep fireplace made of native, unfinished rock; at the right of the fireplace at the south end of the the room, above which were crossed a pair of snowshoes, was a door leading to the kitchen; at its left a narrow open stairway which led upward to a narrow gallery that ran around three sides of the room. From where I stood I could see other log doors along each end of the gallery and judged correctly that there were other bedrooms up there. The length of the gallery ran along the east side of the long room, projecting out over it, as indeed it did on all three sides, and was backed by the rough wall of the lodge, dark and smoke-stained. Not quite midway of the room it swung outward in a sort of rounded balcony at a point where I supposed the stairway emerged. The railing was like the porch railing, made of small criss-crossed saplings. In fact, as Matil bent over a chart the manservant placed in her hand and I looked more closely about me, I saw that there was an evident design to carry out a rustic effect, and the result, to my eyes, was not a happy one. Rough birch tables, with somewhat wobbly legs, chairs and settles of unfinished wood did not appeal to me as being particularly handsome, and when my eyes reached a grand piano that stood under the balcony and found it finished in birch bark I felt personally affronted. I never understood how or why Huber Kingery, a man of taste in many ways, had permitted such atrocities in what otherwise would have been a very lovely room. Its proportions, as I have said, were noble, the rugs and cushioned divans and easy chairs were luxurious and beautiful, and a number of tapestries hanging over the gallery railing and on the wall spaces, with here and there an Indian woven piece picked out in bright colors, were saved from looking hodge-podgy by the size of the room. The fires snapped and crackled and threw glancing lights and shadows, and there were many lights coming, I noted with interest, from numerous lanterns of all sizes and shapes that hung about the room or stood on tables or shelves, some of them in the most unexpected places.

"Pewter lanterns," said O'Leary quietly, following my thoughts. "Mr. Kingery collected them. Get Miss Matil to tell you about them sometime; it's rather amusing."

Matil Kingery seemed to have concluded her calculations over the room chart for she slowly approached the group around the piano, engaging me in some polite conversation about my journey in such a way that I found myself and O'Leary drifting along with her.

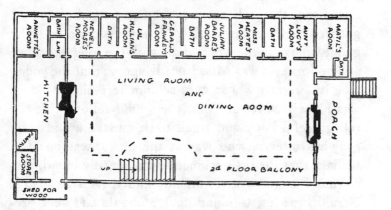

FIRST FLOOR PLAN OF HUNTING'S END

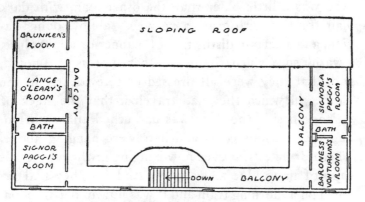

BALCONY PLAN OF HUNTING'S END

Showing a courtesy that many daughters of the rich do not feel obliged to extend a trained nurse, she introduced me, then, all around. At the time, however, I gathered only a few scattered impressions: that the gaunt woman in the wheel chair with the long dark face and hollow eyes was Miss Lucy Kingery; that the young stoutish woman whose eyes seldom left Signor Paggi was his wife, Helene; that the young fellow with the tall graceful body and small dark mustache and lazy, gray-brown eyes, who was at the piano, was one Lal Killian; that the little woman, determinedly blond, was Terice, Baroness von Turcum; and there was also a Gerald Frawley, thin and dark and pale and very precise, and a Newell Morse, blond and broad-faced and sturdy, and a Mr. Barre, whom Matil called Julian and who was a little older than the other man, with dark hair touched with gray, a very easy air of sophistication, and a certain distinction of manner or appearance, I wasn't sure which, that was rather impressive. I noted, too, that they were all dressed quite evidently in the clothes in which they had traveled, that the stack of luggage beside the door was untouched and unsorted, and that various coats and hats were hanging above, where Brunker was even now hanging my heavy nurse's cape of navy blue and scarlet. And yet they had arrived on a morning train and it was now mid-afternoon.

A little burst of conversation had followed Matil's announcement and through it Helene Paggi's voice came rather shrilly:

"I think Terice and I had better take the two gallery rooms on the north, Matil," she said, "since we have to share bathrooms. We always had the two at the north end—that is—at least——" She floundered a little, quite without reason that I could see, and Gerald Frawley spoke quietly:

"That's right. Isn't there a bathroom between every two bedrooms? That's as I remember the place anyhow."

As Matil nodded Lal Killian let his hands fall on the keyboard with a heavy chord or two.

"Exactly," he said rather dryly. "All I ask, Matil, is a next-door neighbor who can remember to take the bolt off my door into the bathroom, when he leaves it." His fingers drifted very lightly into some popular melody and he added dourly: "And who doesn't take more than an hour to shave."

"Speak for yourself, Lal," remarked young Morse. His wide ruddy face looked remarkably vigorous and healthy. "Do you want to get us all settled, Matil? Put Lal and me in the first two rooms." He nodded toward the two doors nearest the kitchen door. "Shall we draw lots to see who gets the bathroom first, Lal?"

"Very well," said Matil. "Aunt Lucy, you will want your old room next to mine, won't you? Then Miss Keate would better have the room adjoining your bathroom." She jotted something on the paper she held. "That leaves the two middle rooms and two gallery rooms."

"Matil." Aunt Lucy's voice was very loud and harsh and curiously deliberate. Every head jerked a little toward her. "Matil," she repeated, "do you mean to say that someone has to take—*Huber's room?*"

Her harsh voice left silence, breathlessness, in its wake. Killian's hands were quiet on the keys. A pine log sputtered and shot blue flame. A wind had risen suddenly and I heard it sweeping against the windows and whispering in the pines. Helene's face looked yellowish, the Baroness gripped the sheet music in her lap with little hard, rather dirty fingers. The very air held a secret and it was motionless and still with fear. Then something dropped with a dull clatter in the kitchen and released us and Julian Barre bent over Matil, looking at the chart. His black hair touched with gray went in crisp waves back from his fine forehead, his rather hard mouth looked softer, his clear-cut features were full of solicitude.

"My dear child," he began—"my dear——"

"I'm sorry, Aunt Lucy," said Matil, her chin up, her eyes black in a white face. "Annette sleeps in her room off the kitchen, Brunker in the west room of the south gallery. That leaves exactly eleven rooms and there are exactly eleven of us. I'm sorry. I didn't think. I didn't mean to distress——"

Even as she said it I knew that she was not sorry; that she had known it all along.

"My dear child," said Barre again, interrupting her, "don't let it trouble you. Any of us will take Huber's room. It doesn't matter in the least. Any of us will take his room."

"I'm sorry," said Matil again. "Who——" Her voice broke a little and Lucy Kingery spoke again, loudly, harshly, staring into the fire.

"Who? Ah—*who* will take it? Take the room where Huber died. Where Huber died. Five years ago this month. That was the last time the lodge was opened. The last time we were here." She withdrew the gaze of her somber, hollowed eyes from the fire, and looked at the company who were one and all looking at her—as, indeed, it would have been impossible not to do, for her manner, to say nothing of her words, was indescribably unpleasant. One by one she searched the still, shocked, secret-laden faces until her gaze met mine. She ran her tongue slowly over her purplish, wide lips. "He died of heart failure," she said definitely. "He died of heart failure."

Another singular little silence held us and in that silence something rather horrible occurred. The collie, who had followed Matil, turned and walked slowly and directly to one of the closed log doors and put his nose to the crack of the door sill. It was curious that no one seemed to stir or breathe while he sniffed. Then all at once he whined, listened, and whined again.

"*Terice!*" said someone sharply. My eyes flew back to the group about me. Terice von Turcum was standing, her hands pressed against her mouth as if to hold back a scream, her eyes wild and terrified above her painted cheeks.

"Terice!" said the voice again, sharply and coldly. It was the man they called Frawley speaking; his white, thin face looked extraordinarily cold and set beneath heavy, dead-black hair and his keen black eyes commanded. She tore her gaze from the dog, met his, and after a moment sank into her chair again. Suddenly everyone was speaking. Killian was at Matil's side, Helene was insisting somewhat disconnectedly that it was only owing to the bathrooms and anyway that's the room she'd always taken, Barre and Killian and Frawley were all offering to take Huber's room, Paggi was shuffling music on the piano with fumbling hands and saying loudly something about his voice and its being a north room but if Matil wanted him to have it he didn't mind at all, and Aunt Lucy was smiling horribly at the fire. I was conscious, too, that O'Leary had said nothing and was fumbling absent-mindedly in his pockets, and that Brunker, standing directly behind him, looked exactly as if he had seen a ghost, for his face was a sickly green and his pale eyes with their dark pupils were nearly popping out from between his lashless eyelids. He caught my gaze and the heavy lids drooped at once and his flat features became dull again.

Then it was all settled. Conventionality, quietly controlled voices, polite smiles were back again; the little wheels of social intercourse were running smoothly. Brunker busied himself with bags; the group broke up with little murmurs of resting and dressing for dinner; Aunt Lucy sent her wheel chair rolling silently down the long room, disappearing at length through a door next to Matil's room; I heard Matil say something to Julian Barre about wines for dinner and he and Brunker went out through the kitchen door; Baroness von Turcum's outrageously high heels clicked lightly on the stairway; and I could see Helene lingering a moment on the gallery saying something to Paggi, to which he paid little attention, his gaze being directed downward over the railing and appearing to rest on Matil's dark head. But through the little stir and confusion I watched carefully to see who entered the room at whose threshold the dog had whined. It was Gerald Frawley.

Matil, O'Leary, and I stood quietly for a moment. I had made a motion to follow Aunt Lucy but a look from Lance O'Leary's clear gray eyes stopped me, so I waited. And as far as that goes I wanted to wait; there is no use denying that I was intensely curious.

"The room is so long," said O'Leary as we heard the door into Helene's room close. "The room is so long that I believe we can talk without being overheard. That divan in the middle of the room looks very comfortable. By the way, Miss Matil, Miss Keate will be very much interested in the collection of lanterns. You must tell her all about them some day. I had no idea the collection was so extensive; it must have cost your father a pretty penny. Take this seat, Miss Keate. Are you quite comfortable there, Miss Kingery? Now if either of you are tired we can put off this talk until morning. No? Very well, then. Will you be so good, Miss Matil, as to repeat and amplify what you told me in my office yesterday? I want to have it all fresh in my mind. And besides, as I told you, Miss Keate is of invaluable help."

Then, as Matil hesitated, he leaned forward a little.

"Tell me, Miss Matil, do the people here to-night comprise the same party who were here five years ago when your father—died?"

"Exactly the same party," said Matil Kingery. "With the exception of yourself and Miss Keate."

"Servants, too?"

"Servants, too. Even Jericho. He belonged to my father."

O'Leary leaned back in his chair. His gray eyes were very clear. As usual he was perfectly groomed, his linen immaculate, his gray worsted suit well fitting, his light brown hair smooth, his expression bland and untroubled. Matil Kingery sat facing him; the flush had died from her cheeks, leaving them rather pale, and her eyes were very dark. Jericho crouched unhappily at her side, lifting his long nose now and then to touch her hand. His brown eyes surveyed us soberly and entirely without the spark of fun and friendliness that lies usually in the depths of a collie's gaze.

"Servants, too," repeated O'Leary softly. "That is really quite remarkable. How on earth did you get them all together? Surely none of them looked upon it as a pleasure trip, in view of what you have told me. Why, then, did they consent to come?"

"It is quite simple," said the girl. "They—were afraid to refuse."

"Afraid to refuse," said O'Leary after a moment. "Well—yes. Yes. I don't wish to harrow you, Miss Matil, but will you please tell Miss Keate what you told me?"

"It doesn't harrow me," replied Matil Kingery steadily. "I have known it for five years. So has everyone else here in the lodge. Five years ago, in that room over there, my father was murdered."

Something inside me had expected it, yet I caught my breath sharply.

"He was murdered," she repeated quite coldly. "And the murderer is here. Now. To-night. Behind one of those doors."

CHAPTER II

ANYTHING CAN HAPPEN

AGAIN in the silence I could hear the wind pushing at the thick walls of the lodge and snow swirling against the window panes. One part of my mind said, "It must be colder. The snow sounds like driving sleet," and another part was repeating at the same time, "And the murderer is here. Now. To-night. Behind one of those doors." How deliberate her words had been, how cold, and how singular it was that I should feel that that very restraint was ominous! The back of my neck twitched and I felt that I must look behind me and up along the gallery at those closed log doors, and I had to hold my neck stiffly to keep from following the almost irresistible impulse.

O'Leary was watching the girl quietly; I'm sure he noted her pallor, the pressure of her hands against the arms of her chair, and the wild flutter of a pulse at her temple that she could not control. Jericho stirred, laid his head on her knee, and looked sadly up into her face.

"It's going to be a bad night," said O'Leary. "Does it snow like this often up here?"

She looked at him slowly and her satin eyelids went up and down heavily.

"I believe so. The old-timers say anything can happen in the sandhills." She paused and added in a whisper: "And they are quite right."

A shiver started about the small of my back and crept upward though the room was heavy with heat.

"If I have it right," said O'Leary, "the situation stands thus: Your father and these—friends had come up here for a week of hunting. One night your father was shot. He was in his own room, just ready apparently to go to bed. The window was fastened on the inside, the doors of the lodge locked on the inside. The sound of the shot was clearly heard——" He paused in a questioning way and the girl's hands twisted a little.

"Oh—*very* clearly heard." She whispered. Her mouth looked a little dry and in her eyes was a five-year-old horror.

"Exactly," resumed O'Leary in a quietly conversational way which was soothing to my nerves. "Exactly. It was clearly heard. You all rushed out of your rooms, and found Huber Kingery dying on the floor of his own room. He died without a word. I'm sorry, Miss Matil, to have to talk of this."

She steadied herself and glanced quickly up toward the gallery as if to be sure no one was watching us.

"We had better smile a little—laugh. Someone might be watching," she said. "I asked you to come, I took the initiative. It is painful, of course, but—I must have an end to it."

O'Leary nodded. His hands sought about his pockets for a moment; he drew out a shabby stub of red pencil and began rolling it between his fingers, drawing it back and forth slowly while I watched with growing irritation. It was a harmless enough mannerism, of course, but it invariably annoyed me.

"Then you sent for the coroner and—made it worth his while to report the case as death from heart failure?"

"Yes. I was only seventeen. Aunt Lucy was ill from shock. They talked it all over—all night long. I can see them yet, sitting over by the fireplace, with my father dead in that room and *the murderer among them*. I sat there, on the settle in that corner." She looked across at the great fireplace and I could see them all, talking—talking through the hours of the night with the dead man in the room beyond and the slim child of seventeen huddled on the bare rustic settle, listening. "Aunt Lucy—couldn't—make a decision. It was a terrible shock. She was devoted to Father; she has never been herself since then. She was not in a condition to consider what course to follow. Julian— Mr. Barre, you know—told me he would try to bribe the coroner; that they could keep the fact that it had been murder a secret among them and that it would be far better to do so. There were social positions to be considered, he said, and told me how sensational the newspapers would be. And he told me—carefully, I suppose, and gently, for he was Father's best friend —that—that Father's private life was such that investigation, such as would follow disclosure of the murder, would be—would be very painful to me and to Aunt Lucy. He said that the public knew Father by his virtues and would be kind to his memory, and that the thing was done and could not be changed, and—it is difficult to say." She moistened her lips, and her hands twisted again on her lap. The collie pushed closer to her as if he shared her distress. "It is difficult to say but he hinted to me that perhaps the murder was justified, that Father might have wronged someone. I don't know how I managed to grasp so much of it when I consider that I was so young. But I did. Then he explained that immediately upon such a disclosure the solvency of the Kingery Trust Company would be questioned; that no matter how definitely it was proved that everything was open and aboveboard, it would be years before the trust company recovered the confidence of the people. He said, too, that things like that —rumors, you know—had caused many failures. And, of course, all my father's money was in the company."

"Had any of the others of the party any money in the Kingery Trust Company?"

"Yes. Julian, of course. And the Paggis. And Lal Killian and Newell Morse and Gerald Frawley were involved; you know, I suppose, that Gerald is vice president, was then. Newell and Lal have lesser positions but I believe both of them own stock. It was to everybody's interest to keep the murder a secret."

"There was no question of suicide?" asked O'Leary softly.

"No. You see, there was no revolver."

"You are sure of that?"

"Very sure. I—I, myself—looked."

And she was seventeen; facing the fact of death for, probably, the first time, and in its most dreadful guise; facing the disgrace of her father's name, the possible failure of the business firm to which he had given the best years of his life. She had looked for the revolver. Truly, whatever Huber Kingery had done or had not done, he had begot a daughter of fire and steel.

"And then?" said O'Leary very gently.

"Then the coroner came; someone, I think it was Newell Morse, went after him. I never knew exactly how the business was settled. I agreed, of course. What else could I have done?"

"You left the hunting lodge—when?"

"That very day. There was—an undertaker, too. From Nettleson."

"Ah—then we can get hold of him."

She shook her head.

"He died, not long ago. I saw a notice in the paper."

"The coroner, then," suggested O'Leary.

"Possibly." She looked at him doubtfully. "Do you think he would admit it? Especially when—I am quite sure no one of the people here will admit it. If I tell them who you are, why you are here, that I have told you the truth, they will deny it. They will tell you I was a child; the shock was too great for me—anything. And remember, Mr. O'Leary—the murderer is among them. I have heard that when a first crime has been committed—" she hesitated and lowered her voice, unconsciously, I think, to a whisper—"a second crime is easier."

I could feel my hair stirring at its roots; after all, we are rather primitive animals. My heart was racing, my skin crawling, my hair prickling, while my reasoning mind tried to convince me that there was no real danger.

"Yes," said O'Leary. "That is quite true. You think then that we stand in rather definite danger."

She nodded. "If your identity is known."

"You hope that by seeing all these people together, in the same place in which they were when one of them killed your father, I can discover the murderer?"

"I—hope so."

"I told you at my office yesterday that it was impossible."

"That is what you said. And I insisted that you come with us. That you—try."

O'Leary looked at her, rose restlessly, walked to a near-by table, fingered idly a heap of magazines, and returned to us.

"My dear lady, it—it simply is not possible."

"Don't say that. You don't understand. I must know."

He studied her for a long moment.

"It must have been a very pressing reason that induced you to come to me, to break the five years of silence. The reasons for keeping the murder a secret are surely just as urgent as they were five years ago?"

"They are."

"Your own money is in the Kingery Trust Company, is it not?"

"All of it."

"I take it that you are not—" he hesitated as if his inquiry were a little difficult—"that you have no reason to doubt its solvency or its officers' integrity?"

"Not in the least."

"And—of course, your regard for your father's memory is as great as it was then."

"Greater," she said very steadily, her eyes steel blue and direct.

"Then—please be frank with me, Miss Matil—why did you make such a decision?"

She did not reply at once.

"It was not easy," she said at last. "It is not easy to tell you. But—you see—among the men here, there is one who I must know is either innocent of the murder—or—" the word came out finally in a husky whisper—"or guilty."

"Why, Miss Matil?" Very quietly.

"Because——" She rose suddenly to face O'Leary. Her slim shoulders were proudly erect, her eyes bravely meeting his looked exactly like bluebells under water—like blue violets with dew on them—like the infinite softness of a blue summer night sky seen through the black lace of trees—— I caught myself up shortly. "Because, I love him."

O'Leary heard her gravely. Her love would be no light thing.

"Do you wish to tell me his name?" he asked very soberly.

"That can't matter, can it?"

There was a long pause. I could hear the soft thud of footsteps in the kitchen, a dish rattle. The pine logs in the two fireplaces kept up a crackling little duel.

"Very well, Miss Matil, I'll try. But I can't promise you success. It is an extraordinarily difficult thing."

"Thank you. You can't know what it means to me. I must know definitely, beyond a doubt. And I realize that to prove any one of us not guilty it must be necessary to prove which one is guilty."

He was looking at her rather vaguely, as if he were seeing quite through her and beyond.

"Now then, Miss Matil, you say the lodge has not been opened since then?"

"Never."

"It didn't seem to take Brunker and your cook long to clean it, set things going, this morning after we arrived. You would think that in five years things would be very dusty, musty, cobwebby."

"The house is built very solidly, Mr. O'Leary, and there is little dust in this country; just sand. The air is dry, too; even the piano was still in fair tune and Annette tells me not a thing in the kitchen has rusted. Although, of course, the place needs cleaning; any housekeeper could tell you that. But it isn't as bad as it might be."

"So you bribed the coroner, had the—er—your father's body taken from here directly to Barrington?"

"Yes." She shivered a little. "On the same train. We all went together. I locked the lodge myself and the keys have never been out of my possession."

"Who, exactly, dealt with the coroner?"

"Julian, I think, and Gerald."

"Gerald? Oh, Gerald Frawley. He is the pale fellow with black hair, isn't he? Looks very precise and cautious. Was it difficult?"

She smiled rather bitterly.

"I told you—anything is possible in the sandhills."

He looked at her curiously.

"I believe you."

"Another thing, Mr. O'Leary. I have rather definite knowledge that the lodge has not been entered during these five years."

"What do you mean?"

"I was only seventeen; I was a child coerced by my elders. But children usually have a keen sense of justice. Also I had twelve hours to think while the others talked. I knew, as they all did, that we were leaving any possible clues here in the lodge. If there were such clues the time might come when I should need them. Oh, it was not to my credit. My father had taken some pains to—to teach me; my father always thought clearly. He saw facts as facts. Anyway, I was the last one out of the lodge. As the others were getting themselves and their luggage into the automobiles, I ran back. Aunt Lucy was hysterical about leaving; they were having some trouble with her, no one missed me. And I—well, I got some flour from the kitchen and sprinkled it lightly over all the window and door sills. This morning when we arrived at Nettleson I rode out here with the driver who brought you, Miss Keate. There was room for only one passenger in his little car. The others followed us in hired cars from the garage. I was fifteen minutes ahead of them. The flour was untouched. Everything was as it had been. I suppose it would have been possible to break into the lodge and get away again without disturbing the little sifts of flour but I don't think it likely. Anyway, Nettleson people always disliked the hunting lodge; the whole town would have known it if anyone had come."

"You could have done worse," said O'Leary. "As you say, it isn't conclusive, but still it inclines me to think that no one has entered."

And she had been seventeen. Huber Kingery, in spite of his faults, must have been a remarkable man; a child does not as a rule travel far to get certain qualities of character.

"You say your aunt showed the effects of the shock?"

"Yes. It was—rather awful for her. You see, she was the first one into his room."

"The first one? Then her room must have been quite near?"

"No. No, Mr. O'Leary. We are using exactly the same rooms now that we occupied then. I remembered perfectly. That is why I was so exact about the room chart a few moments ago. The only difference is that you have the room Gerald Frawley had then, and the room adjoining Aunt Lucy's room, or rather her bathroom, that Miss Keate is to have, was vacant."

This time O'Leary let open admiration come into his face.

"That was right," he said. "Miss Lucy was not at that time an invalid?"

"No. She ran—at the sound of the shot she ran from her room, along this room, until she reached Father's door. She said the door was standing open and Father was on the floor. She saw at once that he was dying.

She said he looked at her and died. He had on his pajamas, no slippers, the bed was open, the lantern above the bed was still burning, and a book was on the table. When the rest of us reached the room she was standing there shaking. She was ill for a long time. She has never walked since."

"Has she—I have to ask these questions, you know—has she property?"

"No." The reply was the first that had showed reluctance. "No. She had once. But when Father—died—it was found that he had willed everything to me."

"Then what became of her own fortune?"

"I—I don't know. She has nothing now; that is, my banking account is open to her, of course, but—I don't know what she did with her own money. I have tried to ask her about it but she will not talk of it. She still has her jewels."

"Is it possible that she still has property of which you know nothing?"

"I suppose it is possible," said Matil doubtfully. "But I think I would know of it. There would be taxes, you know, checks to deposit, business details to see to. And she is quite helpless, never leaves the house unless I am with her. And I know she never receives mail."

"What are her interests?"

"Why—why, the things that go on in Barrington. She broods a great deal. People come to see her very faithfully. Although she does not go out she still has considerable influence. I think she enjoys that."

"Is she religious?"

Matil looked startled.

"Y-yes."

"Yes?"

"In a way."

"Can you explain?"

"Well, she is not orthodox. That is, she doesn't go to church. But she—yes, she is religious, according to her lights. It is a gloomy religion, not very happy."

"Now, Miss Matil, will you see to it that Miss Keate gets that newspaper clipping you let me see? It will tell you something about the other members of that hunting party—and of this one." There was a grim implication in his last words that I'm sure was unintentional for O'Leary has good taste.

"I will," she promised readily.

"I want to look around in your father's room, too, Miss Matil. Though, after the coroner and all, there is likely nothing of interest there. I should have offered to take it for my own use but I was interested in seeing who asked for it with the most convincing earnestness. And who——" He stopped abruptly, put away the little pencil as carefully as though it were set with diamonds, and looked at his watch.

"You said dinner would be early to-night?"

"At seven."

"There's plenty of time then before dinner for a good rest. I'd advise you to get one, Miss Matil, and you, too, Miss Keate. Our conversation has prolonged itself rather suspiciously. I think we would better separate. By the way, Miss Matil, just what did you tell them about me? They must know that I am not a close friend."

"I merely said you were a new acquaintance and I thought they would like you. I didn't 'protest too much.' "

"You don't want yourself to be known, then?" I remarked, speaking for the first time.

"No. Not at present, anyhow."

"But Mr. O'Leary, you are rather well known. Surely someone will recognize you."

"I think not," he said easily. "I'm known mostly in police-court records and not in the society columns where these people flourish."

I regarded him doubtfully. I thought then, and still think, that he was wrong. His mistakes are rare but, since he is human, they do occur, and this one was to cost us dearly. Had he appeared in his proper person, then perhaps—but it is no use speculating. What was to be, was to be.

"It's like this," he said slowly and rather disconnectedly, as if he were thinking aloud and not very lucidly, at that. "The people here to-night are already on a terrific strain. As Miss Matil says, they were afraid *not* to come and it is certainly not a pleasure trip. The murderer will probably wish to convince himself that he left no clues: that will be natural. They are all a little nervous at coming back here, with the memory of the last time they were here so vividly in their minds. It will be difficult in any case—impossible, I'm afraid —but I think that if they should know I am a detective, our problem would be still further complicated. Let me see them as they are, first. At best, it will be a matter of—of non-admissions—of chance." He sighed. "Then, too, there is the element of danger. Miss Matil's word against theirs. You are a brave young woman so I can say that the danger, if there is any, would be to you, for you are actually a witness."

"I am not afraid," she said evenly. "Only—I must know the truth."

"I hope you will know the truth, then."

"There is something that troubles me." She paused, frowning a little perplexedly. "When, after months of indecision, I finally arranged this party and came to you with the story, I felt convinced that I was doing exactly the right thing. I felt relieved of that agony of indecision; I was even a little happier. But somehow, since arriving here at the lodge and opening the door and coming into the place—and—and seeing them all together, the very people who had been here——" Her voice faltered. She left the sentence hanging in the air while she looked at O'Leary with eyes that were dark with anxiety. "I don't know what it is," she went on finally, stumbling a little over her words. "But I— I'm afraid I have made a terrible mistake. Perhaps I should have left things as they were. Perhaps I should let the—the horror of the thing lie in secret, as it has these five years."

"Possibly that feeling is due merely to the associations you have aroused by coming here. It is your own reaction."

She shook her head gravely.

"No. No. It is something deeper than that. I feel as if I had set in motion forces that——" She caught her breath. The collie at her feet whimpered a little. She whispered: "——that are horribly evil. That I can't control."

There was a short silence.

"Nerves," said O'Leary. She looked at him a little indignantly and he smiled. He has a very engaging smile; it lightens his whole face and, though infrequent and very brief, it is extremely telling in its effect. "Call it nerves, Miss Matil. It isn't a pleasant business, but we will do our best."

"And now for Aunt Lucy," said Matil, her face composed once more. "This is one of her good days. I was afraid that coming here would disturb her very much, but I can't see that it has."

Privately I reflected that if this were one of Aunt Lucy's good days I shouldn't like to see a bad one, for it seemed to me that the few remarks I had heard from that old lady were unpleasant in the extreme. However, it did not become me to say so, and I walked along beside Matil in silence. We found Miss Kingery in a very affable mood, telling me to take my time to rest and freshen up after my trip, and visiting in a quite lively fashion with Matil anent the possibility of pack rats having got into the storeroom off the kitchen.

"Tell Annette there's poison on one of the pantry shelves and to be sure to put some out to-night. I don't intend to have pack rats around—nasty things, getting into everything. How is Jericho?"

"All right, I think, Aunt Lucy. He is always un-happy after a train ride."

Aunt Lucy sniffed somewhat audibly. She had a long nose and broad lips whose skin looked very thin; her eyes were set deeply under thick arched eyebrows; her skin was a dark, earth color and very wrinkled and gaunt; her strong Kingery jaw was marked and her chin bore a scant but perceptible gray beard; her hair was iron gray and very thick and vigorous-looking and was waved and twisted high on her head, disclosing large, dark ears with curiously long lobes which were pierced and from which dangled old-fashioned ame-thyst earrings in two long pendants. I cannot remem-ber ever having seen Lucy Kingery without earrings.

"Unhappy! On account of the train ride? Certainly not. Why, don't you remember Huber used to take him everywhere and the dog never minded? It is something else that bothers him. I never saw him so uneasy."

"He's getting old, Aunt Lucy."

"Old! Nonsense. He is just in his prime."

She sat very stiff and straight in her wheel chair and talked on and on in a strident, grating voice, while Matil stood uncomfortably listening and I went through the bathroom into my own room adjoining it. While unpacking the few clothes I had brought, I could hear her telling Matil about a previous time— she figured at some length and to her own satisfaction that it was exactly seven years ago that month—when she and a party had been at the lodge and it had snowed for three days without stopping.

And even through the sputter of the shower and the

closed bathroom door I could hear her heavy words, measured words, going on and on. The bathroom I found to be well equipped; I suppose that was where Huber Kingery had drawn the line at the rustic and favored his own comfort. My room, I surmised correctly, was very much like the other sleeping rooms: it was small, with a birchwood bed, a dressing table of unfinished wood with a mirror above it, a chair or two, and a rustic table. The very wide doors were both made of small unsplit logs and would have been cumbersome had they not been well built and solidly hung so they fitted firmly into the door casing; as it was, they were not unpleasant to look at. The window was small, and upon opening it I found it was protected with heavy shutters made to withstand wind and sand and snow. They were bolted, as, doubtless, they had been bolted for five years. A few fine cold snowflakes drifted through the crescent-shaped slots and such a surprising amount of cold air began to eddy about me that I closed the window again rather hurriedly. There was no way of heating the bedroom that I could see and I foresaw very shivery mornings. An old-fashioned lantern which looked to my inexperienced eyes like early American pewter, with extremely simple and pleasant lines, hung over the bed and a lamp of the same material with a curious metal shade stood on the dressing table.

As I was getting into a fresh uniform Matil knocked at the door that led directly upon the long main room and at my word entered. She carried a magazine carelessly under her arm.

"Did you happen to bring a dinner gown, Miss

Keate? Oh, never mind, it doesn't matter in the least if you have brought only uniforms. I just wanted to assure you that I look upon you as a guest as well as a nurse." She laid the magazine on the table. "The clipping is here. Is there anything you need?"

As the door closed behind her I turned with some curiosity to the magazine, shaking out a picture which was flat and rather limp. I hadn't any more than glanced at it, however, when there was another knock at the door. I shuffled the picture hurriedly under the magazine and answered. It was Brunker, the manservant, carrying a small oil-fed heating contraption somewhat gingerly in one hand.

"Is your room warm enough, miss? This heater will take the chill off."

"Quite warm enough, thank you," I replied, making a motion to close the door.

"Quite warm enough?" he repeated. His pale lashless eyes went past me and all about the room. It seemed to me they lingered at the table on which lay the magazine and the picture.

"That is what I said," I remarked a little sharply, and he murmured, "Yes, miss," and turned, and I closed the door. This time I lifted the rather clumsy bar of wood which constituted a simple but efficacious bolt and dropped it securely into the iron hook that projected from the door casing. I also bolted my side of the bathroom door against a surprise visit from Aunt Lucy, finished putting the cuff links into the starched white cuffs of my uniform, and sat down with the clipping on my lap.

I found it to be a picture cut from the rotogravure section of one of Barrington's newspapers. A note under it said:

Off to Hunting's End. Huber Kingery and his guests about to leave for the famous Kingery hunting lodge in Nettles County. Reading from left to right are——

I bent over the picture with interest. It was remarkably clear, and as I studied the thing I got a much clearer impression than I had had of the people whom I had met so briefly out in the main room upon my arrival at Hunting's End. One after the other I identified them, though I believe I looked first at the tall, handsome man in the center of the picture with the domineering nose and well-defined jaw, who I saw at once was Huber Kingery. Huber Kingery—so vital, so taken up with the matters of this world, so easily smiling—had he had no premonition that he was going to his death? Beside him was—I had to glance at the names below the picture to be sure—Lucy Kingery: tall as her brother, not handsome certainly, her face was too long and dark and gaunt for that, but smiling, fashionably gowned, and wearing a kind of proudly authoritative air that was rather attractive; I could imagine the women who make up Barrington's socially elect fearing her a little, asking her opinions, longing for her friendship or influence. On the other side stood —why, it was the little blond Baroness, of course, but so different to the woman I had met that afternoon: smiling, of course, so carefully gowned that one felt she must be daintily immaculate, her delicate little face as unwrinkled as a girl's, not a shadow of the hard calculative look that now peered from her eyes. It was difficult to see any but the purely physical similarities of height and figure and blondness between the graceful, dainty woman who clung to Huber Kingery's arm in the picture and the painted, artificial woman they called Terice, with the hard lines on her face, the shrewdly sparkling eyes, the dirty, hard little hands. What had so changed her? Had she really loved Huber Kingery? Had she lost with him her hope for money and ease? Had financial burdens been thrust upon her wiry little shoulders? Or was it the possession of a five-year-old secret?

But then, everyone had changed: A laughing youth leaning on his gun case, easily graceful, triumphantly carefree, his dark eyes looking directly into the camera, was Lawrence Killian. A girl beside him, a slim, long-legged youngster with serious eyes and a firm chin, was Matil. A round boyish face, light hair ruffled above a gayly striped sweater, his coat dangling carelessly over one arm, his tortoise-shell-rimmed eyeglasses catching highlights, his expression open and happy and widely grinning at the dog Jericho, whose leash he grasped—that was Newell Morse. The change was marked in Helene, too: she had grown much stouter in the five years intervening; in the picture she was very attractive. She held her hat in her hand and her black hair was parted in the middle and drawn straight, without a wave, to a knot at her neck in a rather effective fashion. Her slender black eyebrows were arched above large eyes which were looking in a somewhat languishing way toward Huber Kingery. Her rather broad body was slender and smartly gowned. Julian Barre stood beside her, a package of books under one well-tailored arm, somehow distinguished-looking even in a group of patently important people. His expression was serene, his mouth hard but smiling a little, his fine eyes discreet perhaps, but only decently so, his crisp hair, only a little touched with gray, waved back from his forehead. Altogether, he and Huber Kingery were quite evidently bred to the same life, the same manners and customs, and, while they did not in the least resemble each other in feature, still there was a very definite resemblance of caste. Julian Barre had changed very little, so far as I could recall what I had seen of him during those brief moments in the main room. And the slight dark man, exactly the same height as Huber Kingery but much thinner and more finely built, whom they called Gerald Frawley, had not changed at all. In the picture he was entirely as quiet-appearing, as cold, as detached, as precise, his hair as dead a black, his face as white, his eyes as unfathomably bright and black and aloof, his mouth as tight as when he had so sharply recalled Terice to her senses a few moments earlier. Neither had José Paggi changed so far as I could see: rotund, thick, deep-chested, he was as buoyant, as vividly and vitally alive, as he had appeared to me on first seeing him. In the picture he was apparently laughing at the woebegone look on the dog's face; his white teeth were flashing, his dark face boyishly gay and candid.

Brunker was not in the picture; neither was the cook they called Annette, whom I had not yet seen.

I remember that I sat there looking at that picture, studying those faces—every one of them, save Matil's, laughing, gay, bent on pleasure. They were going to tragedy. Had none of them guessed that murder was there, too, an unseen, cold-fingered guest at that hunting party? One of those faces must conceal, now, a secret; had had to conceal it for five years.

Surely such a secret would make its mark. Whose face might I find so significantly changed? Upon what face had murder drawn its ugly lines?

CHAPTER III

THE END OF ALL GOOD HUNTING

AFTER a while I roused myself with a little start, reminding myself that I had a patient to attend. I replaced the picture in the magazine. As I stepped into the main room I saw that night had really come, for the windows were quite black. Brunker was replenishing the fires and a long narrow table had been set at the south end of the room, not far from the door into the kitchen. The crystal goblets glittered cheerfully, the silver shone, and tall candles stood about the table ready for lighting. The fires reflected themselves rosily against the filet cloth and the lanterns glowed with mellow light. Curious that the room did not seem more festive; it had a waiting, hushed atmosphere that was oddly threatening.

I had no difficulty in finding Matil's room, for it was the corner one and its door was at right angles to the other bedroom doors. She took the magazine and without comment I went to my patient.

I found Miss Lucy Kingery still affable, talking with harsh and rather grisly gayety of the jewels she had brought with her. She needed no help getting into her dinner gown, she said, but would I please go to the kitchen and put a teaspoonful of baking soda into a glass of luke-warm water and bring it to her? She was very particular about the directions and I forbore telling her that I had probably mixed as many glasses of soda water as she had hairs on her head.

The kitchen proved to be, as I had surmised, at the south end of the lodge. It was a very large room, rather gloomy and dark, though two large lanterns hung from the low ceiling. There was a large fireplace here, also, backing the one at the south end of the main room, and an enormous coal range from which came various appetizing odors. Brunker was standing idly at a window, his nose apparently pressed tight against the glass, and at a table stood a tall woman in a plain blue dress with a large white apron. She seemed to be arranging salads and was singing a curious little song, which was mostly *tra-la-la's* in a high, rather childish voice. "This must be Annette," I thought, and with the thought she heard my step, the song broke, and she whirled to face me, her light blue eyes becoming sharp and looking frightened.

"And who are you?" she said rather insolently. There was a hint of trill in her "r's": a quick little accent that I could not at once identify. I was to find that Annette vibrated between easy English and a kind of patois, a curious blend of Parisian, old Acadian, and Creole French which I shall not attempt to reproduce—which, in fact, I doubt if it is possible to reproduce. Her English, save for the hint of accent, was like anyone's, easy and natural. I think she fell into French only when her emotions got the best of her. She was bulky as well as tall, with a wide pinkish face, a loose mouth, shrewd eyes with little bags below them, and grayish hair which she must have had bobbed once and was just letting grow out, for it was wiry and long and was held back with three combs whose colored rhinestones glittered.

"I want some baking soda, please," I said with dignity. She did not move while she studied me.

"You're the nurse." She had trouble with the "th"; it barely escaped being "z." "You are the nurse!" She put her large hands on her hips, looked me up and down with nonchalant deliberation while Brunker at the window turned and watched, and then flung back her head and began to laugh merrily and in a most disconcerting fashion. "She is the nurse," she said, still laughing, looking at Brunker and at me. "The nurse for Miss Lucy." She sobered suddenly, approached me and thrust her head forward; her breath reeked of alcohol. "Be careful, Nurse; be careful, or our Miss Lucy she—bite off the head. Snap! Like the spider with the fly." She snapped her fingers under my nose and repeated: "The spider with the fly. Listen. I tell you the secret. Her jaws are made of iron."

"You've been drinking," I said coldly. "Get me the soda."

"Ha! Drinking? But, yes. *Certainement.* Who would not? Listen to me, Nurse." The "r" rolled finely. "I drink. Yes. Why? Because—in this house one must drink. A little wine warms the cold stomach, steadies the hands that shake, keeps the eyes from shadows that move, keeps away the ghosts. You dare to look like that? You think I don't know?" She came closer

to me, so that I stepped back a little to escape her hot
breath. She was working herself into a fury, her eyes
were narrowed like a pig's in her fat face. "I—Annette
—*I* know. I know. There is something in this house.
Waiting. Waiting. For five years it has waited. To-
night——" Her mood changed suddenly, became fatal-
istic. She raised her scant eyebrows, shrugged her vast
heaving shoulders. "You will see. To-night."

"Now, now, Annette," said Brunker soothingly. His
lashless eyelids were lowered over cold eyes. "Don't
mind her, miss. She has never liked Hunting's End."

"And why should I like Hunting's End? I hate it. I
despise it. I spit on it. See!" With considerable ac-
curacy she spat directly into the fire. Then she smiled.
"Soda? But certainly. Soda." And she walked, quak-
ing a little like a big blue jelly, over to the pantry door,
and fumbled for the soda, beginning again her absurd
little song. She did not watch me mix it with water,
seeming to think only of her salad and to forget me,
an abandonment of which I highly approved.

And Brunker returned moodily to the window pane.

As I reëntered the main room I saw Julian Barre.
He was standing at the door of Gerald Frawley's room,
the room where Huber Kingery had died. As the door
into the kitchen swung quietly behind me and I walked
along the thick rug I heard Barre say:

". . . don't mind in the least. You take my room
and I'll take this one. Matil needn't know that we exchanged."

Then Gerald Frawley, in a brown flannel dressing
gown which made his white face whiter, his precise

mouth and sharp features sharper and more precise, his dead-black hair blacker, became visible.

"Oh, that's all right, Julian," he said easily. "Poor old Huber's ghost won't trouble me." He paused and added in a rather curious voice, "I'll admit he might haunt someone but—not me, Julian. Not me!" He laughed in an unpleasant fashion and then they both were aware of my approach and turned. As I passed them, only the little rattle of my uniform broke the quick silence, and all the way down to Aunt Lucy's door I was conscious of their combined gaze boring into my back.

Promptly at seven Miss Lucy announced herself ready to go in to dinner. She had got herself into a dark gray gown made of chiffon and lace, in which she looked rather unpleasantly like a great dark spider sitting in her web, waiting to snap up an unwary fly. Which simile, it occurred to me as I held the door open for the passage of her wheel chair, was probably due to Annette's extremely disrespectful suggestion.

From among the quantities of old-fashioned jewelry which she had brought with her, all of it encrusted with dirt around the heavy settings, Aunt Lucy had chosen a particularly ugly set of sardonyx, a stone that I have never liked. She wore on her scraggy neck a heavy collar, bracelets on her gaunt, big-boned arms, and long earrings which I had watched her threading nonchalantly through the tiny holes in the pendulous lobes of her ears with a feeling that was close to nausea. Once on, the yellowish brown stones looked most amazingly like the reddish brown spots and stripes that appear on

certain particularly black and furry and venomous-
looking spiders. All of which heightened the disagreeable effect I have mentioned.

A great fire was snapping and roaring in the fireplace at the north end of the room and chairs and
divans were pulled up comfortably around it. At the
opposite end of the room Brunker came and went,
busying himself around the table, dishes and silver
trays in his hands shining and catching highlights. I
followed Aunt Lucy toward the nearer fire. As we
approached it I saw Newell Morse, already dressed,
leave Gerald Frawley's room and enter his own, nearest the door to the kitchen. Helene Paggi stood at one
of the windows, looking at the shining blackness. Under
the round balcony, Lal Killian sat at the piano, his fingers drifting lightly over the keys. O'Leary, sleek and
well groomed and rather more impressive in a dinner
jacket than in his work-day gray, was enjoying a
before-dinner cigarette in a chair facing the gallery.
After a moment Newell Morse reëntered the main
room and approached us; his thick body sagged rather
wearily into a chair near O'Leary, his ruddy face had a
tired look. His light hair and polished eyeglasses
winked as he turned his face toward the fire and accepted one of O'Leary's cigarettes. I happened to
watch him light the thing and was rather surprised to
see that his pink, healthy-looking hand trembled.

Abruptly Helene turned away from the window.

"Snow, snow, snow," she said discontentedly. "It's a
regular blizzard. Why on earth did Matil take it into
her head to have a houseparty out here at such a time

of the year! We might have expected something like this."

Both men stood as she neared us and she chose a seat on the divan directly before the fire. She wore a flesh-colored lace gown, cut very low over her creamy, opulent shoulders and so remarkably near the color of her skin that it took me an uneasy moment or two to discern just where the skin left off and the lace began. There was, however, a distinct suggestion of rigid corseting about her hips and the soft folds of lace fell nearly to the floor. A large emerald-green velvet bow with long ends was plastered across one side of the gown, below the waist, and made a bright spot of color. Her black, rather coarse hair was drawn as in the picture straight to a knot on her rather large neck. Five years ago she had been an unusually attractive woman and, to a degree, she was yet.

"We could have refused to come," said O'Leary lightly. She took a cigarette he offered. Aunt Lucy gave her head one grimly negative shake at the advanced case, and Helene bent to the light Newell Morse held for her, puffing a little at the cigarette with the hint of impatience and petulance which characterized her.

O'Leary resumed his seat.

"Yes," he repeated idly. "We could have refused to come."

"That's it," said Helene. "That's exactly it. We could not refuse."

I caught Newell Morse giving her a quick look of disapproval but she seemed entirely out of temper and rather reckless.

"That is exactly what we could not do," she repeated rather spitefully, looking straight at Morse, as if to say, "I'll do as I please."

He said nothing and O'Leary laughed carelessly.

"Oh, come now, Signora Paggi. Man is a free agent."

Her green eyes did veil themselves then. But:

"Not always," she said.

Lal Killian rose from the piano and lounged toward us, to stand on the rug before the fire. It glinted on his shining white shirt front, reflected itself in his lazy dark eyes. He was an extraordinarily attractive young fellow, very graceful and well built, his darkish hair brushed smoothly from a good forehead, his features well cut, his mouth rather full and sensitive below its small dark mustache, and he had that clean, well-soaped appearance which is always so attractive to women.

He was looking at some letters carved on the wide stone chimney piece, tracing them with one hand.

" 'The End of all Good Hunting,' " he read slowly, " 'is Nearer than you Dream.' " He stopped abruptly, as if his breath caught a little and then read again and very rapidly: " 'The End of all Good Hunting is Nearer than you Dream.' " He turned to face us in some dismay. "What a gruesome thing! I had forgotten it was there. Why did Huber——" He stopped and Helene laughed. It was a thin laugh of malice.

"Why, indeed, did Huber put it there? *I* hadn't forgotten it." She shrugged, tossed her cigarette toward the fire, and began to smooth the ends of the green-velvet bow between her fingers. Her eyes looking into the fire widened and became a little fixed as she added in a low voice: "*I* had not forgotten. I had not forgotten—*anything.*"

"Helene," said Newell Morse in a warning way, and Lal Killian, kicking into the fire the cigarette which had fallen short, began to hum a little tune lightly as if to cover the queer silence. It was a tune, by the way, that I heard him hum countless times in the next few days; I never could catch more than a phrase of the words but it was something about "taking off your skin and dancing around in your bones" and was singularly ill chosen, it seemed to me, in view of the circumstances, although I believe it was a popular dance song of the year.

As he hummed a door slammed on the gallery. Helene looked up quickly and Jo Paggi ran lightly down the steps, rubbing his hands together joyously as he approached us, sniffing at the odors of dinner. He bent over to kiss Helene's cheek very lightly, which brought a thin smile to her mouth, and straightened up to meet Matil's approach with a bow that was deeper than I should have thought his rather tightly buttoned waistcoat could compass. His olive eyes flared darker as he looked at Matil. Lal Killian said, "Hello, Matil," rather coolly, Newell Morse struggled out of his chair again, the smile left Helene's lips, and I surprised a softer expression on Lance O'Leary's face than I had ever seen there—all that before I turned toward Matil.

I was to find that Matil Kingery was one of those rare women who never approach a group without making a very distinct impression of some sort upon it. There are people, such as Helene, who are accepted casually, passively, whose advent makes not the slightest difference in the atmosphere of the room, not a ripple of change on the faces therein. And there are women who immediately affect a group in some way: a kind of electric tingle seems to run over the faces meeting her and, while they may express pleasure or disapproval or admiration or dislike, still it is a very definite and positive expression of some kind. It just happened that Matil was beautiful; I think she would have had the same effect in any case for she possessed that strange spark of vitality which partakes of magic and which, once met, cannot be resisted.

She stood there for a moment, very slim and erect in her gown of silver tissue which fitted smoothly the lovely long lines of her body, a great ostrich-feather fan looped with a ribbon over one wrist, making a splotch of glorious crimson against the silver, her eyes like sapphires, her soft mouth crimson, and her black eyebrows frowning a little.

"Quite comfortable, Aunt Lucy?" she asked, and as Miss Lucy stretched out a gaunt hand from her nest of cobwebs she advanced.

"Nice gown, Matil," rasped Miss Lucy harshly. "A Hanet? Cost you something, didn't it?"

"Something," replied Matil. Lal Killian's eyes laughed a little at the fire.

"Am I the last?"

It was Terice, blond curls shining, eyes twinkling brightly from between very black and long and sticky eyelashes, skin painted thickly above a decolleté black gown with glittering spangles on it, and a black feather ornament in her hair which looked like nothing so much as an inverted hairbrush.

Then Frawley was there, quiet, severe, meticulously groomed, and Julian Barre, looking amazingly distinguished. There are men who manage to look very impressive and handsome in dinner clothes, and Julian Barre was one of them. Even the narrow black ribbon on his eyeglasses looked unaffected and quite proper. On one lapel was a small scarlet thing that I guessed was some sort of decoration, though I was not close enough to see it clearly. And, so far as that goes, I would not have been likely to recognize it, my experience having run somewhat exclusively to clinical thermometers and hot-water bags.

I shook my head at the tray of cocktails Brunker was passing, having, as I may have intimated, reached an age where I value my digestion. Disapprovingly I watched Aunt Lucy gulp three of them in a rather thirsty fashion, then found myself at the table between Morse and Aunt Lucy.

Dinner was superbly cooked, which was fortunate since it was the only good and ample meal we had during those hideous days at Hunting's End. Under its influence certain moral scruples I hold tottered, and I caught myself reflecting that if Annette could cook like that when she'd been drinking, then I was for her being given a plentiful allowance.

Brunker came and went silently, the candles' flames dipped and wavered and made changing lights as now and then a little current of air sifted through the room, the pine knots crackled and sent up little sputters of flame, the food, as I have said, was delicious, and it would have been a comfortable, pleasant meal if it had not been for a certain door about midway of the room. It did not add to the pleasure of the occasion when Jericho walked slowly, his nose and tail dragging dejectedly downward, to a spot directly in front of his dead master's room, sniffed again under the door sill, and then lay down, stretching his head out on his white forepaws and watching us with dark sorrowing eyes.

Julian Barre and Matil and O'Leary managed to keep a fairly cheerful conversation going, although Aunt Lucy made it difficult, for after the cocktails she lapsed into a morose silence and sat bolt upright in her chair, staring savagely straight before her at nothing and refusing to eat a bite. Terice rattled on and on nervously, falling now and then into a rather ghostly suspicion of baby talk and fluttering with her hard little hands, patting Julian Barre's smoothly fitted shoulder, laying her fingers for a moment on Lal Killian's wrist, at which Barre smiled easily and Killian ate steadily without looking at Terice. Her hands were not any too clean-looking and were loaded with jewels which sparkled a great deal, including a large ring on each forefinger, a place which, according to my view, was not designed by Providence for the wearing of rings.

". . . and it all sums up," Terice was saying when I brought my attention to her words, "to this: How rapidly can you think in an emergency?"

Paggi chuckled.

"Emergency. The whole trouble is you never know when you will be confronted with it. You remember *The Juggler* last season?" Several heads nodded; mine among them as that is a jewel which moves me more than most operas. "Did you ever know that Novello actually sang the entire opera for me?"

"Oh, Jo! Don't tell that!" It was Helene, of course, looking reproachful. "It doesn't matter in the least."

"But I was only going to——"

"It doesn't amount to anything," interrupted Helene sharply. "He fell on the step leading down from his dressing room and thought he'd broken his leg. Rimini Novello, his understudy, sang the whole opera." She smiled somewhat spitefully. "It was Sunday afternoon and only one or two critics were there, and they must have just looked in because——"

"They said I was not in good voice that afternoon," said Paggi, salting his salad vigorously.

"They did not! They said you were in exceptionally good voice."

Signor Paggi darted an unpleasant look at his too-veracious wife and Terice laughed a metallic little ripple.

"And your leg wasn't broken, I gather," remarked Lal Killian, in a way which hinted that it would have been no great loss.

"Not at all, my friend. Not at all. I only tell it to show how quickly one acts during an emergency."

"And not always wisely, one would think," said Terice rather waspishly. "You see, Jo, if you had thought twice, instead of once only, you'd have found you had no bones broken."

Helene's eyes had a lambent green flame.

"You present an example, Terice. You who are so delightfully cool-headed. Never making mistakes."

Terice laughed very gayly.

"Ah, darling, I make my mistakes, but there is this difference between us: I never regret."

"It is a difficult thing to tell just how an emergency will affect anyone," said Julian Barre smoothly. "An emergency savors so strongly of accident, and accident is something that time nor tide nor the affairs of man can reckon with."

"Still," said Gerald Frawley "—No more rolls, thank you—still, one can provide against it."

"How do you mean?" asked Morse. "Salt, Miss Keate?"

"Well, in this way. I, myself, being in a position where my own private records are of some importance feel it obligatory to provide against—" he paused, drank almost an entire goblet of water before he continued—"against accident."

"Accident?" queried Matil, leaning forward. "What do you mean, Gerald? You are not any more susceptible to accident—" she hesitated a little over the word —"than any of us."

He lifted his thin, precise eyebrows; his cold eyes delved rather freely into the blue ones meeting them.

"Do you want me to be quite specific?"

"Why—why, certainly."

"It is only that I have provided against confusion following any accident that might—er—remove me, by leaving very definite and complete records of all my transactions, personal and of a business nature, in a —" he paused again, before he concluded—"in a safe place."

"Gerald! What an idea!" Matil broke off, shrugging with a little distaste.

"Probably in such a safe place that no one could find them and confusion would result just the same," said O'Leary lightly.

"Oh, no," said Gerald Frawley with conviction. "In a place where no one could avoid finding them."

It was just then, I believe, that Brunker dropped the salad plate he was removing. It fell with quite a clatter on the bare space on the floor, and his face reddened as he bent.

"Was that one of the Spode plates?" asked Helene interestedly, peering around the table, oblivious to Matil's faint frown.

"Worse," murmured Matil. "It's Irish Beleek. But we had no business having it out here. It's been here ever since——" She broke off abruptly as Morse cleared his throat.

"They must be very important records," said Morse slowly. He sat directly opposite Frawley and the eyes of the two men met in a long look.

"They are important," replied Frawley precisely. His hand on the stem of his goblet was very still, his whole regular, somewhat sharp face was still, even the dead-black line of his thick hair looked oddly flat and still as if no hurricane that ever blew could disturb its smooth orderliness.

A gust of wind sighed furiously down the chimney. "It's a wild night," said Helene, shivering—as indeed she had good reason to do. "Why did you pick such a time for a party, Matil? If it keeps on like this we will be completely snowed in by morning. It's terrible." She shivered again. Her fat flesh looked white and soft like dough, and I felt that if I put my fingers on her wide upper arm the dents would remain.

"Why don't you wear more clothes?" asked José Paggi rather cruelly, his olive eyes fixed on her bulging shoulders.

A slow, painful flush crept blotchily upward, flooding Helene's neck and face; her eyes looked small and tiny fine lines showed around them, her thin lips drew back a little from her tightly set teeth.

"Oh, come now, Jo," said Morse, rather hurriedly. "That's a smashing gown, Helene. I like it."

She hesitated between rage and vanity. In the waiting silence there was a distinct element of anxiety; then she decided to smile, the flush ebbed away, and Matil shot Morse a look of gratitude, though I thought Terice was a little disappointed.

"Coffee, madame," said Brunker at my elbow.

"Will you sing for us after dinner, Helene?" asked Barre, at which Killian regarded his demi-tasse with sudden disfavor and Helene asked Jo somewhat coyly what he preferred.

"Brunker!" said Aunt Lucy, breaking her prolonged silence with such suddenness and speaking with such peculiar harshness that I think everyone at the table started a little. Brunker clutched rather wildly at his tray. "Poison."

Every head jerked.

"P—poison, madame," said Brunker, his eyes extending themselves unbelievably between their bare lids. Terice gave a little shriek and even Lal Killian looked somewhat perturbed.

"Poison," said Aunt Lucy grimly. Her somber, hollowed eyes traveled slowly about the group. Dinner courses had been carried away untouched while she brooded, and now all at once she seemed to perceive that the meal was over. "Where's the dinner?" she said, as if to herself. "H'mm!" She drew herself straighter, her eyes closed and opened quickly. "Certainly," she said stridently and very distinctly. "Poison." She paused again, in what seemed to me rather grisly enjoyment of our faces, which very likely showed a degree of anxiety. Then, with all the grace and suavity with which one fires a shotgun, she shot out the words: "Pack rats. In the pantry."

"Tell Annette to put some of the rat poison out, please, Brunker," said Matil in an undisturbed way, though her fingers gripped the handle of her small cup somewhat rigidly. "Aunt Lucy is sure that there are some pack rats in the lodge."

"Yes, miss," murmured Brunker, and vanished toward the kitchen with rather more alacrity than the errand demanded.

"There are always pack rats," remarked Aunt Lucy. "Tell him it's on the lower pantry shelf. Did you tell

him that, Matil? Never saw a hunting lodge yet that
didn't have pack rats. Dinner's over. What are we sitting around here for?" She pushed herself away from
the table. Jo Paggi on her other side gave her a look
of extreme distaste as he rose and helped extricate her
wheel chair, and as she started smoothly down the long
room toward the opposite fireplace and a little commotion rose from other chairs being pulled out, I'm sure
I heard him mutter, "You horrible old woman, you!"

His eyes went to Matil in a puzzled fashion and at
once lit again as if the sight of her kindled some fire
in those dark olive depths.

CHAPTER IV

FOUR DO NOT SLEEP

BRUNKER had set up a couple of card tables to which a scattered group drifted, while Helene and Lal Killian sat at the piano looking over stacks of music from which little clouds of sandy-looking dust arose. I heard Helene protesting volubly that she couldn't sing so soon after eating. It struck me that, upon hearing this, there was a little air of relief manifest and no one urged.

Aunt Lucy took up her position at one side of the fireplace where, with her eyes staring out from the shadows to watch us or reflecting ruby lights from the fire, she looked more like a great black spider than ever. Barre began to shuffle the cards lying on one of the tables and to deal them automatically. Frawley and Morse took up the hands. O'Leary shook his head to Barre's questioning look and Terice slipped into the fourth chair, taking the cards eagerly in her hands and glancing avidly through them before sorting them rapidly into suits. Matil, a slim silver sheath, looked on from an easy chair near by, holding her immense crimson fan in one hand to shield her face from the fire, and looking, I must say, extraordinarily handsome, though I think the pose was unconscious. Paggi, who had been lingering over the serving table, hastily set down his small glass and came to lean on the back of Matil's chair and comment idly on the bridge game.

O'Leary, in his rôle of observer, sat not far from Matil, smoking quietly, his gray eyes seeing everything, I had no doubt, through the soft veil of smoke, and I made myself comfortable in a chair quite near Aunt Lucy. Not too near. I may as well say here and now that, while I have had strange patients in my career, from the man who swallowed the spoons and had to be up-ended and shaken to the baby who arrived in the seat opposite me on the elevated during the rush hour, never have I had one like Miss Lucy Kingery, a fact which I count among my blessings.

From the piano we could hear occasional words from Helene and Killian and now and then a phrase or two of music and Helene's voice humming lightly; there was the little whisper of cards falling, and a few words from the bridge players. Paggi's comments to Matil grew lower and lower, and once as his hand slipped lightly upon hers and turned it so that their palms met for a second before she withdrew her own, it seemed to me that a flush rose to her cheeks and lingered there and her eyes began to shine a little feverishly.

Was it Paggi, then? Had she decided to dig up that ugly, five-year-old secret for love of him?

I should have been neither human nor womanly had I not speculated at some length upon the identity of the man she loved. The trouble was that it might conceivably be any one of the men: they were all young with the exception of Julian Barre, and he was at an age which many women find most attractive. Killian and Morse and Frawley were about equally eligible so far as I could see, though I, myself, would not have chosen Frawley, for there was a certain restraint and deliberation about him as if he planned every word and every motion, which was distasteful to me. However, it was Matil's opinion that mattered, not mine. And while Paggi already had a wife, the fact did not appear to restrain his somewhat obvious devotion to Matil.

I could tell nothing from Matil's behavior; her manner was exactly the same to everyone. I know now that she was under a terrible strain, but at the time had no idea of the bitterness in her heart or the thoughts back of those steady blue eyes.

And also, all through dinner and more and more urgently as the night progressed, I found myself studying the faces about me, comparing them with the picture taken five years before. Who had changed? How? Helene was much stouter; was that why her eyes looked craftier, less languishing? The little Baroness had, possibly, had five years of rather difficult financial battles; had it been that which had laid layers of paint on her face and had dyed her hair so crassly gold and had given her hard little fingers that clutching, grasping look? Had that five years alone made Julian Barre's handsome eyes more discreet than ever, or was it the possession of a certain secret? Where had Lal Killian lost the careless triumph of the youth in the picture and become restrained and a little cynical, and why? What had changed Newell Morse from an eager, happy-faced youngster to a weary man with stubborn lines in his face and a careful, calculative look back of his heavy eyeglasses and, despite his evident health, a hand that shook? Was it only the passage of five years' time, or was it something darker? Newell Morse—how much did he know and how much did he guess and how much did he fear?

Aunt Lucy, a fashionable, well-poised woman of the world, a bit opinionated perhaps, and certainly never handsome, but still smiling and authoritative and proud, had become, to quote Paggi, a horrible old woman—with a beard. And Huber Kingery, smiling, alert, positive in the picture, was now dust.

I shivered as my eyes fell on the collie, a gold and white huddle of misery before that closed door.

"Two spades," said Barre in the flat, guarded voice of the inveterate player, and Terice scanned her cards again, eagerly and anxiously, shot a quick look through those sticky-looking eyelashes at the score pad, and then said in a breathless way:

"Three hearts."

Upon which Morse, Barre's partner, passed in an absent-minded fashion which drew a sharp look from Barre. Frawley passed. Barre promptly, but rather carefully, I thought, made it three spades. Terice went four hearts quickly, with an avid glance at the back of Frawley's hand as if she would like to pierce the pasteboard with her gaze. Morse seemed to force himself to study his hand and, after a moment or so, during which Barre watched him steadily and Terice's teeth fretted at her painted lower lip, doubled. After Frawley, Barre, and Terice had passed, Frawley laid down his hand, glanced at Terice coldly, his dark eyes like two hard, shining coals, and then leaned back in his chair. Terice played rapidly, but rather desperately, darting quick sidewise looks to see what cards her opponents would play, worrying her lip with her teeth, and taking in the tricks as if her fingers itched to get hold of the cards. She made her bid and the rubber. The stakes were already a penny a point, and as the game progressed Terice became more and more eager, her small painted face showing hard anxious lines as she began to lose. At the end of an hour or so, during which Helene and Killian had joined the group of watchers, she flung down her cards, said something rather furiously gay and shrill about luck going against her, promised to pay her losses the next day—"No need to climb the gallery steps just for that!"—and left the table. Frawley, with the cold, still look that seemed habitual to him, paid her losses as well as his own, I believe, and the game stopped.

"Want a game, Lal?" asked Frawley.

"Aren't we going to have some music?" suggested Lal Killian. "How about it, Jo?"

Paggi shrugged.

"I'll sing if my wife will accompany me," he said. "I don't want you, Lal."

"How do you know I was going to offer my services?" asked Lal Killian lazily. He was standing beside Matil's chair, looking rather fixedly at the feather fan. It now trailed extravagantly over her arm, making the soft flesh look whiter than ever by contrast. "As a matter of fact, I was not. Though you might do worse."

"And I can do better," said Paggi ungraciously. "You make everything sound like a dance tune, Lal. You're like—a hand organ playing *Il Trovatore*."

"That's one opera," murmured Lal, just loud enough for Paggi to hear, "that a hand organ, with a good lively monkey attached, distinctly improves. Don't you agree with me, Matil?" His lazy eyes laughed a little at Paggi's back.

Helene said over her shoulder, "America has no reverence," and sat down at the piano and ran her supple fingers lightly over the keys.

It is curious how vividly and distinctly I recall the smallest events of that long evening: how Paggi sang first an opera air or two and then more sentimental songs, with his lambent eyes going constantly to Matil; how smoothly Helene accompanied him and how oddly bulky and strong she looked bent over the piano.

"She's got a peasant's back," murmured Aunt Lucy, rather more loudly than she ought to have done. "Never could understand what Huber saw in that woman. Never understood what he saw in any of his women," she continued, addressing me somewhat to my embarrassment. "That Terice—any woman could see through her. Scheming little hussy. Smirking, lying, posing. She's no good. She needed money and was only after Huber's pocketbook. He saw through her, though, at the last. Refused to marry her." She paused, much to my relief, for Terice sat on the divan not far from us and I felt quite sure that if the music stopped suddenly, as it often does, Aunt Lucy's booming undertones would carry on relentlessly. Julian Barre was regarding her somewhat apprehensively; he sat fairly close to me and probably heard every word the dreadful woman uttered.

Paggi's songs were getting stickier and stickier in sentiment. During the prelude to a song about pale hands crushing out life, or some such nonsense, Gerald Frawley moved quietly to Matil's side, saying something in a low voice. Lal Killian's lazy eyes awoke suddenly to ugly life; I thought likely he, too, had noted the curious little air of possession with which Gerald Frawley addressed the girl. I remember that Frawley picked up her crimson fan, playing with it, smoothing the soft feathers with his slender, cold-looking hands, appraising it with an air that somehow savored of proprietorship. Was it Gerald Frawley, then, whom she wanted to marry?

It was just then, I believe, that Paggi stopped singing.

"No more to-night," he said abruptly, stopping almost in the middle of a word, while Helene's fingers automatically followed the phrase along and she stared at him in some astonishment.

"Why Jo——" cried Terice.

"No, no," he repeated. "No more to-night. We have had enough music. Perhaps too much." He was clearly out of temper.

"But aren't we to hear Helene?" asked Killian, his eyes veiled and his face lazily good-natured again.

"Come on, Helene," urged Morse, coming out of his abstracted silence. "Sing for us."

"No!" said Jo Paggi. "I said no more music."

"You needn't accompany me," said Helene. "Lal can do——"

"No, no, no! When I say no more music I mean no more music." He was bent on being disagreeable.

Helene slammed the sheets of music together and tossed them on the piano top.

"Very well," she said, her voice rising and shaking a little. "Very well. Since you don't want to hear me——"

"Oh, Helene, don't," remonstrated Morse uncomfortably. Paggi shrugged, approached the fire, and stood with his back to it. His well-developed singer's figure looked powerful.

"This is a horrible place, anyhow. I don't see why you insisted on us coming, Matil. It's cold as a barn. I shall probably get influenza or something and not be in good voice all winter. It's a regular blizzard outside."

Helene, having apparently decided not to make a scene after all, followed him. She looked cold, too, and a little pinched. Her strong supple fingers were red.

"You have no idea how cold it is over there under the balcony. There's a draft from somewhere."

Terice withdrew her brooding eyes from the fire.

"I hate this place," she said viciously.

Barre stirred.

"O'Leary, here, will think we are ungrateful guests," he remarked.

Terice shot O'Leary a quick look: one which scanned him from head to foot. It was clear that he puzzled her slightly; also it seemed to me that a certain calculative look came into her eyes.

Aunt Lucy roused.

"You liked it well enough one time," she said to Terice. Her voice sounded like two rough surfaces rubbing against each other.

Terice's twinkling eyes shot venom; she was about to reply when Helene lifted her hand.

"What's that?" she cried sharply.

For a moment there was only the wild tumult of the wind outside and the sighing of flames in the fireplace. Then we heard, rising thinly and clearly above the rush of wind and snow, a sort of wail. The small sound slid upward and dwindled to nothing, and everyone was standing save Aunt Lucy, whose hands gripped the arms of her chair. Her face was livid, and she whispered hoarsely: "What's that?"

For a long moment we stood there waiting for the sound to be repeated. Jericho stirred, walked toward us, and stopped, listening, uneasy and curiously intent.

The sound came again, sharper in a little lull of the wind, and Lance O'Leary moved suddenly, breaking into a laugh that sounded forced.

"It's a cat," he said.

None of us moved. I think none of us quite believed him until he strode to the heavy front door and opened it, holding it with some difficulty against the surge of wind and fine particles of snow.

Through the snow advanced truly a cat. It was a

starved-looking creature, unbelievably thin and bony, with a mottled coat which was wet and glistening, and it stared at us with rapacious, greedy eyes.

O'Leary got the door shut again and bolted it.

"Whew, it's a wild night!" He returned, shivering, to the fireplace. "I don't blame the cat for wanting in. Here, kitty, here. Come over here and get warm." The cat refused, however, to come farther into the room. It sat down suddenly on its gaunt haunches and started to lick itself with a long, thin scarlet tongue. Jericho regarded the creature without much interest, somewhat to my surprise, for I had expected him immediately to give chase. Instead the collie dropped down on the floor again and sighed unhappily.

We must have sat for another hour or longer in growing uneasiness about the fire. Once or twice Brunker came silently into the circle and replenished the fire. Conversation languished and there was a growing disposition to cast quick and furtive glances toward the closed doors and gallery and corners of the great room. Once at least Matil hinted that it was getting late, but no one stirred and a certain tension of nerves tightened. And I did not like the behavior of the dog: while collies are, of course, extraordinarily sensitive, ecstatic at a smile, broken-hearted at a frown, still I did not think that losing his master five years ago could quite account for the dog's extraordinary unhappiness and disquiet. He was very restless, lying in one spot for a few moments and staring with wide eyes out into the room, his ears moving at every whisper of the wind, then rising, pacing slowly about the room, paying no attention at all to the cat, sniffing uneasily at the doors, and coming back to Matil's feet to whimper a little in his great throat and look up anxiously at her face as if for reassurance. I must say his uneasiness did not impress me favorably.

"Ugh! What a night!" said Lal Killian, shivering as a draft sighed wildly in the chimney, swooping the flames out toward the room a little and then sucking them furiously up the chimney again. "Sounds like all the witches in Christendom are out to-night, riding high." He glanced at the cat. "I'll bet that damn cat fell off a broomstick."

All of us looked at the cat.

It was unfortunate that just at that moment it finished scrubbing an ungainly long hind leg, rose, sniffed the air a little, and started toward the kitchen. And exactly in front of Gerald Frawley's room the thing stopped, its thin tail became stiff, its ears flattened a little, then it calmly veered its course around something *that was not there at all*—and went serenely on to the kitchen door.

It was then that Terice shrieked, a horrible high-pitched scream that brought us all out of our chairs and Brunker thrusting his flat face from the kitchen doorway. And it was at that scream, I learned later, that Annette bolted her door and started on her second bottle of sour red French wine.

Tumult arose within the lodge. Terice screamed as if she could not stop. Helene's teeth chattered furiously and she simply stood there staring and shaking and chattering. Aunt Lucy kept repeating over and over again in her loud harsh voice, quite as if Terice's shriek had released some spring in her: "It's Huber. He is here. It's Huber. He is here. Huber! Huber!"

And the men, helpless as men always are in the face of hysteria, were moving confusedly about, offering Terice water, brandy, a chair, and the fire tongs simultaneously. I never knew for what purpose the fire tongs were intended, and am under the impression that Morse, who offered them, did not know either.

Then I reached Terice, pushed away the crowding black shoulders, and simply clapped my hand over her mouth. She writhed and struggled to pull away from me, her eyes glaring rather frantically from between those sticky black eyelashes, and I think she tried to bite me, but everyone knows how impossible and extremely unpleasant it is to try to bite the palm of a hand. Her skin felt oily and rather like warm putty. Gradually her struggles quieted, she began to gasp a little, and as she relaxed at last I relinquished my clasp about her wiry shoulders. A scent of her heavy perfume clung to my white uniform as I stepped back.

Matil, white to the lips, but very straight, dominated us.

"We are all very tired," she said evenly. "I think we need rest." She paused, and added in as matter-of-fact a way as she could achieve: "Aunt Lucy, shall I ask Brunker to make your bedtime sandwich?"

Aunt Lucy, who at the cessation of Terice's screams had lapsed, herself, into a bleak, brooding silence, tore her still gaze from Huber Kingery's old room and said to Matil, more meekly than I had ever heard her

speak: "If you please, Matil." Then she stared somewhat savagely around the group until she came to Terice, when her great eyes became fixed and glaring.

"You—you hounded Huber to his death," she said,
suddenly harsh and loud and rasping again. Her wide
purplish mouth looked hungry; her eyes were incred-
ibly ugly. "It is because of you he—he had to die. You
and your threats! You and your hopes! He would
never have married you."

A choking sound came from Helene: it was something between a laugh and a sob and a scream. The
old woman whirled toward her.

"Or you either," she snarled. "You were both just
playthings. You needn't have been so jealous of each
other. Playthings! Bah!"

So remarkably vehement was her scorn and her
hatred that I really think that for a rather dreadful
moment no one dared move or speak. Then O'Leary
took up the little brass hand bell on a table near by.
Its clear little tinkle was in strange contrast to Aunt
Lucy's loud violence. Brunker entered so promptly that
I surmised his flat nose had been at the crack of the
kitchen door.

"Miss Lucy's sandwich, please, Brunker," said Matil through stiff lips.

"Determined to put me to bed, huh?" said Aunt
Lucy. "Well—I'll go. I'm a tired old woman and I'll
go to bed." She sent her wheel chair spinning smoothly
along the floor. We stepped back silently for her passage. At the door to her room she turned, gaunt and
black and menacing in her gray web.

"I'm stronger than any of you now," she boasted, and then said something that has rung in my memory ever since.

"And as for Huber, remember this: He deserved to die. He well deserved to die." She shook her grizzled head and gray beard with a grisly hint of triumph and vanished.

I don't remember much of how we separated. I think we were dazed with ugliness and the fear that had lurked about us all evening came boldly out and gripped us, so that our good-nights, our regret at leaving the warmth of the fires, Brunker's appearances with extra blankets, Matil's polite hope that we should rest well —all the little remarks and exclamations that courtesy demands—were strange and unfamiliar and very unreal. Nothing seemed real but the wind and the restless dog who was still pacing about and the ugly tirade we had just heard. I do remember that the cat returned silently from the kitchen so gorged with food that its sides stuck out and sat complacently on the hearthrug, staring knowingly at the black window panes.

When I went to my patient I found her sitting quite comfortably with a tray on her lap. Her abstinence in the matter of food at dinner was at once explained, for the innocuous-sounding bedtime sandwich was only a myth, and she was eating great slabs of bread and meat and cheese with gusto, her iron jaws working regularly and her eyes fixed avidly on a thick slice of what looked to be a suet pudding that was waiting for her.

"I'll just pound with my cane against the wall if I need you," she said as I left her. She nodded toward a cane that leaned against the head of the bed; it was a thick black stick, remarkably stout-looking. I adjusted the window, and as I closed the bathroom door had a last glimpse of Aunt Lucy looking as spiderish as ever, her face a dark earth color against the white pillow and the outing-flannel nightgown she wore—which was gray and white striped and entirely hideous—contriving to suggest enfolding cobwebs. Her eyes were staring from black pockets at nothing.

"Bolt your door to-night, Miss Keate," she rasped suddenly. "This is—" she dropped her voice to a stertorous whisper which made my skin crawl—"this is a bad place—a wicked place. The devil himself is loose in it."

I closed the two bathroom doors somewhat hurriedly between us. But I could not shut out the echo of that hoarse whisper.

For a good hour I rolled and tossed, quite unable to sleep. The company gathered at Hunting's End marched tirelessly through my mind, Aunt Lucy's unpleasant conversational efforts repeated themselves again and again in weird monotone, Matil's white face and feverish eyes looked at me and looked at me.

My very flesh ached with turning and twisting, and finally in desperation I rose, shivering as my feet met the icy floor, and got into slippers and my thick, quilted green dressing gown. I have never been a nervous woman but that night I had left a light burning in my own bedroom. It was only one of the lanterns, of course, whose wick I had turned very low, and I took the bail in my hand, lifted it from the hook, and went into the living room. It had occurred to me that if I could find some milk and heat it the drink would soothe me into sleep which I sorely needed. I did not know that I was to get no sleep that night.

Two lanterns, one above the stairway, one about midway the length of the room, were burning dimly. The fires had burned to red and gray ashes. The cat dozed, her shoulders and haunches and pointed ears making grotesque shadows along the rug. Jericho was nowhere to be seen. The room stretched emptily before me. I wondered where Annette kept the milk— probably in the pantry, since they could have brought only canned milk among the supplies.

I was hoping I could find a can opener as I passed the door to the room which Gerald Frawley was using. I stopped suddenly. Through the log door I caught distinctly a little murmur of voices.

I have never known what impulse led me to forego my errand to the kitchen and decide so suddenly to remain in the living room and see just who came out of that room. Surely there was nothing out of the way or unusual in the fact that Gerald Frawley and some other member of the party desired a little private conversation. Lay it to what you please—my curiosity, my lack of good taste, my restlessness or meddlesomeness, anything—the fact remains that I simply turned and walked back to the fireplace at the north end of the room where the ashes looked reddest.

As I neared the fireplace I found I was not alone in the room. Signor Paggi started from the depths of an armchair drawn up to the fire, then settled back again, mumbling something under his breath. He looked fat and thick in his florid silk dressing gown; his shirt front loomed dimly white in the semi-twilight.

"Oh, it's you," he said. "Couldn't you sleep either?"

"No," I replied shortly. I set my lantern on a table, walked to the fireplace, and sat down not far from Paggi. We were in the shadow there but the log door to Gerald Frawley's room was directly in the mellow little area of light from one of the lanterns. The long room was cold and the shadows were black in the corners and under the balcony and beneath the stairs.

At least a quarter of an hour dragged by and still no one emerged from Frawley's room. José Paggi glanced at his wrist; a watch crystal caught for an instant a red reflection from the fireplace. As I said nothing and the moments prolonged themselves, Paggi became restless, squirming a little in his chair, worrying an unlighted cigarette, turning up his silk collar and turning it down again. It occurred to me that he might be waiting for something—an idle notion which only his extreme uneasiness put into my head.

It was just then, I believe, that a soft whispering sound caught my ears. I sat upright, and saw Paggi stiffen in his chair.

At my questioning look he mumbled: "I thought—I heard something."

And I was sure I had. A curious little froufrou of motion. Could it be very light footsteps above our heads? On the gallery?

In another fraction of a second I would have turned to look toward the gallery railing. But just then, without any warning at all, a crash of sound shook the world.

It shattered the silence of Hunting's End. And amid the shock of the reverberations came a sluggish heavy. sound as of something falling—something heavy and inert.

Paggi and I were standing, staring into each other's eyes as if frozen. I saw him run his tongue over his lips; his eyes looked terrified. Then we both whirled toward the bedroom doors.

The door into Gerald Frawley's room was open. We both ran toward that room.

Gerald Frawley was lying on his face on the floor, a foolish inertly sprawled figure in yellow-striped pajamas. His feet were bare. A light burned over the bed.

Paggi squatted down, turned him over. He gasped something that sounded like "Kil——" and died. He had been shot exactly through the heart. It was Gerald Frawley: his features were unmistakable. But his head, resting against Paggi's arm, was bare and shining and white. A toupee, the hair very thick and black, was lying on the dressing table.

CHAPTER V

ON THE GALLERY

THE whole thing was terrible to see, so ugly, in fact, that I simply cannot bring myself to describe it, though I can still see it in every detail. Seasoned to ugliness though I am, having served in the operating rooms for more years than it is necessary to mention, still the sight turned me a little sick and I leaned against the dressing table, while my head whirled dizzily, and I could not drag my eyes from the torn thing that Paggi held on his knee and arm.

A little rustle under my fingers pulled my gaze automatically that way. "Matil, my darling," leaped at me from a letter lying there.

One's mind works curiously in a crisis. If this letter were meant for Matil, far better it should reach her through my hands than pass the rounds of the whole party. I could hear frightened voices and outcries now rising from the bedrooms and living room and gallery; footsteps were running. My fingers closed over the two pieces of paper and thrust them into the capacious pocket of my dressing gown as Julian Barre burst into the room. I was sure that neither he nor Paggi saw me.

Barre had got into a bathrobe; Morse, who followed him closely, had flung a blanket around him; they were both kneeling beside Paggi, staring at the burden he held, when O'Leary appeared. He, too, had tossed a blanket over his pajamas; it occurred to me briefly that even in his dishevelment he looked somehow cool and collected. He gave the huddle on the floor one sharp glance, Paggi, Barre, and Morse another, shot one look at me, stepped lightly past the body, which lay between bed and dressing table, and edged over to the window. He stood there for a second or two, not touching anything, then went to the door leading to the bathroom. It was closed and bolted securely on the bedroom side.

"What is it? What's happened?" Women's faces, such masks of white terror as to be scarcely recognizable, were staring from the doorway. A dull heavy pounding was coming from somewhere. Brunker, his cold face colder, one hand clutching at his trousers to hold them up, was looking over Helene's shoulder.

Then Matil was there, brushing aside Terice's clutching hands and Helene's bulk. She looked tall and straight in her long white satin negligee; her eyes sought the thing that Paggi still supported as if he could not relinquish it.

The pounding grew more furious.

"What's happened?" It was Killian pushing past the crowding faces at the door.

"Frawley has been killed," said O'Leary. His clear voice cut into the confusion. Things suddenly became less blurred. The kaleidoscope seemed to whirl all at once into focus and to right itself.

"Frawley has been killed," repeated O'Leary. "And someone in this house killed him."

Terice opened her mouth as if to shriek but perhaps her throat was dry. In the silence rose a dog's howl. It was a long, gradually descending chromatic, inexpressibly weird and chilling.

My knees began to tremble; I leaned heavily against the dressing table. If I could only cover that shining dead head with the black toupee that lay there, perhaps I should feel better; less sick. Then I knew that the pounding was from Aunt Lucy's cane, and that the howling dog was Jericho, of course.

"Miss Lucy," I mumbled through oddly numb lips, and the others moved aside dazedly, as if they did not know what they were doing, to let me pass.

"Get me into my chair," commanded Aunt Lucy; her voice was harsh and shaking. She seemed to know without asking what had happened. I obeyed and had so far recovered myself as to take one of the blankets and bundle it around my patient's feet. It was icy cold.

"Give me that shawl. Who is it?"

"Frawley. Gerald Frawley."

"Dead?"

"Yes."

"I heard the shot. Who did it?"

I shook my head. Her gaunt hands were trembling. Her purple lips kept moving, forming words that were without sound.

She motioned toward the living room and I pushed the chair through the door. After that she grasped the wheels herself, as usual, and sent the chair smoothly toward the figures huddled at Frawley's door.

The dog howled again, long and clear and in a fashion that made my heart stand still. He must be close at hand, likely in Matil's room. I opened the door and let him out into the living room, though he did not seem anxious to go, walking past me with his head down and his tail dragging. The window was open a few inches, and a shutter was open and blown back by the wind, and snow was sifting in. I crossed the room, closed and bolted the shutter and closed the window. Already the silver slippers Matil had worn that night were soaked through.

Jericho followed me along the living room. Aunt Lucy had pushed her chair directly into the doorway. They seemed to have recovered their voices for they were all talking at once, excitedly, fearfully, anxiously. As I reached the door I heard Lance O'Leary's quiet voice.

"Since you ask me, Miss Matil, I will. It is not a suicide. That is clear. There is no revolver. Someone must do it, and, as you say, better a stranger."

"That is exactly the trouble," said Killian. "You are a stranger. The only stranger. Your own con- duct——"

"Please, Lal," interrupted Matil pleadingly. Killian returned her gaze coldly, blankly, almost as if she had not spoken, and just then Paggi sneezed, and sneezed again. It was rather horrible because the body slipped a little, and Terice gave a half-stifled scream.

"We'll let it lie here on the floor," said O'Leary.

"Here, Paggi. Let me help you. Gently, now. That's better." Paggi rose stiffly, still looking downward.

"On the floor?" remonstrated Morse. "Why, that's brutal. Let's at least put the poor fellow on the bed." He looked terribly shaken; he had left his glasses off in his haste and his face looked thinner and haggard and had a dazed expression.

"If you'll give me a towel . . ." I said. O'Leary, I think, handed me one and my fingers shook as I tied it carefully around Frawley's jaw, knotting it on top of that bare, shining head. There was a little fringe of black hair above the ears and along the back.

"Miss Matil," said O'Leary abruptly, "you said wisely that someone must take charge of this affair until we can get the proper authorities here. You asked me to do it. Did you mean that?"

"Yes," said Matil, without taking her steady eyes from O'Leary's face.

"Very well. Listen." O'Leary strode to the window. In the silence we could hear the wind and snow surging wildly outside. "A man could not last ten minutes in this storm. We can't possibly go for help till morning. You must give me authority to do as I think best —at least till we can get help."

"Matil——" cried Killian.

"Matil, my dear child——" began Barre.

She silenced them with a motion of her hand. Aunt Lucy's mouth was very grim and set.

"I may as well tell you," said Matil steadily. "Mr. O'Leary is—is a detective." I could not tell whether O'Leary approved of her announcement or not. Certainly his gray eyes were enigmatic. But there was no doubt but the others disapproved and that very vigorously.

"What do you mean?" cried Killian.

"A detective! Why did you bring a detective?" flashed Helene sharply. Her eyes were two green slits in her white face. One and all stared from O'Leary to Matil and back again; anger, suspicion, distrust, and above all stark fear looked out of their pallid faces.

"My dear Matil," remonstrated Barre, "you should have told me of this. You should have let me advise you." His words hissed a little clumsily, and his face looked oddly shrunken about the mouth. I looked more closely; gaps appeared here and there in his upper teeth; probably the gentleman wore what is called a partial plate, and in his hurry and confusion had forgotten to place it in his mouth. I reflected that only a Julian Barre could yet appear suave and poised without his teeth, and then O'Leary stepped past the huddle on the floor and horror swept over me again.

"Why did you bring a detective?" cried Terice thinly. "Matil Kingery, why did you bring a detective *here?*"

"Huber——" muttered Aunt Lucy. "Huber. He was murdered here, too. In this very room. He had on his pajamas. His feet were bare. I found him. He lay right there."

Hysteria threatened us all. The very air trembled.

Matil pointed to Frawley's body.

"You ask me why I brought a detective?" she said. Her voice was so cold and so brittle that one felt it would break, shiver into screaming fragments. *"That is reason enough."* With an effort she steadied herself, turned and led the way from the room.

We must have made a strange procession. O'Leary was the last one to leave the room. He closed the heavy log door carefully.

We all huddled over the north fireplace where the chairs we had sat in during the long evening were still clustered. Brunker worked at the fire, pausing now and then to hitch up his trousers, and we watched him and huddled closer, and shivered.

I caught myself looking at the bluntly carved words in the stone above the mantel. "The End of all Good Hunting is Nearer than you Dream." The end of all hunting had come to Gerald Frawley. Had he dreamed it was so near? Only a few short hours ago he had sat there, smoking, talking, shuffling cards; had he had no premonition, no fear?

"Call Annette," said O'Leary quietly to Brunker. "Call her at once. Stay here, please, everyone; I shall return in a few moments." He disappeared into the kitchen; returned shortly, went from bedroom to bedroom, finally up the gallery stairs, and at last returned to the silent group near the fireplace. He must have stopped long enough in his own room to hurry into some clothes for when he came back he wore trousers and a coat over his pajamas. No one had spoken. This struck me as curious until I recalled that the ghost of that other murder, of that shared secret of five years ago, had likely risen in everyone's memory.

The dog had retreated to the farthest corner of the

room and was huddled there, his eyes never blinking and fastened on that closed door. Presently the door from the kitchen was pushed open again and Annette followed Brunker toward us. She was an extraordinary, disheveled figure in a faded blue kimono which did not conceal her entire vastness and was augmented with a quilt from the bed which dragged behind her. Her hair was hanging in wild gray shreds about her face, which was red and swollen, with her eyes puffy and looking bleary and the pouches under them red. She was not a pretty sight. But none of us was that. Brunker must have told her what had happened for she asked no questions.

Brunker lit a few more lanterns; the place was lighter, the fire began to send up fitful little flames.

"There is one course that will save us all much trouble and anxiety," began O'Leary in his clear, quiet voice. "As I have said, a man couldn't live in the storm to-night. By morning perhaps some of us can get through to Nettleson. The person who shot Gerald Frawley is here among us. There is no one concealed in the lodge. Doors and shutters and windows are all closed and solidly bolted. And moreover the storm itself prohibits the possibility of anyone making his way to or away from the lodge. The murderer is here." He stopped, looked slowly around the circle of blood-drained faces. His eyes were very clear, so curiously clear and lucent that you felt he could see your very bones. "I am speaking to you, the murderer of Gerald Frawley. Will you confess?"

My heart leaped into my throat and dropped back

again. Did he dare—would anyone speak—would one of those drawn, ghastly faces break up, mouth words? Lance O'Leary took out his watch.

"I'll give you three minutes to decide," he said slowly and very quietly. "Think well. And remember —you can never escape yourself."

And he looked steadily at the shining little face of the watch.

In every person's lifetime come moments of crisis, moments of unbearable suspense and anxiety, and I have known my share. But I had never experienced, and hope I never shall again, such a three minutes. Knowing that the murderer was one of that huddled little group; knowing that one of those still, awful faces concealed blood-guilt; knowing, as the seconds ticked softly one after the other, that at any second that confession might come—knowing all this, those fateful three moments of breathless, waiting, *listening* silence were ghastlier, more unspeakably ugly, than anyone who did not experience them can possibly realize. I think they made a mark on all our lives.

Just when the strain was unendurable and I felt that my taut nerves would snap, that I should scream out, in spite of myself, and I knew I wasn't guilty, O'Leary looked up, replaced his watch, and let his eyes travel slowly about the group. I can still see them: the men desperately composed with tight, drawn faces, Matil white and cold, Terice biting her finger nails, her crassly gold hair in her eyes, Helene a lump of fat yellow dough wrapped in flowing black silk, Aunt Lucy ugly and black in her chair. Annette's features were losing their blunted look and her eyes were beginning to be less vague, shrewder. And all of them, so unlike, were yet made akin by the fear that stamped itself on every face.

"Very well, then. Take what comes." O'Leary's eyes were hard, gray, like the water of a northern sea.

"Who was the first one in the room?"

I looked at Paggi, he looked at me; we spoke simultaneously.

"You were sitting by the fireplace? Here?" went on O'Leary.

"Yes," replied Paggi. "I was cold in my room and didn't feel sleepy. I came down here to get thoroughly warm. I was sitting here when Miss Keate came out of her room, walked down toward the kitchen about as far as Frawley's door, stopped all at once, and came back and sat down right there in that chair."

O'Leary looked at me inquiringly.

"I was on my way to the kitchen for some milk. As I passed Gerald Frawley's door I—heard voices."

"Voices!" shouted Aunt Lucy, leaning forward.

"Voices?" said O'Leary in a still way. "Then— who came out of the room?"

"No one."

"I don't understand, Miss Keate," said O'Leary after a pause.

"It's just as I told you. I heard voices. I decided to sit by the fire for a moment or two; it was very cold. This gentleman—Mr. Paggi—was already here. But no one came out of that room, either before or after the sound of the revolver shot."

O'Leary looked at me thoughtfully.

"Which way did you face? Arrange the chairs as they were then, please."

"My chair faced the fireplace. Not directly; it was more at an angle—like this." Helene rose from it somewhat reluctantly and moved to another chair.

O'Leary measured it with his eyes, turned and looked in the direction my vision would have embraced.

"You could see the bedroom doors from Miss Matil's down to Mr. Barre's without turning your head. Frawley's door was on the edge of your vision. Right?"

"Y-yes," I agreed hesitantly. "That is, Mr. Frawley's room was, as you say, on the edge of my range of vision, but I'm quite sure any movement at the door would have caught my eye."

"Can you swear to that, Miss Keate?" asked O'Leary softly.

"No," I said, vexed with myself. "No, I can't swear to it. However, I *can* swear to this. We were sitting here when the sound of the shot came. We both jumped to our feet. It was only a second or two before we turned to look toward his door. And I am sure no one was there."

O'Leary considered this a moment in silence.

"The door into Frawley's room was closed, of course," he said.

"No," said Paggi. "It was open."

I nodded.

"It was open. I suppose that is why we ran immediately to that room."

"You couldn't tell from what direction the shot seemed to come?" O'Leary was looking at me and I answered.

"No. No. It seemed to—fill the whole place."

"And the bedroom door was open?" repeated O'Leary musingly.

"Yes."

"And you saw no one besides Paggi in the living room?"

"There was no one," I answered definitely.

"How much time elapsed between the sound of the shot and your turning to look directly at that door? You have hinted that you did not turn at once."

I recalled that frozen second or two of suspense during which Paggi and I had faced each other, and looked at Paggi in some perplexity.

"Not more than a second or two," he said, frowning. "In fact, my recollection is that we turned at once. And I am sure that there was no one to be seen."

"And you, Miss Keate?"

"I—really, I can't say. You see, we heard the shot; it was loud and unexpected. We jumped to our feet and looked at each other, and it seems to me we stood dead still for a second or two, then we both turned. And the room was empty and the door was open."

"Could not someone have come out that door and got out of sight before you turned?"

I shook my head decisively.

"I am sure I should have seen any movement. I have a strong impression that there was none."

"This room was fairly light?"

"There were lanterns, three, I think, burning: one that I had placed on the table, one in the center of the room, one at the foot of the stairway. It was shadowy over here by the fireplace but the door into Frawley's room was not in the shadow."

O'Leary looked meditatively in that direction.

"Your room is the first door to the right of Frawley's room, isn't it, Barre? And yours to the left, Killian? Killian's room is the nearest. Now then, Miss Keate, could not someone have got to Killian's door before you——"

"See here, what do you mean by that?" broke in Killian.

"—before you turned?" finished O'Leary blandly.

"I was alone in my room," said Killian.

"I don't doubt that," replied O'Leary. "How about it, Miss Keate?"

It is not O'Leary's way to try to beat down impartial testimony and I was a little surprised that he kept harping on that point; however, at the time I did not know what he knew.

I shook my head again; I was becoming a little irritated. Heaven knew I had not asked to be there in full view of that sinister door when a murder occurred behind it; inwardly I cursed the impulse that had led me toward hot milk.

"There was no one in this room save myself and Mr. Paggi," I said stubbornly. "There was no movement, no sound——" I stopped abruptly. The moment before the shot had crashed in upon the silence of Hunting's End returned to my memory, and with it the susurrant froufrou that sounded like silk and soft footsteps on the gallery.

"What is it, Miss Keate?" asked O'Leary softly, his eyes shining a little as if he had known that eventually something would come out.

I turned to Paggi.

"That sound on the gallery!" I cried. "There was someone there."

Paggi looked at me uneasily. I could see something glistening on his swarthy forehead though the room was still cold.

He said nothing.

"Don't you remember?" I prodded, my irritation growing as he looked stupidly at me. "Just before we heard the shot, you said you heard something, and we both listened and heard light footsteps on the gallery?" I looked speculatively at Helene and Terice; surely one of them would admit to being out of her room and on the gallery. Terice, her face unbelievably haggard and looking years older, was nibbling at one hard forefinger, and Helene simply sat, a lump of yellow-white terror, and stared at me.

Paggi looked perplexedly from me to O'Leary.

"I don't know what she's talking about," he said. "I didn't hear any noise."

Well, of course, he didn't know that Lance O'Leary happened to know me rather well. And while I have my faults, I have never been afraid to tell the truth. I did not scruple now.

"You did," I said flatly. "I don't know why you are lying about it. I have the best of memories. You said,

'I heard something,' and we both listened and heard something on the gallery. I was just about to look when—I heard the shot."

Aunt Lucy opened her mouth as if about to take a bite and then snapped it shut again, eyeing me with a kind of grim approval.

O'Leary was fumbling absent-mindedly in his pockets; I knew that a silly, shabby stub of pencil would be forthcoming, and it was. It was the only eccentricity O'Leary allowed himself, and I had time for a fleeting wish that he would lose the pencil before Paggi again astonished me. He looked straight at Lance O'Leary and, in the smoothest voice in the world, reaffirmed his complete ignorance of any sound or any footsteps.

O'Leary's eyes were apparently fascinated by the little red pencil which he slipped forward and backward through his fingers.

"You thought it was a woman?" he asked me quietly, unheeding Paggi's denial. That gentleman flushed a deep dark red and Terice moved restlessly. Evidently O'Leary had not missed my inquiring glance at Helene and Terice, who were the only women who had rooms on the gallery.

"Why, yes. That is, it was a sort of whisper like —silk." I hesitated, finding it difficult to describe and impossible to identify that elusive, fleeting little sound, so suddenly and terrifying erased by the crash which had followed it. Which had followed it! I rose at once, and looked upward at the gallery; the little rounded balcony where the stairs emerged was directly opposite Frawley's door—that door *which had been open!*

Lance O'Leary met my eyes warningly. I stopped the words that were on my lips and sank back into my chair, which was not difficult for my knees were shaking again. Had it been Terice? Had she stood on that balcony? Was it close enough to Frawley's room for her to aim and fire a revolver with so deadly a precision? Could it have been Helene? And above all, what had there been about that little rustle of movement that was so convincingly feminine?

O'Leary seemed to have followed my thoughts.

"You said it sounded like very light footsteps and the little rustle of silk," he said meditatively. "Do you have any idea when the door into Frawley's room opened?"

His question was so very gentle, so very quiet and restrained, that I knew it was important.

"I only know it was open when I turned," I said slowly, weighing every word. "But I don't know when it opened. I know that I had heard no sound of anyone leaving that room and I am sure I would have heard it as that was what——" I stopped in some confusion.

"Was what you were waiting for?" finished Aunt Lucy grimly, but looking at me in an approving way.

"But, Miss Keate," said O'Leary, "if you heard voices in that room and there was no one there when you entered but the dead man, someone *must* have come out that door."

"There's the window," I hazarded uncertainly.

"Which was closed and fastened and its shutters

bolted when I entered the room," said O'Leary. "And
I presume neither you nor Paggi bolted it after you
found the dead body."

"We did not," I assured him. "But there's the adjoining bathroom. It leads to another room, doesn't
it?"

"It leads to mine," said Julian Barre promptly but
a little uneasily.

"Frawley's door into the bathroom was bolted, too,
on his side," said O'Leary. "Luckily for your peace of
mind, Barre."

Barre did look relieved and I can't say that I blamed
him. Even I, who knew myself to be innocent, still had
felt a certain pleasant security in the fact that José
Paggi had had his eyes upon me when the shot was
fired and thus I had an unshakable alibi; this was a
primitive feeling for, of course, in spite of the horror
the night had held and the hysteria that threatened us
all, I yet retained common sense enough to realize that
no one would suspect me. At least such was my earnest
hope.

Then my attention flew back to what O'Leary was
saying. Paggi began to look more and more uncomfortable under O'Leary's searching questions and finally hedged a little, mopping his forehead with his
gay silk sleeve and at last guessing that someone might
come out of that door into the living room without our
knowledge.

But I stuck to my original belief, though I was much
troubled about it and inclined for the first time in my
life to doubt the evidence of my own ears and eyes.

"See here, Miss Keate," said O'Leary finally. "You say you heard voices in Frawley's room, that no one came out of that door, that no one but the dead man was there when you entered the room. And yet, murder was done and the only other exits closed and bolted. It—well, it simply doesn't add up."

CHAPTER VI

THERE IS MURDER IN THIS LODGE

"I can't help that," I said sharply. "The adding up is your business. I only know what I saw and heard. But I know that."

O'Leary looked at me in some exasperation but apparently decided to let the question drop for the time being; at any rate, he began to inquire of the others, one at a time in a very searching and detailed fashion, as to their hearing the sound of the shot, where they had been, how they had got to the murdered man's room and exactly what they had seen on getting there. He stressed the latter point a little, although they all seemed somewhat confused. Helene only remembered that she met Terice in the gallery outside her room and that they were just a few steps behind O'Leary in getting down the stairs. Morse said that he and Barre collided in the living room and both gasped, "What is it?" before they saw us in Frawley's room and Barre and then Morse entered. Brunker said in a cold, unpleasant voice that he'd been asleep, the sound of the shot had awakened him, he had heard the commotion and followed the others to the door of Frawley's room. And Lal Killian insisted that he was sound asleep, and though the crash of the shot must have awakened him,

he didn't realize what it was until he heard voices in
the next room. And all save Paggi professed to have
been awakened from a sound sleep by the revolver
shot. Not an insomnia victim among them!

O'Leary appeared to take an interest in Killian's
statement for he questioned the young man at length;
and I, myself, thought it odd that Killian, with only a
wall between him and Frawley, should have been the
last one on the scene. He had heard no voices, Killian
added with much decision, until after the shot was
fired. He repeated this with a defiant look at me. It
was just there that Paggi stirred and cleared his throat.

"I've just remembered something," he said in an
apologetic manner that did not seem quite genuine.
"I—it doesn't mean anything, of course, but you
know Gerald Frawley died—on my arm. We got there
just as he died." He did falter a little there but he
went on composedly enough; it even seemed to me
there was a touch of satisfaction in his voice and in the
oblique glance he cast toward Killian. "And just as he
died he gasped something." He stopped again.

Killian regarded him with an indifference that, I believe, was a little forced, and O'Leary said coldly:
"Well?"

"It was just a syllable. He didn't live to complete
the word. He gasped 'Kil——' and died." Paggi
pulled his bright dressing gown tighter around his deep
chest and smoothed down the lapels before he added
casually: "Probably tried to say he'd been killed, poor
fellow."

Killian's face had darkened furiously and he jumped

up, took a quick step toward Paggi, and tripped on the folds of the blanket he had clutched about him. As O'Leary said quickly, "Did you hear that, Miss Keate?" Killian sat down again—rather more abruptly, I think, than he had intended—and cast a look of baffled rage at the blanket.

"Did you hear that also, Miss Keate?" repeated O'Leary.

"Yes, I did," I snapped; I longed to deny Paggi's statement as he had mine but could not. It did not lessen my irritation to see a faint, complacent little smile hover upon Paggi's full red lips.

"What was your impression regarding it?"

"I was in no state of mind to receive a clear impression," I said acidly. "*I* was completely bewildered and taken by surprise."

"Still you managed to see quite a little," murmured Paggi wickedly. "Certain papers on the dressing table, for instance." He scrutinized his finger nails, smiling faintly in a maddeningly satisfied way, and while I have never entertained murderous desires, still at that moment I could have choked the singer with the greatest pleasure. My fingers itched with longing, especially as I noted the singular silence that greeted his words. Everyone was looking at me—everyone, that is, except Paggi and Annette, who was staring at the fire. And it seemed to me that those converging eyes shared a certain secret conjecture; I could only comprehend that that knowledge existed among them. Have you ever put your foot on ground that looked solid and found it was, in fact, marshy and that curious ripples and waves followed the pressure of your weight and spread out and out and out as if the quicksand were alive under your touch? Well, that is something the sensation I experienced then, though I am not in the least a fanciful person.

"Papers," said Newell Morse slowly, his troubled eyes searching my face. "Did you—were there—what——" He turned from me to Paggi. "What do you mean, Jo?"

"Ask the nurse," advised Paggi, shrugging his bulky shoulders.

Terice's hard little hands were opening and closing greedily at her sides; Matil was leaning forward, blue eyes like swords piercing mine; Killian's eyes swerved suddenly from me to Morse's anxious countenance and narrowed thoughtfully; Aunt Lucy shot out a long, outing-flannel arm toward me—happily I was just out of reach—and she said hoarsely:

"Were there papers? What are they? Where are they?"

I glanced at O'Leary in indecision. Should I hand over the letter to him at once or put off the questions as best I might?

"Did you see any papers?" he asked quietly.

"Yes. There was a letter on the dressing table. Here it is." I reached into my pocket, drew out a sheet of paper and passed it to him. In the act of passing it I realized that, of the two sheets, I had given him only one, which he was already glancing through. Apparently everyone was watching O'Leary intently and I felt stealthily in my pocket to be sure the other piece was still there; a tiny crackle of paper reassured me and I resolved to give it to him later. There was entirely too much interest displayed by those haggard, fear-ridden faces to suit my taste.

No one moved while O'Leary looked swiftly through the note, though I could hear Aunt Lucy breathing heavily and Paggi, for all his complacence, was watching O'Leary's face furtively but intently. Morse rose and took a step or two toward O'Leary, though he did not seem by nature an impatient man.

"What is it?" he asked, in a voice that was husky with suspense. "I—is that for me?"

"Yes," replied O'Leary quietly. "It seems to refer to a conversation you had with Frawley before dinner last night."

"Then give it——" He checked himself and said more mildly but as anxiously: "May I have it, then?"

"Why, certainly." O'Leary handed him the slip of paper. It must have been a very brief note for Newell Morse read it at a glance and then let his eyes linger on a portion of it while his lips moved unconsciously as if he were memorizing some part of it.

Then without warning he took a quick step toward the fireplace, tossed the paper lightly upon the flames, and turned to face us rather defiantly, his body braced and his hands clinched tightly and outflung a little as if he expected active resistance. But the only real resistance came, surprisingly enough, from Aunt Lucy, who thrust her wheel chair forward in a quick swoop.

"Newell, what are you doing? Give me that! Quick! It's going to burn," she demanded with strident vehemence. I heard Terice gasp and Matil rose, twisting her hands and looking at O'Leary as if for help.

"No, Miss Lucy," said Morse firmly. "It is mine and I——"

"Get out of my way. You are crazy! Quick! It is burning." A tiny flame shot up from the paper and seemed to infuriate Lucy Kingery for both her gaunt hands clutched madly at Morse. "You are out of your mind!" she cried wildly. "Can't you see? It's Huber I must know about. The truth about Huber. Someone knows. It may be—it may be——" She was gasping incoherently and Newell Morse resisted with some difficulty the iron clutch of her hands. The whole thing was extremely unpleasant, so ugly in fact that I felt I couldn't endure it. I reached out, took hold of the bar across the back of the armchair, and simply pulled chair and Aunt Lucy and all backward away from the fire. She dragged Morse a step or two with her but finally relinquished her grip, and he straightened up, looking very uncomfortable, and shot me a look of gratitude.

The paper that had caused the furor was now a brown crisp and O'Leary thrust the toe of his bedroom slipper into the flames and broke its crispness so that it disappeared among the burning logs. A smell of scorched leather crept over the room.

Aunt Lucy twisted her long neck, gave me a venomous look, growled, "Oh, it's you, is it?" and O'Leary said quickly:

"Sit down, Miss Matil."

I glanced about. Every pair of eyes was riveted on

the spot where the paper had burned; I strove to read those eyes, and those strangely intent faces, but I could not. They were too guarded, too secretive, too wary of observance.

Then all at once Terice sighed and leaned back in her chair and crossed one knee over the other; her bare ankles, emerging from the somewhat wilted negligee she wore of belaced pink satin, looked cold and hard and were not pretty; she let a soiled pink mule dangle from one toe and her exposed foot, though small enough, was thick and flat-instepped. Apparently she had not washed her face that night for there were still patches of white paste and brilliant dabs of rouge adhering to her cheeks which, in the last hour, looked old and rather sunken. She'd have looked better in more clothing for the negligee did not accomplish much in that direction, but it did not become me to say so.

"Well," she said, sharply flippant, "that's that. Newell isn't going to give us a chance to know what was in his precious note. How about you, Mr. O'Leary? You read the note, and I think it is our business as much as Newell's to know what Gerald Frawley said. Will you tell us?"

O'Leary contemplated the small red pencil in his hands. Was he going to tell them? Surely he remembered every word of the note; otherwise he would not have let it burn.

"There was nothing secretive about it," he said easily. "Just a reference to some conversation between Frawley and Morse and a number. What was the number, Morse? I can't just remember it."

Silence, breathlessness—the very air palpitating with eagerness.

If we had only known then what we were to know later!

Morse cleared his throat.

"It was just—just an errand Gerald Frawley asked me to do for him in case——" He stuck, cleared his throat again and went on: "Just an errand. But he asked me not to tell. Not to tell anyone." His voice faltered again.

O'Leary's clear eyes went back to the pencil; I longed to know what lay behind his clear, cool gaze and his thoughtful, clear-featured face.

But without going further into the matter of the note, O'Leary began again to question us as to our exact locations at the moment of hearing the shot. It was then, I believe, that Matil directed Brunker to bring the room chart, which she placed in O'Leary's hands and to which he referred now and then, though I was sure that every room and every door and every window in the lodge were etched as sharply upon his mind as if he had spent years of his life there at Hunting's End.

He questioned us at such length that I, myself, grew restive and ill at ease, and I could see that the others were similarly affected, for Helene's green eyes began to flare wildly and her supple, strong fingers twitched; Killian lit and smoked innumerable cigarettes, rapidly, one after the other; Julian Barre kept running his hands over the crisp wave in his hair, touching his mouth with a handkerchief, changing his position rest-

lessly, lighting and immediately throwing away cigarettes, and watching Matil anxiously as if he feared
for her collapse. But Matil only grew whiter and more
and more like a frozen, horror-carved little statue.
And when the collapse came it was in an unexpected
quarter.

Though, as to that, I think we were all about at the
breaking point; in my long acquaintance with Lance
O'Leary I had never known him to be so deliberately
cruel in his nagging repetitions. Afterward I comprehended that it was because he hoped to wring out a
confession but at the time it seemed needlessly cruel
and harassing. Even Annette lost her shrewd self-
possession and grew hysterical, lapsing into staccato-ed
French as she reiterated the facts of her retiring to her
own room off the kitchen after Brunker had helped her
with the dinner dishes. Upon pressure she admitted to
two bottles of wine and insisted that her bedroom door
was bolted and she had gone to sleep and had known
nothing until the sound of the shot aroused her. Then,
she said, she was afraid to come out, and muttered
something, with a side glance at Aunt Lucy, about having expected some such thing.

"What do you mean by that?" asked O'Leary
coldly. "Do you mean you expected someone to be
murdered? Why should you expect murder? What do
you know of it?"

"Nothing. Nothing. I know nothing about it," cried
Annette, her pale blue eyes, like bits of opaque blue
glass, darting here and there and returning always to
O'Leary.

"Then why did you expect it?"

"I—I——" She made a helpless gesture with her wide hands. *"Je ne sais pas."*

"But you must know. You say you expected some such thing. Come now, just what did you mean by that?" insisted O'Leary. "Or—were you only talking?"

Annette drew herself up, vast and enormous and proud in her quilt and flesh, cast one defiant look at O'Leary, a less defiant one at Aunt Lucy, and all at once shrunk back and her shoulders sagged and she began to tremble as if she could not stop.

"I knew it was coming. I knew it. I knew it because —because there is——" She tried to control her shaking voice and the words when they came were husky and deliberate and carried the strangest feeling of impending fate. "There is murder in this hunting lodge. It has waited five years. There is murder in this hunting lodge."

There is murder in this lodge.

It was then that the collapse came, and it was from Terice, though every one of us was near it. She uttered a curious sound that was halfway between a giggle and a shriek and a cough and savored of all of them and went immediately into a fit of hysterics that seemed very real and threatened to infect us all for our nerves were tight to the breaking point. Aunt Lucy grasped the arms of her chair and mumbled harshly to herself and stared at Gerald Frawley's door, and Helene began to sob loudly and wildly, and Matil and I, our hands cold and shaking, tried to bring Terice out of her spasm, and Annette clutched her quilt around her and shook, her mouth wavering and loose. Even Brunker's cold face looked discomposed and the wide black pupils of his eyes shone and glimmered under their bare lids. And Barre and Killian and Morse were all talking at once though, through the turmoil- I could distinguish no words.

Then O'Leary's clear voice controlled the confusion by its cool, unhurried simplicity.

"Look here," he said. We watched his slender figure make its way to one of the windows. He threw off the catch, opened the window, unbolted and leaned out to open the shutters. Terice quieted for a moment and Helene's racking sobs arrested themselves. The cold gray daylight of early morning filtered into the room and with it snow.

"It is still snowing steadily," said O'Leary. "There has been wind, too, and the snow is badly drifted. A man could not live ten minutes in that storm. It will be impossible to get to Nettleson."

It was very still in the lodge. Gradually we grasped the import of his words.

"Do you mean—*Will we have to stay here?*" screamed Helene.

"Not only that," said O'Leary rather grimly. I think Morse was the first to catch the significance of that grimness. He went a kind of gray white and stepped toward O'Leary.

"Why, then, if that's so, then he—then Frawley——" He faltered to a stop.

"You mean we can do nothing?" asked Barre, his voice cracking.

"Nothing but wait," said O'Leary slowly.

Lal Killian, his blanket pulled tightly around him and his hair still tousled, walked to O'Leary's side and looked out at the swirling, smothering torrents of wind and snow and shivered. An icy draft crept over the floor from the opened shutters.

"*C'est faire le diable à quatre,*" muttered Annette, shuddering under her quilt.

"It may last three or four days," said Killian in a stunned way. "Here in the sandhills—anything can happen."

"Three or four days," repeated Aunt Lucy, whose great, long ears heard everything. "Three or four days," she said. A rather terrible speculation peeped out of her hollowed eyes which were glaring at the closed door into Frawley's room and she added harshly: "It's lucky it is so cold in that room."

A very paralysis of horror held us still for a moment.

Then Matil gasped: "*Aunt Lucy!*"

And Terice shrieked again and Helene gave a hysterical *yoop.*

"Stop that!" ordered O'Leary sharply. As Terice, her mouth still open, stared at him and Helene nearly strangled on a sob, he added:

"See here, we are in a rather terrible situation. It is something that cannot be helped. We will simply have to make the best of it. It is quite possible, as Killian says, that this storm will last two or three days or longer. In any case, it may be some time before we are able to send to Nettleson, get the coroner—" he paused—"do what it is necessary to do. It will not be pleasant waiting."

"Pleasant!" wailed Helene.

O'Leary surveyed her sternly.

"Tears and hysterics will only make matters worse. We must employ as much self-control as we are individually capable of. As I say, it is not easy or pleasant—but we can't help ourselves."

"What can't be cured must be endured," offered Aunt Lucy with a harshly sententious air that grated on my nerves. "At any rate, it looks as if you will have plenty of time to question us all to your heart's content, Mr. Detective."

"It looks that way," agreed O'Leary imperturbably. "But just now I'd advise you all to go to your rooms and get some clothes on and rest."

"Rest," said Helene with a kind of moan. "Rest! With—*that*—in the bedroom there, and some-one——"

"Be quiet!" O'Leary's eyes flashed though his voice was calm. "Brunker, can you and Annette get us some coffee? We'll rest the better for it," he added, as Annette stirred, rose, and made her way toward the kitchen. In spite of her bulk she moved as lightly as a feather; Brunker, following her, seemed very heavy-footed and awkward.

O'Leary glanced apologetically at Matil.

"That was quite right, Mr. O'Leary," she said, with

a wan smile. "Don't hesitate to do anything you think advisable."

"Thank you."

Morse, who had been regarding O'Leary with some disfavor, turned suddenly to Matil.

"Matil, why did you bring a detective here? I thought this was only a house party here at Hunting's End. None of us wanted to hunt. I thought you probably asked us all along because you—you dreaded opening the lodge and wanted your best friends with you. Had you any other reason?"

Everyone was listening closely.

"If you are my best friends——" began Matil, her voice breaking and the storm that leaped into her steel-blue eyes threatening to have its way. Then she lowered her satin eyelids, took a deep breath, and said steadily: "I can't tell you that, Newell."

"Can't tell me! Why, Matil, I don't understand. What do you mean?"

Julian Barre was watching the girl closely.

"She is very tired," he said abruptly to Newell. "Can't we leave things for a while? Don't worry, Matil; it will be all right." He looked at O'Leary. "I think we should all be the better for a little rest," he said in a slightly commanding fashion, which was a little marred in effect by his lisp.

He seemed to realize at that instant that he had forgotten his teeth for he looked puzzled, put his hand suddenly to his mouth, said something that I could not understand, and rose. O'Leary did not stop him and he walked hurriedly but with undiminished self-possession and ease to his own room, the door of which stood open. Next to it, with the width of the bathroom intervening, and a panel of ducks and rushes and water in blues and grays, was the closed door into Frawley's room. Barre was back again immediately, his cheeks filled naturally and his teeth an unbroken rim of white. I remember thinking that only a Julian Barre could have remained unshaken at a discovery which might well have destroyed the aplomb of a lesser man. Although, as to that, the thing that confronted us was such as to dwarf all small anxieties.

"I agree," O'Leary was saying as Barre rejoined the group. "We will drink some hot coffee and go back to bed and try to get some sleep which we all need rather urgently."

We waited in almost unbroken silence until Brunker appeared carrying a tray from which floated a delicious, steaming fragrance. I reached quickly for my cup. The coffee was hot and very good.

I suppose the sight of Brunker with his tray of coffee cups stirred a recollection in Aunt Lucy's mind for she said between sips:

"Poison, Brunker. Did you put out poison for the rats?"

Brunker's shoulder jerked. A little coffee splashed over onto the tray.

"I am not sure, madame. I'll ask Annette."

"Well, ask her then," advised Aunt Lucy impatiently. "Take your coffee, Julian, and let the man go."

Julian Barre reached for his cup and Brunker vanished. I could hear Aunt Lucy gulping her coffee and

O'Leary was staring somewhat thoughtfully into the depths of his cup. It was a moment or two before Brunker returned, and when he did I could see Annette's shrewd cobalt eyes peering out from the kitchen doorway. The nondescript cat, whose presence I had forgotten, drifted like a thin, black shadow after Brunker and took up her position at Aunt Lucy's feet.

As Brunker did not speak I shifted my gaze to his face. It was a sort of yellow-white like wax, his eyes had shining black pupils between their lashless lids, and his flat features were working curiously.

"Mercy on us!" rasped Aunt Lucy. "What ails the man? Speak up, can't you?"

"Pardon me, madame," said Brunker jerkily but quite clearly at last. "Pardon me——" He stuck.

"Well, what is it?" urged Aunt Lucy. She took a long gulp of coffee and held out her cup. "More coffee, please," she said. "And what's the matter with you, Brunker?"

"It's the poison, madame," said Brunker. "The rat poison. It—it's gone."

Aunt Lucy eyed the man dazedly. I could hear a little tinkle from somewhere as if a cup was being placed hurriedly on its saucer.

"Well, what of it?" said the old woman at last.

Brunker looked far more affected than he had at any time during the horror of the night.

"Just—" he swallowed with some difficulty—"just this. It was there yesterday when I unloaded the supplies. You put it on the pantry shelf yourself, madame. I saw you. And—now it's gone. And all I want to know is this, madame," went on Brunker, gathering courage. "Where is that poison now?"

Silence followed his words.

Then Aunt Lucy's gaunt hand, outstretched with the cup in its grip, began to shake. The cup and saucer rattled against each other. She withdrew her staring eyes from Brunker's lashless, terrified gaze, looked at the cup as if seeing it for the first time, then drew it back slowly and placed it on the arm of her wheel chair.

"I—guess I don't want any more coffee," she said in a mumbling way.

CHAPTER VII
A BLACK TOUPEE

IT IS strange how grim tragedy and a kind of dreadful humor walk together. A wild tremor of laughter swept over me, even as I, too, set my cup down rather more hurriedly than was necessary.

Helene surged to her feet. She must have simply let go the coffee cup for it crashed thinly to the floor, spilling coffee as it shattered.

"I can't stand this," she wailed. "It's terrible. Why did I come? Why did you make us come, Matil? It is all your fault. I know why you've got this detective here. It's your father's death you want to know about. Well, you never will. You never, never will!"

"Helene, stop that." It was her husband speaking, his dark face flushed and unpleasant.

"You never, never will," she repeated, as if taking satisfaction in the phrase. Her thin mouth was drawn downward, away from her teeth, her eyes were green slits, and her supple fingers twitched and worked. "I'm going to leave. I can't stay here. It's a horrible place. With that in the next room—for days and days. I'm going to leave."

"You can't," said O'Leary, without much concern.

Helene whirled on him; her wide flat back looked enormous under the flowing black silk negligee. As she moved a fold of the black silk fell back, and under it I saw quite distinctly creamy lace and a flare of vivid green; she still wore, then, the dinner gown she had worn the night before. I merely noted it and thought little of it at the time.

"I can and I will," she cried furiously. "You can't keep me here."

"You can't live in the storm," O'Leary said in a dispassionate way that was much more effective than bluster. "You'd lose your way in two minutes. We couldn't possibly save you. But go ahead if you like."

She met his eyes for a moment, then her own wavered and went to the closed log door across the room. Her set face broke, became blurred and blotched with red, and an ugly, retching sob forced itself between her teeth.

"Come now," said O'Leary briskly. "We will all have some rest. I'm quite sure this coffee is all right. There's nothing to be alarmed about. That rat poison was likely just misplaced. Anyhow, it's painfully evident that the man in there was killed by a revolver shot, not poison. Waiting for help under the circumstances will not be easy but there's nothing else to do. There's one thing—the murderer can't escape."

Helene sobbed louder. The sound clashed on my already hair-trigger nerves. I rose.

"Stop that!" I cried. "Things are bad enough without your making them worse. If one of us goes to pieces all of us will. And it's enough like a nightmare as it is without your making it a—a madhouse," I ended up lamely but with considerable vehemence. Matil gave me a grateful look and Signora Helene, in surprise, I think, stopped sobbing, slid her green eyes toward me, and passed a wide black silk sleeve over her blotched, tear-stained face and swollen eyes.

"The nurse is right," said Terice suddenly. Every so often a hard little stratum of common sense, engendered possibly by years of none-too-happy contact with the world, bobbed up amid Terice's superficialities. "I'm going back to bed. And I'm going to bolt my door. And if——" her hard, jeweled hands gripped the chair back with a kind of defiance—"if anyone disturbs me I will scream with all my might."

That was for the murderer's ears. And the murderer was sitting there, one of us, perhaps Terice, herself. Indeed, she looked a very Jezebel in the remnants of her paint, with her glittering eyes and her soiled pink satin garment.

I moved my shoulders impatiently and tried to shake off the weight that revolver shot seemed to have brought upon me.

"May I help you?" I asked Aunt Lucy.

She did not reply. I think she did not hear me. Her great eyes were staring so widely and fixedly from their dark, hollowed sockets that ugly white rims showed. She sat bolt upright and did not turn or question me when I laid my hands on the bar of her wheel chair.

Well, somehow I got her into bed with several blankets over her and a hot-water bottle at her icy-cold feet. When I went to the kitchen for the hot water, I noted that the disheveled, nightmarish group about the fireplace had broken up, although Barre and

Morse and Killian were standing before the fire, talking in low voices.

Brunker was going automatically about his cleaning and setting things to rights and in the kitchen Annette was getting breakfast, she told me grumpily, though it occurred to me, in the interval of waiting for the water to heat, that she was doing a deal of prowling in various cupboards and store closets from which she would emerge, her face pink, her bare forearms shining with cold, and an anxious, thoughtful look in her shrewd eyes, only to delve into another. Her mouth had lost its loose look and was set tightly and her eyes were a bleak, sharp blue and were very guarded.

Not the least unpleasant feature of the days at Hunting's End was the fact that every time an errand took me to the kitchen I had to pass directly before the closed door into the room where lay that pathetic, infinitely ugly figure. I always felt, unreasonably, that the door was about to open and that something, I didn't know what, was about to drift silently out of the room. It was only a feeling, absurd, of course; I had an impulse to shy around that door much as the cat had done. And speaking of the cat, I had an irrational but disturbing feeling about her, too. I knew the creature was only a half-starved and nearly frozen female cat whose instinct had led it to warmth and food. But there was an air of knowingness about the creature: a certain crafty sang-froid. I did not like the way she sat before the hearth, not far from the dark spot where Helene had spilled her coffee, and licked her gorged stomach with a thin red tongue and sent cool glances from her slitted eyes at Jericho. She seemed to know that the collie was plunged in misery, and not only that but to know also, which was impossible, the reason for that misery. Killian's suggestion as to the cat's origin recurred to me and pointed out my own absurdity and I went on my way. But I never liked the cat.

Jericho had padded after me, and as I pushed open the door to Aunt Lucy's room he thrust his nose, which was hot and dry, into my hand. His dark eyes were troubled and anxious and seeking.

"Poor old boy," I said. His dainty ears dropped, his plumy tail hung dejectedly, and he turned away from me, looked listlessly at the cat, and went to curl up on a rug. I noted that he dropped his slender nose on his small white forepaws and his deep-set eyes went at once to the door of Gerald Frawley's room.

As I say, I got Aunt Lucy into bed, and with the hot-water bottle at her feet she seemed to grow drowsy and I left her.

My own room was dark and very cold. I opened the shutters to let gray daylight drift into the room. The covers on the bed were tossed exactly as I had left them—what for?—oh, yes, I had gone for hot milk. And I had found a murdered man.

And there is no shame in admitting that I looked under the bed and bolted my door before I sat weakly on the bed and pushed my hair wearily from my face and rubbed my tired eyes.

Then I seemed to arouse from the torpor of acceptance that horror and shock had thrust upon me. Up till then, from the sound of the shot until I bolted my own door, the whirl of events had caught me; I had been numbly acquiescent and unquestioning. Now the thing the night had held became sharply significant and real. It was exactly as if I opened my eyes from the horror of a peculiarly grisly nightmare and found reality more gruesome than the nightmare had been.

Not far from me lay a dead man, murdered by one of his supposed friends. And that murderer was there, must be there, must be one of that smiling group that, not so long ago, had eaten and talked, had amused itself with music and cards, had smiled and smiled, and ill the time murder had walked and smiled and talked, unseen and perhaps unguessed among them.

And the memory of Gerald Frawley's unexpectedly bare and glistening head troubled me; I wished I had made myself cover it with the toupee that lay on the dressing table.

Something rustled under my sharply impatient gesture. It was the paper that was still in my bathrobe pocket. I drew it out, and at once my incipient hysteria vanished. I dare say I shouldn't have read the thing but the few words on it stared up at me so boldly, so plainly written, that I couldn't have helped grasping their sense.

> MATIL, my darling [it said]: Please permit me to announce our engagement while we are at Hunting's End. Regardless of what you say I must insist upon doing so.

And it was signed simply "Gerald F."

I sat looking at the thing for some time. Gerald

Frawley, then, was the man whom Matil wished to marry. He was the man she had wished to clear of suspicion. And he was now dead—murdered.

No wonder she had seemed so frozen in horror, so desperately quiet and still.

And yet—was it grief back of her unfathomable dark blue eyes?

I don't know how long I looked at the note before I began to wonder just where my duty lay concerning it. My first impulse was, naturally, to take it immediately to Matil Kingery. Then other considerations began to present themselves, as I believe they always do when some catastrophe releases us from conventionality.

In the first place, since that note had been written, the situation had changed definitely. In justice the note should be placed in O'Leary's hands, who would, of course, give it to Matil. But Matil had herself expressed a reluctance to tell O'Leary the name of the man she loved.

And all at once I recalled Matil's soaked silver slippers, and the open window and shutters in her room that I had closed. True, the window into Frawley's room was bolted on the inside; moreover, I felt sure Matil had not killed him. She had been engaged to marry him and Matil Kingery was not a woman to engage herself to a man she did not love. And, a much-quoted ballad to the contrary, the things one loves are protected and cherished, never dispatched with such graceless expedition. But after some very thoughtful moments I decided to keep the note in my own possession; at least, until I knew better where my duty lay concerning it.

I put the troublesome scrap of paper in the pocket of a fresh uniform that I presently, after a shower that was too cool for comfort, donned. If only there was a possibility of a stranger being involved in the affair, some outsider making his way into the lodge! Such an eventuality would do away with the thing that, I already saw, was to make those days ghastly in their suspense; the knowledge that the murderer was one of us, coming and going, eating and perhaps sleeping, sharing in every aspect but one the grim business of Hunting's End. The thing that one did not share was the horror of uncertainty, the suspicion and doubt, and the grisly feeling of insecurity, of not knowing what might happen next.

But thanks to that ill-timed storm, there was no other possibility. I remember that I went wearily over the list of people who composed the party; it was all too brief.

There was I and there was O'Leary; I knew I had not shot Gerald Frawley and I knew O'Leary had not. And I knew José Paggi had not done so, because he had been under my eyes at the instant the shot was fired. But there my exact knowledge ceased. Lucy Kingery, a half-paralyzed invalid; Annette, drunk; Terice, tawdry and hard-eyed; Julian Barre, anxious and toothless; Morse, troubled, worried, burning the note from Frawley. Wearily my thoughts went from one to another. Had Helene Paggi leaned over the balcony railing and aimed a revolver with so deadly a precision—and if so, for what possible motive? Did Killian's lazy, enigmatic eyes conceal murder? And if so, again, what possible motive was there? And Brunker, with his stolidity breaking under his anxiety as to the whereabouts of the rat poison—I could not conceive of him possessing other emotions than the strictly limited ones dictated by his instinct for self-preservation. I have heard of automatons but Brunker was the first man I had ever seen who might approach that definition. And anyway, include him though I must in my list of suspects, again the question arose, what possible motive could he have had?

As the last question bobbed up again and again I began tardily to perceive that it was one of considerable importance.

And at once a thought wormed its ugly way into my mind: whatever that motive had been I was obliged to hope it had been successful and that murder would not again be at large in that hunting lodge.

The homely little rustle of my starched white uniform brought me back to the things of everyday life. I looked at my watch, saw with a distinct sense of shock that it had been only some eighteen hours since I had arrived at Hunting's End, and put on a fresh white cap, arranging it carefully so as to conceal the gray streak in my rather nice, reddish hair. I looked pale and there were blue lines around my eyes but my mouth was firm again. And I reflected that if, by any evil chance, there had been poison in the coffee, it would have had time to take effect, upon which my spirits lifted a little. Though that is not saying I was at all cheerful.

I found, on entering the main room, that there had apparently been little rest on anyone's part. Matil and O'Leary and Paggi stood talking near the fireplace, Matil in a blue wool frock with a soft white silk collar above which her head rose gracefully and proudly. Helene and Terice sat on the divan, both fully clothed and smoking with nervous little puffs and saying not a word. Killian, Morse, and Barre were standing at one of the windows, watching the thick swirls of snow that blotted out all other worlds.

With daylight and properly donned clothing and Brunker coming and going laying the table for breakfast, the nightmarish aspect of things had gone a little and there was a semblance of conventionality and naturalness. But it was only a semblance, a sort of crust that might crack and break through at any time. One felt that in meeting those desperately controlled eyes, in hearing those carefully guarded voices, as much as in permitting one's self to recall a certain closed log door and what lay behind it.

Breakfast was a ghastly meal. In the first place, the empty space where, the night before, Gerald Frawley had sat was singularly inescapable; every way I looked my eyes were drawn back to it. And in the second place, while I was intensely hungry, still I did not feel any particular desire to eat. I shook my head to orange and grapefruit juice and muffins and a cooked cereal, took coffee with some reluctance and a slice of dry toast; just then Brunker passed a large dish of boiled eggs still in their shells and I believe I took three of them, though as a rule I detest boiled eggs, especially in the morning.

It was disconcerting to find that all the others seemed to share my taste that morning. While everything else remained almost untouched, the eggs diminished with astonishing dispatch.

And I recall that I watched O'Leary covertly, and only when he had completely, and with every evidence of pleasure, drained his coffee cup and was being given more, did I touch my own to my lips.

There was practically no conversation. Helene stared at the table, her face still a cold, yellowish lump of fear, and Terice smoked feverishly between cups of coffee, her eyes twinkling strangely from between those sticky black eyelashes and her gayly striped orange and black sport dress looking flamboyant and garish beside Matil's severe simplicity of tailoring. They all looked haggard, drained of color and vivacity and life, and there was a growing tendency to turn at sudden sounds, to dart quick, somewhat furtive glances at each other, and to stare at the snow from weary, underlined eyes. The men smoked as if they could not leave off, save for Paggi, whose voice seemed to be always his first consideration, and who looked decidedly liverish in the cold light of morning. And we all ate eggs.

As I recall it, the day then beginning was chiefly notable for its long, wearily monotonous hours. So far as I know nothing of any particular interest occurred, although Lance O'Leary must have gone quietly and thoroughly about his business, for every so often I would see his slender gray figure moving with a deceptively unhurried air here and there about the lodge, and several times I saw him engaged in low-voiced conversations with one or another of the party. Aunt Lucy kept to her bed all day, with me in rather constant attendance, and the others drifted in and out of the long main room, thumbing magazines, smoking nervously, eyeing each other, saying very little, and watching the snow.

And I must say I have never seen the like of that snow in all my life. It was not an honest, out-and-out snowstorm which comes down cheerfully and rapidly and is over with. There was something unbelievably sinister about that relentless, smothering fall of snow and the swirling of wind and the bitter cold. It surrounded us, threatened us, held us helpless and immovable in its menacing, stifling white folds. As early twilight finally came on and there was no letting up of that merciless onslaught I began to feel that existence itself was merely a matter of waiting and waiting in bewildered, numb suspension in a dizzy white fog.

The thought frightened me a little; such fancies, with me, and I suspect with many, only occur after having eaten something indigestible. I was in the main room at the time, having a brief respite from the musty atmosphere of Aunt Lucy's room; Brunker had brought a little portable heater to her room which smelled most vilely. I rose abruptly and got my knitting. Not that I like to knit for I do not, but it keeps one's hands busy, and when I returned to the fire in the living room the click of my long steel needles sounded rather cheerful in contrast to the other sounds—the occasional low-voiced word or two from the men, Terice's sharply scratched matches, and Helene's slow sighs.

Brunker went around lighting the lanterns very early, which was most thoughtful of him for our eyes were already beginning to slide to the darker corners of the room. And I believe Matil had a slight altercation with Annette for I saw her come out of the kitchen with her eyebrows black and straight, her cheeks scarlet, and her Kingery jaw firm and go swiftly to her own room, whence she presently emerged with a bunch of keys in her hand and returned to the kitchen. But if she locked the wine cupboard Annette had forestalled her, for when I went to the kitchen for Aunt Lucy's soda water, about tea time, I found Annette flushed again and loose-mouthed, singing her little song and padding uncertainly here and there. I think that that night she had shared with Brunker for he looked faintly flushed himself, less cold and machinelike, and refused to meet my eyes.

After her tea Aunt Lucy roused herself and with my help got into the gray lace gown again. She downed the soda water with a gulp, selected some heavy jet jewelry, and sallied forth in her chair to a corner near the fireplace where she moodily watched the others finish a desultory tea which consisted of extraordinarily thin sandwiches and tea which cooled with distressing rapidity. Her face was darker, the hollows of her great brooding eyes deeper and blacker, but otherwise she gave no evidence of the shock of the previous night.

Gradually the living room became empty as one by

one the others drifted to their rooms to dress for dinner. It struck me then, and does yet, as being curious that one and all clung rigidly to little customs of everyday life. There we were, marooned in an immovable world of snow and cold and fear, bound to that thing that lay in the room so near us and to the horror that permeated the very walls and rugs and air itself, and yet—beards must be shaved and studs inserted in stiff and shining shirt fronts and dinner jackets donned; and the showers must sting and lace and silk go on over shrinking flesh and shoulders and backs must be powdered and bared to the cold and pale cheeks must be rouged and the black marks under weary eyes carefully covered. And above all there must be smiles and a little patter of quiet talk and a pretense of eating. Well, that is living, I suppose, and I must not forget the rather disturbing incident which occurred during that hour while the living room was deserted of all save Aunt Lucy and myself and occasionally Brunker.

It was deep dusk, I remember, dark enough for lights in the living room and still barely light enough so that I could see the spindrifts of snow outside the yet unshuttered windows. O'Leary, who had scarcely exchanged a word with me during the whole day, appeared suddenly at my elbow.

"Busy, Miss Keate?" he said, and as I looked up quickly he added, for Aunt Lucy's ears, I think: "Do you mind coming into Frawley's room with me for a moment or two? I want you to help me."

I let my knitting fall at once on the divan and accompanied him, my heart leaping as he swung open that heavy log door and we entered the bedroom. He closed the door behind us at once. The shutters had been thrown back sometime during the day and the room was very cold and still and there was only the dusky twilight coming in from the window. I had braced myself to see a huddled figure on the floor, but it was on the bed, covered mercifully with a sheet. A white chalk mark outlined an irregular patch on the bare floor where he had fallen.

"I want to talk to you alone, Miss Keate," said O'Leary quickly; I think he saw the sick horror which must have been in my face. "I haven't had a chance to-day. And I haven't accomplished anything either! This is not an easy case; if I could only get some of them to talking it would help, but I can't. They are as mum as so many oysters. It's easy to see why, of course: Huber Kingery's death is hanging over them. They all seem to be afraid of getting implicated not only in the murder of last night but in that murder of five years ago. Funny—I don't fancy there's much love lost between them."

"The ties that bind them together are not of love," I said somberly. "You can see that with your eyes shut. It's a matter of 'I won't tell if you won't.'"

"Exactly," said O'Leary. "With your customary sagacity you have hit the nail on the head."

"But haven't you made any progress?" I asked in some disappointment.

"Very little. In fact none of any significance. Unless you would call it significant that—there's not a revolver on the place save this one." He drew a glittering thing from his pocket. "And this one is mine! You'd think that on a trip to a hunting lodge there would be all kinds of guns, but Miss Matil tells me that no one desired or intended to do any shooting. Odd, isn't it, Miss Keate? Looks like an—anti-shooting complex." He paused, looking at his own revolver, balanced on his palm. "Mine is the only revolver in the lodge; and I didn't shoot Gerald Frawley."

"But what was done with the one that shot—" I glanced at the bed and something made me whisper— "that shot—him?"

O'Leary shrugged but he looked sober.

"Heaven only knows—out in some snowdrift likely. And another thing——" He paused. "How are your nerves, Miss Keate? Steady? You see, it's rather gruesome."

"Steady enough," I snapped. My heart had given an unexpected jump which was unsettling. "What is it?"

He eyed me a moment before he replied. Then he said very slowly:

"It's—the toupee. The toupee that lay there on the dressing table. Sometime between lunch and ten minutes ago it vanished."

As I turned involuntarily toward the dressing table I caught an unexpected glimpse of myself in the mirror above it. My face loomed as ghostly white in the dusk as my cap and I met my own eyes with a feeling of strangeness and unfamiliarity. I could hear my heart thudding, thudding. The wind surged against the window and moaned eerily around some corner. I took a deep breath. The toupee was certainly gone from the dressing table. I don't know why the disappearance of the thing should have affected me so disagreeably, but it did.

"I had already gone through the pockets of his clothes," said O'Leary. "There was nothing of any particular interest there. And I looked at the toupee, but, so far as I could see, it was simply a thatch of black hair. The fact that he was not wearing the toupee when he was killed raises a rather nice problem, by the way, Miss Keate; you see, the number of persons before whom he would appear without the toupee is— well, extremely limited. Whoever was in this room talking to him must have had a very close and intimate relationship. And yet—" he paused, frowning— "things don't fit. A toupee or the lack of one certainly changes a man's appearance," he went on, looking thoughtfully at the rigid outlines of the sheet. "You'd scarcely have recognized him when—— I beg your pardon, Miss Keate. Am I harrowing your feel——"

I didn't hear the rest of his sentence. I was staring over his shoulder. Surely something was moving beyond the window pane—something white against the darkening twilight, something reaching—reaching—— It was certainly a hand—reaching toward the sash.

I have never tried to account for what I did, beyond admitting that my nerves may have been a little shaken. But without a word, or, in fact, a thought, I snatched O'Leary's revolver out of his hand, pointed the thing at that clutching hand, and pulled the trigger.

It made a hideous racket, there was a crash of shattered glass, an incredulous exclamation from O'Leary, and the hand was gone and snow and wind were pouring through the broken window pane.

O'Leary had whirled but had seen nothing, for he turned to me again, took the revolver gently from my hand, looked at it strangely, restored it to his pocket, and said in a soothing way that was maddening:

"Don't you think you'd better get some rest before dinner?"

My mouth felt numb and my tongue kept trying to move and failing, and fright and anger were seething so furiously within me that I could only glare at him and try to get my breath past the pounding thing in my breast.

"Was there really something at that window?" he said quickly.

"There was," I stammered. "A hand reaching up toward the sash——" He was at the window before I had finished.

"Nothing there—snow, storm—it's too dark to see anyway. I'll go——" At the door he paused to give me a look that was part admiration and part a kind of awed apprehension. "You act with such remarkable enterprise," he said, and was gone.

I followed at once; immediately, in fact, without lingering for a moment in that cold, death-ridden room. Two men had come to their deaths there. I closed the door very carefully behind me.

And it was as I stepped into the main room and walked slowly toward Aunt Lucy, seated near the fireplace, that one of the most peculiar things about the whole affair occurred. Or rather it did not occur; that was what was peculiar.

No one questioned that revolver shot!

Not a door opened. Not a voice cried out. Not a sound came from anywhere in the whole lodge. Instead there was a singular silence, a breathless, frozen hush, an absolute lack of motion or sound. But the question in that silence was almost palpable; the very air seemed thick and tremulous with inquiry. It was as if the lodge itself became one silent, palpitating demand and yet shrank from a reply. And Aunt Lucy, leaning forward from her wheel chair, her great straining eyes upon O'Leary, her steel mouth moving soundlessly, fixed and made definite that question.

Then O'Leary flung back over his shoulder to Aunt Lucy, almost in a shout for he was at the kitchen door, "An accident—nothing at all. No one hurt," and disappeared, and I dropped weakly on the divan while Aunt Lucy leaned slowly back in her chair and shut her mouth. And the spell over the lodge seemed to take a long breath and break itself. Someone walked quickly across a gallery room, a door closed stealthily, a shower was running, and the little stir and breath of motion began again.

Aunt Lucy said nothing, just stared at me, and I, not to be outdone, stared at the fire and thought of that hand. I could not have been mistaken for I have good eyesight and am not a nervous woman. That is, as a rule I am not nervous. But whose hand could it have been? Who could have been outside in that driving snow? And why?

O'Leary came back presently but looked sober and to my fuming impatience said nothing, the others drifted into the room, Aunt Lucy gulped her three cocktails and became immediately sunken in morose, brooding silence, and dinner was served. It was a horrible meal, noticeable chiefly for the failure of various attempts at polite conversation and the lack of appetites. The soup, a clear soup with a delicious fragrance, was untouched, I am sure, though I believe the salad, which was made unmistakably of vegetables, received some attention. And the worst of it was we were all hungry; Paggi's eyes on the mushroom sauce were pathetic but he shook his head decisively. O'Leary was the only one of us who ate with any degree of satisfaction and I was inclined to suspect that that was pure bravado, such as O'Leary, being young, is sometimes capable of. And all through dinner I was preoccupied; I had never in my life before aimed a revolver at a living target and pulled the trigger and I'm bound to say it is an extraordinarily disagreeable experience. I kept watching the hands of those at the table—would one be bandaged?—would one show a red wound? It seemed quite impossible that the requisite number of hands should be still attached to their proper persons about that long, narrow table. But so it was. I even eyed Brunker furtively and after dinner manufactured an errand to the kitchen, whence I returned, shaken in body and spirit. Annette's wide shining pink hands were, also, quite intact.

But just before we retired for the night—which was early, owing as much, I think, to the fear that stalked among us, painting on each face a stiff, white mask, as it was owing to our natural fatigue—something happened which drove the hand from my mind.

For I found the toupee.

Yes, I did.

It had been thrust down between the cushions of the immense over-stuffed chair in which I sat. I dropped my knitting needle and when it slipped into the crack I reached for it. And found the toupee. I shall always marvel over the fact that I did not cry out, and that I did not attract any attention from that singularly silent gathering. But I did manage to extract the thing —the hair was dry and dead feeling—under cover of the scarf I was knitting and, presently, to convey it to my own room.

After I had seen Aunt Lucy through an unwholesome lunch and into bed, and bolted my own door, I looked the toupee over carefully. My fingers shrank from it, and it was not a pleasant thing to touch and examine, but I found nothing about it of any significance. However, before I went to bed I put the toupee and the note to Matil, which I still had, under my pillow. I did not enjoy the proximity and it was no wonder I could not go to sleep but there was no other safe place in the room.

But finally, after counting several thousand sheep jumping over fences and repeating as much as I could remember of Rabbi Ben Ezra backward, I did fall into an uneasy sleep.

I have never known what awakened me.

It may have been a current of air on my face, a rustle, a feeling of movement, but whatever it was I awoke very suddenly, with my heart standing quite still and then leaping madly.

Someone was in the room. Someone was standing beside the bed. Something under my pillow was moving.

I was frozen. I could not raise my head. I could not scream.

That hand I had shot was under my pillow. I knew it—it must be. And I think my own hand must have clutched under the pillow, too, for I knew suddenly that that other hand was hot and—curiously sticky and wet.

CHAPTER VIII

A SCRAP OF LACE

THEN it was gone. And I still heard nothing.

For a few delirious moments I think I must have been quite paralyzed with fright, and I remember that I kept thinking, "It must be a dream—it must be a dream—I must rouse myself," and all the time I knew that it was no dream. I could not move and I could not scream. And I felt that something must be done.

Resisting a desire to pull the covers over my head and simply lie there and hope with all my heart that whoever was in that room would leave me untouched, I very carefully turned my head, listening intently.

There was no sound; not a breath of movement. It was dark; evidently the light I had left burning had been blown out. Gradually I became convinced that whoever had visited my room had gone, as silently as he had come.

But when I pulled myself upward in bed I did so very cautiously, with my heart racing and my skin prickling.

Nothing moved; no hand clutched at my throat; no revolver shot crashed through the night. Presently I drew a breath, swung my feet over the bed, and as nothing seized me, I got boldly out of bed, groped

about the room—feeling all the time and most unpleasantly that that hot, wet hand might seize me at any
instant—and found a match. The tiny flame wavered
and flickered.

There was no one in the room. But the door into the
living room which I had left bolted was standing wide
open. The main room loomed dark and menacing beyond and if Brunker had left lights they had burned
out of oil. Nothing moved; no shadow loomed darker
than another.

Could I have dreamed it, after all?

I went to my bed, and grasped the pillow and turned
it over.

The toupee was gone. The note was gone. And the
white linen was still white and blank and empty.

I should have given that note to Matil or to O'Leary
at once; I realized that perfectly. And, to make a long
story short, the conclusion was forced upon me that
O'Leary should know of the whole affair at once. I
lit my lantern—my hand shook, which made it difficult
—and seized dressing gown and slippers.

The living room was a cavernous, echoing blackness,
my lantern lighting up only the circle about me and
leaving shadows that seemed to move and waver in a
fashion that was shattering to my nerves. Once up
the narrow stairs, which creaked and whispered under
my steps, I had no difficulty in finding O'Leary's door,
which was the middle one on the south gallery, and I
first tried the latch and then knocked very lightly.

O'Leary was either awake or an abnormally light
sleeper for he was at the door before I had time to

knock again, and I heard him lift the bolt, and the door opened.

"What is it?" he said in a sharp whisper.

"I—something has happened——"

"Come in." He drew me inside and closed the door. "Here, let me take that lantern. What's the trouble? Don't shake like that."

It did not take long to tell him.

"It was the note—to Matil," I began, trying to keep my teeth from chattering from the cold. And in as few words as possible I told him of the note and what it said and why I had kept it a whole day in my possession—a reason which did manage to sound rather unconvincing though he only gave me a sharp look, pulled a blanket around him, and said merely:

"I thought you knew me by this time, Miss Keate. Good Lord, it's cold in here! Go on. So Frawley was the man she was to marry. Somebody took the note from under your pillow?"

"And the toupee."

He stared at me, then, and the slightly reproachful look was crowded out of his face.

"The toupee!" he exclaimed. "You don't mean to say you found the toupee?"

"That's exactly what I did," I replied. "And it was no pleasant thing to find either. But—well, it's gone, now, too."

"You didn't even scream?"

"I couldn't," I replied with candor.

"You are an amazing woman," he said, then. "Look here, are you sleepy?"

"Sleepy!" I said indignantly. "Do you think it likely?"

He looked at his watch.

"One o'clock," he said. He reached for a little flat package done up neatly in a linen handkerchief and placed it in a pocket of his dressing gown. "Quite a conventional hour for hands groping under pillows. See here, I've been wanting to talk to you undisturbed for some time. We were interrupted yesterday. Suppose we go downstairs where it is warmer and talk awhile?"

When I think of Hunting's End I always think of that hour or two, in the middle of the night, with the secrets and silence of the lodge lying thick about us, and a log crackling now and then, and the moaning sound of the wind outside.

We went to the kitchen. O'Leary whispered that in the living room we could easily be seen from the door of one of the rooms and in the kitchen there was only Annette's door to guard against. Not that it would matter, he added, still whispering, as he pushed open the swinging door into the kitchen and I preceded him into the room, but it would certainly draw attention to our acquaintance.

"And so long as no one here has any idea of your—er—remarkable powers of observation, there is no need in putting the thought into their heads," he concluded cheerfully, if obscurely, and drew a chair up to the fireplace, where a bank of coals shone redly.

"I'll just add a log or two," he went on. "Should you like some coffee or tea? You look a little pale——"

"And who wouldn't!" I broke in bitterly. "I didn't come out here, Mr. O'Leary, to—to almost see a murder and have toupees thrusting themselves upon me and having to shoot at hands through windows and then have them coming back to crawl under my pillow. I came to nurse a sick woman."

He laid a log lightly on the coals and took the fire tongs. He was smiling; his hair was tousled, the first time I had ever seen it so, I think, and his heavy gray dressing gown was turned up at the collar, giving him a boyish, youthful look.

"Oh, come now," he said blandly. "You know very well you didn't come to nurse a sick woman. You came because—you expected excitement."

"I didn't expect—murder," I said with vehemence.

He sobered at that.

"No," he agreed. "Neither did I." He had stirred the coals into reluctant flame.

"Nice comfortable chairs," he said, pulling another to the fireplace. "Do you suppose kitchen chairs are made so hard to keep the cooks from sitting down too much? But at any rate it's warmer. Was your door bolted to-night?"

"Why—yes."

"There's a bathroom between your room and Miss Lucy Kingery's; was your door into that bolted?"

"No. Of course not. My patient might have wanted me."

"How about your window?"

"I left the shutters barred, but the window was open

a few inches. Not much, for even with the protection of the shutters it was very cold in the room."

"I believe you," said O'Leary, shivering. "Do you think that log is going to burn?" He took the fire tongs, leaned over to adjust the log, and said quietly over his shoulder:

"Looks like your patient took a notion to have that toupee."

"My patient! Why, you forget she can't walk."

"Oh, can't she," he said in a disinterested way. He leaned back again in his chair, his clear gray eyes on the bed of coals and darting little flames he had stirred into life. "Are you sure of that, Miss Keate?"

"Why—yes. That is—what do you mean?"

"Nothing. It's only a matter of expediency. Was her door bolted, too?"

"I—think so. Surely it was."

"You don't remember bolting it yourself?"

I hesitated.

"No, I can't remember. But surely she bolted it, before I helped her out of her chair."

"Is she difficult to care for, Miss Keate?"

"I have had worse patients—and better," I said grudgingly.

"See here, Miss Keate," said O'Leary, changing the subject quite suddenly. "I've been on queer cases before and I'd hate to confess how many times I've been completely at my wit's ends, but I've never felt just like this. I guess I am too accustomed to the police paraphernalia, the enormous amount of routine work they accomplish, the very important assistance they give you. Not to mention matters of technicalities—you know, laboratory facilities and all that sort of thing. Why, it took me most of the day to make only a few routine inquiries of various of the people here, and look for a revolver that I didn't find and a package of rat poison that apparently has vanished off the face of the earth." He rubbed his hands over his face worriedly and then plunged them deep in the pockets of his dressing gown. "How I will appreciate certain blue coats, hereafter," he said wistfully. "And what wouldn't I give for some of them right now! Well, there's one thing," he added a bit more briskly. "Exactly one day has taken a nice lot of conceit out of me."

"You have never——" I began, and stopped. I have never flattered a man and, I hope, never will. "I shouldn't worry," I said dryly.

"I believe I've got the circumstances of the murder fairly clear in my mind. I mean the circumstances under which the body was found. That's one of the things that took so long. And I find that you and Paggi, sitting there in the living room, were the first into Frawley's room. Barre and Morse came out of their rooms almost at once, collided at the door of Frawley's room in their haste, and entered. I, myself, saw Madame Paggi and the little Baroness come out onto the gallery. Miss Matil was among the last, and she, herself, saw Brunker come out of his room there beside mine on the gallery. Then Killian arrived on the scene and you went to get Miss Lucy and later we sent for Annette. So that's all straight—and so far as I can see offers not much opportunity for the concealment of a revolver. Yet—sometime that revolver was disposed of and disposed of very thoroughly. Of course, everyone denied the possession of a revolver, but I expected that." He made a restless motion. "It's this damn snow that messes things up," he said. "I suppose that revolver is out somewhere in a snowdrift. The easiest thing to do would be to walk to a window and throw the thing. But surely someone doing so would know that eventually it would come to light. By the way, Miss Keate, when we were talking of the fact that all doors and shutters and windows in the lodge were apparently bolted on the inside—and these bolts are nothing to make light of—there was a look on your face that I— well, I seemed to know. Just what did it mean? Have you private knowledge to the contrary?"

"Why, I—yes, I have, Mr. O'Leary. You see, just after the murder was discovered, when I went to my patient, the dog was howling. He seemed to be shut in Matil's room so I opened the door to let him out. And —well, the shutters were open and the window open a little. I, myself, closed the shutters and the window. But I don't see how it could possibly mean anything," I went on, warming to my work and reminding him that Matil, herself, had been one of the last to come to Frawley's room, therefore no one could have got into the lodge through her room without her knowledge.

"But one might—with her knowledge," remarked O'Leary very softly. And as I uttered a sound of protest he smiled. "There, there now, Miss Keate, I'm inclined to think you are quite right and the shutters being open was only a mischance. And there's another argument in your favor," he added. "Do you remember who was the last one to come to the door of Frawley's room and inquire what had happened? It was this young Killian. But Signora Paggi remembers seeing him come out of his own room; so that rules him out. However, that is interesting. The stumbling block is, though, that Frawley's own shutters were quite unmistakably barred and his window still closed. There would be no point in anyone's being outside. No, the shot must have come from the inside."

He fumbled about in his pockets, reaching absentmindedly inside his dressing gown as if for a vest pocket and encountering, I suppose, only pajamas, for he uttered a disgusted exclamation.

"Are you looking for that silly little pencil?" I asked crisply. "Because if so, Mr. O'Leary, I should consider it a personal favor for you to cure yourself of that little mannerism."

He was looking somewhat amazedly at me; I found myself irritated.

"I know I'm not being polite," I snapped. "But I'm thoroughly sick of seeing you roll that pencil around; I'll give you a fountain pen."

"Why—why, Miss Keate!" His surprised eyes sharpened and softened suddenly and he leaned over and placed his hand on mine. "I'm sorry to have let you in for all this, Miss Keate," he said. "But you are so confoundedly resolute and loyal and——"

It was just then, I believe, that the door into Annette's room opened.

The French are an immoral people; I have always
felt it and never more strongly than when I looked
around and saw Annette standing there smirking at us,
her hair in two short gray pigtails and her eyes knowing and sly.

O'Leary was quite equal to the occasion; he let his
hand remain on mine, said rather sharply to Annette,
"Make us some coffee, please," and finished his sentence to me "—and altogether fine"—before he relinquished his clasp. Then he leaned back in his chair
again and.looked at the fire with gray eyes that shone
and danced.with repressed mirth. And as for me, I was
so torn between two desires that I actually did nothing: one was to smack O'Leary's ears smartly and the
other was to tell Annette in no uncertain words exactly
what I thought of her, of her faded blue flannel
kimono and of her nation in general. And at the same
time I must admit that I felt a warm little glow inside; I am not accustomed to approbation.

It did not take Annette long to make the coffee,
which tasted very good. She added to my discomposure
by going into her own room and returning with a flat
bottle nearly full of a liquid that was colorless but
somehow dynamic-looking, which she set on the table
beside us with an indescribable air of having done us a
favor. O'Leary dismissed her rather sharply upon that,
though his eyes were laughing, and she retreated to her
own room, where I have no doubt she remained with
her salacious ear at the door for some time. But if so,

it did her no good, for the kitchen was enormous and we spoke in low voices.

After that things went more briskly.

"And so, Miss Keate," resumed O'Leary, "since we are positive the shot came from the inside, and since you are equally positive that no one came out of Frawley's room—" he hesitated there in an inquiring way, and as I shook my head decidedly, continued—"that leaves us in a rather difficult position. About the gallery, Miss Keate. You were sure you heard someone on the gallery. Now, as you have doubtless noted, the balcony where the little stairway emerges, leans out quite a way over the main room. And this balcony is exactly opposite Gerald Frawley's room."

I nodded.

"Yes. I thought of that. But can't you tell something about the distance at which the shot was fired?"

"Something," he said thoughtfully. "However, it might interest you to know that there was someone on the balcony." He glanced at Annette's door, which remained closed, and reached into his pocket, drawing out the flat little package done up in a handkerchief. I watched him unwrap the thing. It contained two small objects. One was a scrap of fine, flesh-colored lace. The other—I caught my breath a little as I leaned forward —the other was a tip of a flat crimson ostrich feather, uncurled, broken sharply off. And part of it, blotched and stiff and ugly, was a darker red: a color that I know well.

"Blood!" I whispered. And added: "That's a tip of feather from Matil's fan."

O'Leary nodded soberly.

"Where did you find it?"

"Under Frawley's body, when I moved him," said O'Leary slowly. "Yes, it's blood. Frawley's blood. But don't ask me how it got there. The lace, now, I know something of; it was caught on one of the projecting ends of the rustic railing of the balcony. It looks like it was torn from that dinner gown that Signora Paggi wears. In fact, I'm sure it came from there because I found the torn place, which was on the side of the gown just above her right hip." He paused and added slowly: "She might have braced herself against the railing—or she might not. But I know this: such was the excitement of the instant when it was torn that she did not know her gown was caught or had been torn. She still does not know that bit of lace was torn or she'd not have worn the thing again to-night. Am I right about that, Miss Keate?"

A memory flashed over me.

"She had that dress on, under her black negligee, immediately after the murder occurred. I'm sure of it, because while we were all there together and you were asking us questions her negligee fell a little apart and I saw that she still wore the dinner gown she'd worn during the evening. So evidently she had not gone to bed and asleep."

"Good for you, Miss Keate. Of course, that doesn't prove anything—I mean, the torn bit of lace—for I can't be sure just when she leaned against that railing. But it is something to consider. And even assuming that someone stepped out on the gallery—and remember that, so far as we know, only Brunker and Signora Paggi and I and the Baroness were in the upstairs rooms at the moment—and went to the balcony rail and shot Frawley, how on earth would it happen that he opened his door at exactly that moment and stood there, making a target of himself? And if you are so sure that no one passed through that door, how is it that you do not know exactly when the door was opened?"

He was looking directly at me, his gray eyes lucent, clear.

"I—I don't know," I faltered as I strove to recall the exact moment of hearing that revolver shot. "I—I simply don't know, Mr. O'Leary, when that door opened. I feel that it must have been just at the moment that revolver went off, although—well, I just didn't see it, that's all. But at the same time, contrary though it seems, I am perfectly certain that if someone had come out of that door and moved as he must have had to move—either to the gallery stairs, thus across that end of the room, or to the kitchen door, some twenty feet, or to one of the bedroom doors—I should have seen him."

He studied me for a long moment.

"And yet you heard voices in Frawley's room and then a shot. Someone must have come out. Killian's door is the closest, and on the other side, with the width of the bathroom intervening, is Julian Barre's door. Now you are certain that neither Killian nor Barre could have got from the open door of Frawley's room to his own room. Not a long distance, remember."

"I am positive," I said firmly. "Neither could have done so."

I think he was still a little disappointed for he rubbed his fingers over his hair, felt again absent-mindedly into his pajama pocket, gave me a rather guilty look, and let his hand fall.

"Barre would be the likeliest," he said meditatively. "But the door from Frawley's room into the bathroom was very securely bolted on Frawley's side. If there were any way that it could have been bolted from the other side—but there isn't. Not with heavy log doors and wood bolts, such as these. Crazy notion, anyhow," he added resentfully. "Nothing but a little iron latch on the outside of the door and those heavy wooden bolts on the inside. I can't even lock the door into Frawley's room now, for there's no way to lock it from the outside."

"I don't think you need worry about that," I remarked somewhat acidly. "So far as I can see, that room is the most unpopular place in the lodge. No one is going into it just for the pleasure of the thing. Even the dog has stayed away from it."

"He watches it, though," said O'Leary in a low voice. "Do you know, that dog gives me the creeps, Miss Keate. And I'm not exactly a subject for the creeps, either. But he—it's not natural—or rather it is too natural. He knows too much of what's going on."

"Dogs do," I said. "Especially collies. They are

extraordinarily sensitive to—to things that we think
are beyond their understanding. Sometimes I wonder——"

O'Leary shrugged impatiently.

"Nonsense, Miss Keate. They can't know. Let's get
back to the subject. We know the general circumstances
of the murder: door open, no one emerging from the
room, shutters and bathroom door barred, someone on
the balcony, no revolver"—he was touching his fingers
as if checking off certain items—"everyone but you and
Paggi claims to be asleep, we have found a tip of a
feather fan, Matil was engaged to the murdered man,
someone in the lodge wants that toupee and also has
found the note you—er—harbored"—he shot me a
peculiar look but said nothing further of the matter,
though I still felt a little uneasy on that score in spite
of having acted, as I say, to the best of my judgment
—"Signora Paggi left a scrap of lace on the spot where
the murderer may have stood and—and that's about
all. Save that the murdered man said, dying, a syllable
which may mean anything. Just what was your impression of that, Miss Keate? How did it sound?"

"I only heard him gasp, 'Kil——,' like that. I don't
know what he was trying to say." I shuddered and
pushed my chair closer to the fire. "He may have been
trying to say 'Killian,' as Paggi hinted. Or he may have
been trying to say something else entirely. It was distinct enough. But that is all."

"Probably didn't mean anything," said O'Leary.
"We'll never know for a certainty. But still——"
Whatever his thought was he kept it to himself.

There was a short silence; I was seeing again that rather hideous death. O'Leary's gray gaze was thoughtful.

"By the way," I said at a sudden recollection. "I overheard a scrap of conversation between Frawley and Julian Barre just before dinner. Not that it means anything," as he looked up hopefully. "It was just that Barre offered to exchange rooms with Frawley." As briefly as possible I repeated the few phrases I had overheard.

O'Leary looked thoughtfully at the fire.

"Thanks, Miss Keate," he said after a moment.

"Funny that Killian lied about hearing those voices in Frawley's room just before he was killed," he went on presently. "If you could hear voices through the door, Killian could hear through the single wall that separated his room from Frawley's."

"Unless he was asleep."

O'Leary shot me a quick look.

"Just what do you think of this Killian?"

"He seems a nice enough young fellow," I said slowly. "To tell the truth, I don't know that I particularly like any of them. And Killian—he's very good to look at, and has a rather nice way. I think that he's quite capable of keeping any thoughts he has in reserve. But as to that, any of them are. And Mr. O'Leary, you didn't mention that note that Morse read and burned." I stopped in a questioning way and he smiled a little.

"Do you want to know what it said?"

"If you care to tell me," I said, trying not to appear eager.

"It said this:

> "Morse: Here's the number so you can't forget it: 30A594. Remember what I asked of you this afternoon."

"Why, that sounds as if Frawley may have killed himself!"

O'Leary shook his head.

"No. I think it was only that he knew he was in danger. I couldn't get any admissions from Morse. That number is the number of a safe or of a safety-deposit box, I suppose. Remember the broad hint Frawley gave at dinner as to how he had his affairs arranged? It struck me at the time that he was saying it rather more earnestly than the nature of the talk demanded. Now I know that he was defying—someone. And his defiance, poor fellow, only sealed his death warrant."

"Then—that was the motive?" I asked a little diffidently.

"The motive, Miss Keate, is the only clear thing about this business. Evidently Frawley knew something, had a definite, written record, that one person in this lodge did murder to keep a secret. Morse may be in an exceedingly dangerous position. So might I be unless everyone assumed, as I most earnestly hope they did, that I couldn't possibly have memorized those numbers in the brief glance I gave that note. Fortunately I did, and if we could get back to a city I could make use of them. This way my hands are tied for Morse refuses to tell me what Frawley told him."

Something—some phrase he had used sounded a little odd. What had it been? Oh, yes!

"Why do you say Morse 'may be' in a dangerous position? And didn't you warn him of his danger?"

"I warned him, of course, but he couldn't see it that way. And I say 'may be' because Morse is as apt to be the murderer as anyone. He talked to Frawley late in the afternoon, was in his room for some time before dinner. He was very evidently troubled and paying little attention to what went on; I never saw a man play a hand of bridge with so little care. And he certainly does not feel that he is in danger. He may be just stubborn; but he may have good reason not to fear."

"What was that knowledge that Frawley held?"

O'Leary moved restlessly in his chair, got up, poked at the fire, and stood with his back to the flames.

"I don't know. It may have been the truth as to Huber Kingery's death. That affair seems to be hanging over everyone threateningly. Or it may have been something else entirely. We'll find out if ever we get to a city. And if someone else doesn't get there first. I wish this infernal snow would stop!"

"I have wondered whether there is any connection between this crime and that one five years ago. I had nothing to do all day but massage Miss Lucy and watch the snow and think, and, of course, I thought of all kinds of things," I added rather apologetically.

"I don't know," said O'Leary, slowly and thoughtfully. "I'm inclined to think, why I can't tell you, that when—or if—we solve one crime we will solve the other. My first duty is, of course, to the man who lies dead here in the lodge. But I think that both crimes— interact. It's an interesting situation, isn't it, Miss Keate?"

"I shouldn't call it interesting, precisely," I said with some asperity. "It is not my idea of entertainment."

"Of course not," replied O'Leary soothingly. "Nor anyone's. By the way, the voices you heard in Frawley's room: are you sure there were two voices?"

"Yes. That was my impression."

"Both men's voices?"

"I'm not sure. It was just a murmur, you know, but it was—conversation. Not a monotone."

"He wasn't talking to himself then," said O'Leary, less flippantly than it sounds. "You are worn out, Miss Keate. And I'm keeping you from your rest."

"I am tired," I admitted.

"Think you can go back to sleep?" he asked.

"Certainly," I replied with some dignity. "I am not at all nervous."

"That's good," he said, as blandly as if he hadn't known I was in a panic of fear. "I'll just be sure you get to your door unmolested."

He took my lantern, turned down the wick again, and we left the warmth of the kitchen.

"By the way," he said in a low whisper as we went through the doorway, "have you ever seen anyone taking shorthand?"

"Why—yes, I think so. You mean those wriggly little marks?"

"Exactly," he said. "Well, keep it in——" He broke off abruptly. "What ails that dog?" He whispered sharply. I think his breath caught and I'm sure mine did.

The dog, his gold and white coat outlined sharply in the area of light cast by my lantern against the blackness of the reaching shadows beyond, was standing at the door of Frawley's room.

He was standing quite still, his head lowered, his ears alert—and his ruff was standing on end, every hair electric. He did not appear to note our presence. And all at once he turned, his body low to the floor, and fled into the darkness. "Fled" is the only word. And a collie is afraid of nothing human.

I was trembling. And I think O'Leary was a little shaken in spite of the direct way in which he hurried to that door and opened it.

He held the lantern high and I peered over his shoulder. The room was icy cold. A sheet had been hung over the broken window and the snow on it had frozen so that the cloth was quite stiff.

On the bed, beneath another sheet, lay that still figure.

O'Leary advanced quickly to the bed and jerked the sheet backward.

I stared, leaned forward, and pressed my hands against my teeth to hold back a scream.

The black toupee covered that head. The towel had been carefully reknotted above the hair.

There was a long silence. I could hear my heart

beating and rather irregular breaths coming from
O'Leary.

Then he pulled the sheet upward again, and sighed.
"Hell!" he said. "If this keeps up I'll have to camp
on a chair outside this door!"

CHAPTER IX

THE POISON AGAIN

THE rest of the night passed somewhat lengthily and not any too well. Twice I roused uneasily, only to listen anxiously and then force myself to settle back into a light sleep again, and once I was sure I heard the dog growling outside in the main room. However, morning did come at length and with it more snow and a settled depression. My patient was decidedly cantankerous that morning, I remember, and kept to her bed again, staring at the gray window pane from eye sockets that were black and deep-sunken, and explaining her symptoms to me at some length—which included, if I am not mistaken, a neuralgic headache, shooting pains in her left arm, a buzzing sensation in her chest and a heavy feeling below her heart. I surrounded her with hot-water bottles, forbore to suggest a connection between the heavy feeling below her heart and the nightly meal of cheese and meat, and sent Brunker in with her breakfast tray.

I don't know whether O'Leary made good his threat to camp before Frawley's door or not; I am inclined to think not, although he was already about when I came out to breakfast, gray and immaculate and imperturbable, with the clearest of eyes. My own felt tight and weary.

It was strange that as the others gathered, warming themselves about the fireplaces, haggard, hollow-eyed, staring at the windows, and avoiding each other, nothing was said about the weather. No one mentioned the continued storm; no one expressed surprise, no one hoped audibly that it would soon stop. Yet I was perfectly sure that the continued storm, and our resultant isolation, was uppermost in everyone's thoughts, and it was not nice to see eyes going in a furtive way to that closed door and then being hurriedly withdrawn.

Appetites were heartier that morning; I think our hunger overcame to some extent our discretion, and when the boiled eggs ran out, as they did early in the meal, muffins and a cooked cereal were resorted to, though somewhat languidly and with many covert glances about the table. I believe Matil asked Brunker for more eggs, for I saw him shake his head and heard something about supplies and the man from Nettleson. After breakfast she went at once to the kitchen and had a prolonged conversation with Annette, whence she returned looking anxious, and I heard her telling Helene Paggi that the supplies were getting a little low.

"There's enough for a day or so, if we aren't particular as to variety," she added.

"Matil Kingery, do you mean to say that you've brought us out here without enough food?" cried Helene indignantly.

"I'm really awfully sorry," replied Matil. "I had arranged to have fresh fruit and vegetables and all sent out from Barrington to Nettleson and a man there was to bring them on to Hunting's End. I never thought of it storming like this. In fact, I didn't dream that there could be such a storm, ever—anywhere."

"You should have thought of it," bristled Helene, whom I judged to be rather fonder of her food than is quite discreet. Her eyes looked tearful. "Jo," she called complainingly to her husband, "Matil says there's not enough food for more than a meal or two. This horrible storm may keep up for days and days. Really, I think it's bad enough to be shut up in a house with a dead body without being starved to death, too."

"Helene!" said Jo Paggi sharply. His olive eyes looked ugly. "Don't be a fool. Matil can't help it."

"She could have," flashed Helene, getting herself into a nice rage. "She'd no business having us out here. She might have known something horrible would happen. This lodge is haunted!" She flung herself petulantly into a chair and let tears roll down her agitated cheeks. "There's a devil in it. Don't look like that at me, Jo. I'm not afraid of you. I'll say what I please. I tell you there's a devil in this place. Who knows what's going to happen next!"

"*Helene!*" Paggi leaned over her. His face was flushed darkly red, and if, as his wife said, there was a devil in the lodge, it certainly looked out of Paggi's eyes for just an instant. He closed his hand on his wife's fat arm so firmly that she looked up in the middle of a sob, her mouth fell a little open, and her eyes flickered and wavered, and finally met his for a long moment.

"I'm sorry Helene said all this, Matil," said Paggi,

then was suddenly buoyant and smiling again. His white teeth flashed pleasantly. "She is a little upset, I think; a little forgetful."

Killian had lounged across and was standing at one side, tall and easy, his eyes narrowed and lazy but holding a spark somewhere in their depths.

"You aren't making it any better, are you, Jo?" he said indolently, smiling a little. "Matil, do you want me to try to get to town?"

"Oh——" Her breath caught a little quickly and I saw Paggi's eyes glint and that lambent flame leap into them. "*Lal—you can't!*" She paused and continued less vehemently: "No one could. Not in this storm."

Killian looked deeply into the girl's eyes; Paggi's smile became fixed.

"One might try at least," said Killian finally. Morse had strolled up to the little group in time to hear the last.

"Try what?" he asked abruptly.

"Try to get to town," said Killian in an expressionless voice.

"No one can," repeated Matil. "It would be—death. A horrible, slow death." Her slim hands began to twist a little. Killian's eyes lingered on them and he half extended his own hand, only to withdraw it hurriedly and reach into a pocket for a cigarette. His lighter did not work at once and he said something impatiently under his breath, though his face was as unmoved and his eyes as lazy as ever.

"Well," he said easily, "there's no need for any of us to make frozen offerings of ourselves. This snow will be gone in a day or so; it can't last forever. Most of us are fairly sporting about the thing, I think; might as well be. And as for Helene——" He looked at Helene, letting his gray-brown eyes sweep her slowly from head to foot; only then did I realize that he was furiously, wildly angry beneath his air of nonchalance. "Helene's got too much flesh anyway," he said cruelly and casually, and strolled away, his shoulders graceful under his brown tweed coat, his dark head arrogant.

"Pig!" cried Helene shrilly. "Pig! Jo, did you hear him? He is a barbarian."

"You brought it on yourself," said Jo, none too pleasantly.

Morse took off his horn-rimmed eyeglasses and began to polish them nervously, and Matil stared after Killian for a moment, her hands still working, her blue eyes dark in her white face.

"Never mind, Matil," said Morse clumsily. "Don't look like that, dear. This isn't your fault. Don't blame yourself."

She turned her eyes slowly toward Morse so that she looked directly into his face. He met her gaze steadily; I can still see his rather thick body, his smooth light hair, the bleak, harassed look in his eyes. In a day and two nights his face had lost its ruddy look of health; it was pale that morning—but then, so were we all—and there were anxious little lines about his eyes and rather nice mouth.

"You are quite right, Newell," said Matil, all at once very steady and cold. "Whosesoever fault it is, it is certainly not mine. And I am possibly the only one of you who can say that with honesty."

"Why—why, Matil," said Morse, taken aback, as well he might be, but still kindly. "You don't mean that, Matil."

She moved her shoulders impatiently.

"Oh—perhaps I don't. I don't know what I mean." She spoke wearily and then suddenly flared into a queer little outburst of temper: "And really, Helene, when I consider everything I'm not at all concerned about your starving to death. Go ahead and starve!"

She finished in a voice that made no doubt of the matter and walked away. And just then I became aware that Aunt Lucy's cane had been pounding for some time, and I, too, left the little group around the fireplace.

As I opened Aunt Lucy's door I glanced back. O'Leary was looking at the small red pencil in his fingers; Helene, her face blotchy and agitated, was taking a cigarette out of her case with long fingers that trembled; Killian was lounging on the piano bench, rubbing Jericho's ears, who crouched beside him, his eyes intent through the little cloud of blue smoke that surrounded him; Paggi had made a motion as if to follow Matil, but thought better of it; Morse appeared to be plunged deep in thought; and Terice, laying out a game of solitaire at one end of the tables and winking through cigarette smoke, was smiling with a spiteful pleasure.

That day, although it was as long-drawn-out in its monotonous hours of waiting as the first one had been,

still seemed to arouse us from the torpor of the preceding day. There was some attempt at normal, everyday living. The horror of being shut in with the body
of a murdered man, and, moreover, with the murderer
himself, was no less—indeed, it grew uglier with every
moment of waiting—but still we had roused a little
from the numb inactivity of shock. It was not, however, any pleasanter than the preceding day, for with
awakening, strained nerves grew impatient, querulous,
sensitive to small irritations, and all the time that
primitive fear of death and the dead which lurks in
the depths of everyone's heart was present, ready
to grip us and shake our very souls every time the
wind shrieked around a corner of the lodge, or a log
cracked loudly, or someone moved suddenly. I have
seen the whole group, O'Leary included, start up when
someone scraped his chair along the floor—start up
with darting eyes and tensed nerves, only to drop back
again and take hasty refuge in cigarettes, or talk, or a
restless stroll up and down the long room. And always
they watched the snow.

It was still quite early when O'Leary presented himself at Aunt Lucy's door and received her hoarse per-
mission to enter.

"Don't go, Miss Keate," he said, as I made a half-
hearted motion to leave. "Your patient might need
you."

I had no objection to remaining, of course, and sat
down at the foot of the bed with my knitting in my
hands.

"Sit down," said Aunt Lucy. "You look all right this

morning, young man. So you're a detective? Well, who shot Frawley?"

"I don't know, Miss Kingery," said O'Leary quietly. "How are you this morning?"

"So-so," replied Aunt Lucy, and promptly detailed her pains. O'Leary listened with the most deceitful solicitude, and when she had finished he suggested that she didn't eat enough at dinner. Upon which Aunt Lucy cast me a very queer look, pulled down the sleeves of her gray knitted bed jacket, and lapsed at once into silence.

I think O'Leary did not know how directly he had touched the source of her indisposition, for he went on blandly:

"I was afraid you were too upset to be troubled yesterday. Do you feel like helping me a little this morning?"

"Just what do you mean?" said the old woman, lowering her thick eyebrows suspiciously.

"By answering some questions."

"What kind of questions?"

"Well, for one thing—" O'Leary reached into his pocket and then drew his hand out hastily, without the pencil—"for one thing, just who is the little blonde woman who calls herself Baroness von Turcum?"

"She *is* Baroness von Turcum," said Aunt Lucy quickly, as if in defense. Then she lowered her voice to a sudden rasping whisper, and her eyes looked malicious: "And she's a painted hussy, if you ask me."

O'Leary cleared his throat vigorously before he continued.

"Is she an old acquaintance?"

"Too old," said Aunt Lucy, frowning. Then she deigned to explain. "She came to Barrington about six years ago, I think. Was a good friend of Helene Paggi's until—they fell out. They still kiss when they meet, but if they had their way about it they'd bite each other instead. Oh, yes, I've seen a good deal of Terice von Turcum, one way and another. Had to while Huber—" she paused and her eyes looked suspicious—"while Huber was alive," she finished slowly.

"Huber—that's your brother?" asked O'Leary.

"Certainly. You know that."

"And he—died here?"

"Of course. Don't hedge. That's what Matil brought you here for, wasn't it? To find out how Huber died?" She had bent forward a little and now she leaned back against the pillow, her face like clay against the white linen and her expression complacent. "But you never will."

"Possibly not," said O'Leary quietly. He looked at the white window for a moment and then said rather unexpectedly: "Just what is your opinion of that affair, Miss Kingery? You must have some explanation?"

She peered at him warily, as if she were about to crawl back into her cobwebs and hide herself.

"I don't know a thing about that, young man. Don't forget. I don't know a thing about it." She stopped as if she were going to say not a word more, and then continued without warning: "Any man who lived like Huber did must be prepared for a sudden taking off."

I must say the words shocked me a little, coming

as they did from the man's sister, and, moreover, a
sister whose devotion had been so intense that the
shock of his tragic death had made her an invalid for
five years. That, or—I added to myself—her un-
bridled fondness for rich foods.

"You did not approve of your brother's way of living?" asked O'Leary, very quietly, very gently.

"Approve!" The old woman snorted; it was a definite and extremely vulgar snort, such as only aris-
tocracy may permit itself, and she seemed to think it
expressive enough without amplifying it. And, indeed,
she was quite right.

"You indicate that Signora Paggi and the Baroness
are no longer friends. Do you know why?"

Aunt Lucy nodded her grizzled head a great many
times but said nothing.

"Trouble over Paggi, I presume," said O'Leary.

Her great eyes flashed.

"Paggi, nothing!" she said. "Trouble over Huber.
That was it. Terice thought she'd got him fast, when
Helene stepped in. Helene was much handsomer then
than she is now and Huber was quite mad about her.
For a while. It wouldn't have lasted. Yes," repeated
the horrible old woman with a kind of complacence,
"Huber always had good taste about his women. He
used to say beauty and brains didn't go together and
he preferred beauty. Easier to manage," she added
with a most disagreeable chuckle.

"At just what stage was his—er—interest in Madame Paggi when he died?"

"At the height," replied Lucy Kingery, with a candor which I considered in remarkably bad taste. "Yes, Helene was quite nice-looking. Terice was always scrawny; I dare say that's one reason Huber tired of her so quickly. She wanted marriage, too; she was tired of being a penniless widow. But Huber never thought of marriage, not after having had Matil. That's Matil's mother, of course; if she had lived things might have gone differently." A kind of hurt look came over the dark lined face and she said rather simply: "Yes, things might have gone differently. Something went out of Huber when she died; it was as if he had lost his soul." Then her face darkened again and she said vigorously: "But don't you forget it: Huber was bad. Huber was bad."

"But a good brother," said O'Leary rather daringly.

She looked at him intently.

"No," she said slowly. "He was not a good brother. I always thought he was that, at least until——" She stopped abruptly, as if on the verge of letting out something that was better reserved, and clamped her iron mouth shut with a metallic snap.

"Was Paggi jealous?" asked O'Leary, after waiting a moment.

"Paggi?" Aunt Lucy laughed. "If he was the tables are turned now."

"Tables are turned now?" repeated O'Leary.

I think Aunt Lucy felt that she was growing unwise in her revelations but her feverish mood for talking prevailed; it would be followed, I knew, by a prolonged spell of melancholy brooding but just now talk she must.

"I should think it would be fairly clear," she said unpleasantly. "Helene realizes she is growing older and isn't so handsome as she once was. And she knows women run after Paggi; they do pursue an opera singer. He makes quite a lot of money, and he has got tired of her—oh, it's an obvious enough situation. Helene is afraid she'll lose him, now."

"And was Signor Paggi jealous of his wife and your brother?"

She nodded again vigorously but said nothing, though there was a look in her eyes as if she might have said a great deal, had she been so inclined.

"Does Miss Matil—er—favor Paggi?"

Aunt Lucy gave O'Leary a sharp look.

"Not choosy with your questions, are you?" she said rather nastily. "Well, I don't mind telling you that Matil——" She stopped, leaving her sentence hanging in the air for a moment before she concluded abruptly: "Ask Matil, if you want to know. Paggi is a nice enough fellow. Women always like him. It's the way he sings. And then he is very popular, asked everywhere, people are mad about him."

"Miss Lucy," said O'Leary suddenly, leaning forward, "why did you want Frawley's toupee?"

If he had hoped to take the woman by surprise she was more than a match for him. Her great eyes surveyed him blankly.

"Frawley's toupee?" she repeated. "I don't want the thing. Why should I? What do you mean?"

"I mean," said O'Leary, quite unabashed, "that Gerald Frawley's toupee disappeared. Someone must have taken it and——"

"So you thought I did!" Her putty-colored face grew livid with sudden rage. "Well, let me tell you, young man, I've got hair enough of my own without taking anybody's toupee, let alone that from a dead man's head. Besides," she said craftily, calming a little and leaning back against the pillows again, "besides, I'm helpless. I can't walk."

"That's right," said O'Leary. "You've been an invalid for some time, have you not?"

She nodded.

"Haven't walked since Huber's death. Everybody knows that. The shock of his death caused it. There aren't many sisters who love their brothers as I did. Not many who never recover from the shock of their brother's death. Yes, I've been an invalid ever since."

O'Leary looked at her quietly. My own thoughts were far from respectful. Loved her brother, indeed! She'd hated him, or I was no judge of human kind.

O'Leary arose.

"May I come in again and visit, Miss Lucy?" he asked, letting that very winning smile come to his lips for an instant.

"Certainly," said she. "I like young men. But if you think you are going to find out anything about Huber's death, you are wrong. All wrong. You can't do it."

"But Miss Lucy, I've been told he died of heart failure," said O'Leary.

"H'mm!" she grunted noisily and very scornfully.

"Don't try to deceive me. I know why you are here. I'm tired, Miss Keate. Fix these pillows, will you?"

"Ah, Miss Keate," said O'Leary, "you can take shorthand, can't you?" And as I made a startled motion which might have meant anything, he said to Miss Lucy, "May I borrow your nurse awhile, Miss Kingery?"

"Certainly. I'm going to sleep. Go ahead, Miss Keate. I'll knock with my cane if I want anything."

Nothing loath, I left my knitting on the chair, shook up Aunt Lucy's pillows, put some fresh water on her bedside table, and followed O'Leary into the main room.

"Nevertheless I think she took that toupee," said O'Leary quietly. "And she's got the note to Matil right now. She was about to tell us that Matil had been engaged to Frawley. Did it strike you that she made rather a point of being so affected by her brother's death? Well, let me see. There's Julian Barre over by the window. Suppose we chat with him awhile. Here's some paper, Miss Keate, and a pencil."

Not long ago in my desk I ran across that yellow page on which were a higgledy-piggledy of queer little hooks and curves which looked like nothing so much as the efforts of a baby or a lunatic. I looked at the thing and recalled that snowbound day, the leaping of the fires, the bleak white window panes, the enormous room with its silence, its secrets, those pale faces and furtive, watchful eyes—and myself in my white uniform with that sheet of paper on a magazine on my lap, listening with all my ears to the questions put by

O'Leary and making silly little marks to justify O'Leary's implied statement that I was taking down the inquiry in shorthand. No one objected, though Julian Barre looked at me rather askance and hinted that, isolated and cut off from help as we were, O'Leary might have his own way, but had we been back in Barrington things might have been different. Which was quite true but not exactly as Mr. Barre meant.

He was very willing to talk and replied definitely and without reluctance to all of O'Leary's inquiries, though it seemed to me that he was more willing to talk of the present party at Hunting's End than of that other one. I caught myself studying the man rather closely and once or twice forgot my meaningless little pencil marks and had to be recalled by a sharp look from O'Leary.

Julian Barre admitted at once and without hedging that Huber Kingery had not died of heart failure.

"Yes, he was shot. There in the same room in which poor Gerald Frawley met his death. There's no use trying to keep it from you for I presume Matil has told you the whole thing." His voice, which was even and rather pleasant, lifted inquiringly at the end of the sentence, as if he would like to know exactly what Matil had told O'Leary, but O'Leary was oblivious to the implied question.

"See here, Mr. Barre," said O'Leary, with that frank little manner which made him so many friends and which so frequently covered thoughts of an entirely different nature. "You were here, were you not, when Kingery was killed?"

Julian Barre's eyes narrowed a little. He had rather nice eyes, but his mantle of tolerance and sophistication cloaked any earnestness he might have displayed and made me doubt his sincerity.

"Yes," he replied.

"What was your opinion of that affair?"

"Well—I shall be quite frank with you, Mr. O'Leary. I was Huber's best friend, I think; his tragic death was a severe blow to me. But I thought, and I still think, it best on all accounts to leave the matter untouched. You see, Huber was highly thought of in Barrington, and—well, to be brutally frank, an investigation of the peculiar circumstances of his death would bring before the public certain phases of his life which were unsavory. Unsavory, to say the least."

"But surely you had an impulse to avenge your friend." O'Leary's clear gray eyes were watching the steady snow outside the window pane. "To find and bring to justice your best friend's murderer?"

"No," said Julian Barre with the utmost ease. "I had no such impulse. I much preferred protecting my friend's memory. And saving his daughter as much as possible."

"Then you must have considered Kingery's death was—er—justified."

"That is a terrible thing to say, O'Leary. And it is a dreadful thing to admit. But—it is quite possible that it was justified."

"Then, if you believe that, Mr. Barre, our problem

is quite simple. Who among this party here had such a real and desperate grievance against Huber Kingery?"

There was a long silence. Barre's handsome clear-cut features were composed, his eyes thoughtful. He ran a large, well-shaped hand over his hair, shifted his position a little, reached for a cigarette case, offered it to me and then to O'Leary. I refused, having been brought up in the days when silk stockings were doubtful, rouge suspicious, and cigarettes conclusive; O'Leary accepted and bent forward with a light, and in its tiny flare I studied the face of the man before me.

His straight nose, his well-cut chin and rather hard mouth, his unshaken ease and polish were all very attractive and I began to wonder why Matil had not fallen in love with him. True, he was a friend of her father's, but daughters have married, yes, and loved, their father's friends before now, and I, myself, should have much preferred him to Gerald Frawley.

"That is a question that it is almost impossible for me to answer," he was saying thoughtfully, his eyes squinted to escape a little eddy of smoke. "All these people are my friends. I can't turn suspicion upon one of them. You must understand that. Besides, in spite of my affection for Huber, as I have said his death might —mind I say *might*—have been justified."

"Do you mean that you have definite suspicions?"

"No—no. I can't say that."

"Then do you mean that, of all these people, each one might have a motive?"

Julian Barre surveyed O'Leary soberly for a moment before he spoke.

"You are determined to make me answer, aren't you? Well, I'll go this far. I know that I had no motive. I know that Matil had no motive. If either of the servants had a motive, I don't know what it was. And there you are."

"You mean then that Paggi, his wife, Baroness von Turcum—each had motives to kill Huber Kingery? That these three young fellows, Morse and Killian and —yes, and Frawley, each had a motive? Even that Miss Lucy Kingery, Huber Kingery's own sister, had a motive?"

"No," said Barre, a little sharply. "No. I meant nothing of the kind. Do you think that Gerald Frawley's death is connected in any way with Kingery's death of five long years ago?" he asked suddenly.

"Do you think so, yourself?"

"I—don't know," replied Barre soberly. "I don't see how it could be. If I were sure of that—— See here, O'Leary. You are a decent enough fellow. Why stir up anything about Huber's death? You'll only make trouble for all of us. He is buried and his faults forgotten and his memory respected. And his daughter ——" He paused and O'Leary said softly:

"Not happy, Barre."

"Well, perhaps she is not happy," granted Barre slowly. "But happier than she would be if all the truth were hashed about in courts and in the newspapers."

"And, moreover, as you suggest, it would mean trouble for all of you," remarked O'Leary very gently.

Barre made an impatient movement.

"Why, of course it would mean trouble for all of

us. And I, for one, am not anxious for it: the publicity, the grinding inquiry, the long-drawn-out routine of the law which can be so blind. I think no one has ever come out from a murder trial as he went in. It leaves a blight—a certain soil—a scar."

"Are you still thinking entirely of Miss Matil?"

A slow flush crept into Barre's cheeks.

"No. I'm thinking of myself, too: my position in Barrington, the trust company of which I am president, the responsibility I hold. And I am not the only one who would be injured. There are social positions. Business matters. Paggi, for instance, will be ruined if all this comes out. He knows it."

"I thought publicity of that kind was good for a singer," remarked O'Leary idly.

"Not for one in Paggi's place," said Barre definitely.

"But I had the impression that the Paggis were rather—well fixed. That Signor Paggi could be quite independent of the public's favor. Hasn't he stock in the Kingery Trust Company?"

Julian Barre studied his cigarette for a long moment before he spoke.

"Well," he said finally, "yes. He has some stock. And I'll tell you—the stock he owns was given him by the late—" he scrutinized the tip of the cigarette closely—"by the late Huber Kingery."

O'Leary did not speak for a moment or two. Then he said in an expressionless voice:

"You are suggesting, I suppose you realize, that this—er—gift was actually in the nature of a price."

Barre shrugged.

"I am suggesting nothing of the kind. I have said too much. I actually know nothing about it. But—well, you can understand that none of us would relish an investigation of Huber's death."

"Do you mean that you think Gerald Frawley's death was a result of Kingery's death, and that inquiry into one entails inquiry into the other?"

"I did not say that," said Barre evenly. "But since you ask me—I think it possible."

"Do you mind telling me why you think that?"

"Not in the least. It has probably already occurred to you. Frawley must have got hold of something—some dangerous knowledge."

"It must have been very dangerous knowledge," said O'Leary. "Frawley was a vice president of the Kingery Trust Company, was he not?"

"Yes. First."

"And Killian and Morse are connected with the company?"

"Yes. Have been for some time."

"Are they in positions of importance?"

"Well—yes. They are both in the investment department. Fine young fellows, both of them."

"How are the company's finances?"

"What do you mean? You can go too far, O'Leary. There is no more solidly organized company than the Kingery Trust Company. All my money is in it, and I have always insisted upon the most conservative of investments. No, if you are trying to find something wrong with the Kingery Trust you will fail. These murders are, in my opinion, from very private and personal reasons."

Brunker was standing suddenly at O'Leary's elbow. His advance had been so silent that I had not seen him and started nervously as he spoke. He addressed me, however, somewhat incoherently.

"The dog," he said. "The dog—perhaps the nurse would look at him."

"Why, what's the matter with the dog?" asked Barre. "Is he sick?"

"The dog—I think he's poisoned," said Brunker.

CHAPTER X

I ENTER A ROOM

BRUNKER was quite right. The dog was poisoned and most thoroughly. We found him stretched out on the floor of the storeroom for wood and coal at one end of the kitchen. His eyes were glazed slightly, his legs already numb. Someone told Matil, and when she followed us Jericho tried to get up and walk over to her, but his front legs were stiff and his back legs dragged helplessly and he collapsed on the floor and closed his eyes.

"It's strychnine, I think," I said. "Heat some lard, Annette, quickly."

We worked over the dog anxiously, with everyone I think but possibly Aunt Lucy drifting in and out of the crowded little room to lend a hand or to stand and offer suggestions. We used all the hot lard Annette had and by noon he was distinctly better. It was a close call. If he had had more strychnine or less we could have done nothing, but we poured the hot lard down his throat valiantly and finally left him, when Brunker announced lunch, weak and sick, with grease all over his ruff, but his eyes were wide open and intelligent again, and as Matil stooped over him he lifted his tail in a feeble wag.

Directly after lunch, which was a strained and silent meal, we returned. By that time the dog was much better and I felt sure he would recover.

"You are sure it was strychnine, Miss Keate?" said O'Leary in a low voice as we bent over the collie, and as I nodded affirmatively he turned to Annette.

I think she had been expecting a few questions for she seemed to brace herself a little and her keen blue eyes were very shrewd.

"Do you know anything about this?" he asked directly.

Brunker turned quickly from the silver he was cleaning to watch with cold, dispassionate eyes, and Matil, who had followed us from the lunch table, sat down in one of the straight, hard kitchen chairs, glancing from the dog to Annette and O'Leary.

"Not anything," said Annette. "The first thing I know, Brunker says, 'The dog, he is sick.'"

"Certainly," said O'Leary. "But—what had you fed the dog to-day?"

"To-day?" she said, with an air of one striving to recall. "I think he did not eat much to-day. But this morning—this morning a large part of some roast in the pantry was gone. I think the poison might have been given him on that."

"You think then he was poisoned during the night? How about it, Miss Keate? Wouldn't the poison have taken effect sooner if that were true?"

"Not if he ate poisoned meat quite early this morning. It's hard to say definitely just how soon it will affect a dog; so much depends on the dog's strength and the amount of poison he got. Strychnine works rapidly. Of course, this may have been a mixture of some kind. It may have been——" I stopped suddenly.

O'Leary finished for me:

"It may have been the rat poison? That's exactly what it was; evidently given to him during the night."

"Oh!" said Brunker suddenly. "I think—I think someone was about the lodge during the night." He addressed O'Leary. "This morning I found the fire had been built up and there were two cups on the kitchen table. They were empty but smelled as if they'd had coffee in them."

"Indeed," said O'Leary soberly, and Annette looked at me with such disconcerting and approving knowledge in her sly eyes that I rose abruptly.

"I think the dog will do now," I said, and beat a retreat with such dignity as I could muster.

I went at once to my patient, who had to know immediately and with detail why we had all spent so much time in the coal room; upon my informing her she lapsed into rather enigmatic silence.

I believe that O'Leary remained in the kitchen for some time talking to Brunker and Annette, but he gained nothing by it, he told me later, save a feeling that both servants knew more than they pretended about affairs in the lodge. But he added that that was quite natural.

"The devil of it is," he said abruptly, "I can't find that poison. And I've been over this place with a fine-toothed comb. Busy now, Miss Keate? You are getting on splendidly with your shorthand. What was your impression of Barre this morning?"

"I hardly know," I said slowly. We were standing near the fireplace, O'Leary bending over with the tongs to adjust a log, and I with my knitting in my hands. Aunt Lucy had intimated her desire to sleep, which left me free for the moment. A desultory bridge game was going on at a table not far from us, Barre and Matil playing against Helene and Morse; Terice was sitting on the arm of Barre's chair, leaning, one felt, rather purposely against Barre's shoulder; Paggi was sitting near Matil, his olive eyes following the game, and Killian was sitting in a chair by the window reading a magazine, upside down—at least the cover, which I could plainly see, showed a girl's head at an angle which nothing in the world was ever painted.

"The trouble is," I said, "Barre is the logical one to suspect, as his room was next to Frawley's and connecting with it."

"Also next to and connecting with Huber Kingery's," said O'Leary rather grimly.

"Is there no way that bolt can be worked from the wrong side?" I asked.

O'Leary smiled.

"Are you trying to pin the guilt for both murders on Barre?" he asked, still smiling. "Well, I'm sorry. He may be guilty, anyone may be. But that bolt could not be moved from the wrong side of the door. And while anyone in a connecting room would certainly be a subject for suspicion, still—Frawley himself must have bolted that door."

I nodded listlessly, my gaze upon the faces around the bridge table. I am bound to say I never saw four such faces ostensibly enjoying a game. They were without exception haggard and drawn and yet there was a ghastly pretense at naturalness, smiles that were mere motions of pale lips, guarded eyes that held horror in their depths. Morse drummed constantly on the table with his fingers and stared at his cards with eyes that did not see them, Barre covertly watched Matil and Paggi, Helene kept looking around her quickly with a sort of nervous jerk as if something were approaching her on stealthy feet, Terice's hard twinkling eyes had deep black rings under them and her heavily painted mouth continually tightened and then relaxed, tightened and relaxed, in a kind of spasm.

"A good time to see if Killian is a little more communicative," murmured O'Leary, and as he approached that gentleman O'Leary added under his breath: "I'm not nervous, but if I had to watch that bridge game very long I'd be a candidate for a sanitarium. Busy, Killian? Miss Keate finds she can take shorthand; I hope you don't mind if she does so now."

Lal Killian gave me no welcome look.

"She can take anything I have to say," he said grudgingly. "I've already told you, O'Leary, that I know simply and absolutely nothing about this business."

"You might know something of it without realizing just what bearing it had on the matter," returned O'Leary blandly. "Good story?"

Killian glanced at his magazine, noted the angle at which he held the thing and flung it on the floor.

"Well, what is it?" he asked somewhat savagely.

"This note which Frawley wrote to Morse, evidently intending to deliver it to him—have you no idea what that may mean?"

"No more than I had the last time we talked of it," said Killian. "I suppose, of course, it is the number to some safety-deposit box or something of the kind. And, judging from Frawley's remarks at dinner about leaving his affairs in shape in case something happened to him, I should say that probably that's where his papers are. But if Morse knows about the whole thing, and I suppose he does, he hasn't seen fit to take me into his confidence."

"Do you think Frawley expected something like this?"

Killian's lazy eyes sharpened suddenly, then he dropped his eyelids.

"If he had, surely he'd have taken some precaution against it," he replied smoothly.

"Still, it's curious that he should have said just that."

"Very curious," agreed Killian impassively.

"You are some official in the Kingery Trust Company, aren't you?"

Killian nodded briefly.

"What's your—er—office?"

"Well, they call me a third or fourth vice president, I believe. It doesn't mean anything. I actually handle some of the investments."

"I hope you'll answer me honestly, Killian, when I ask you if, in your opinion, the affairs of the Kingery Trust are entirely sound or not."

Killian opened his mouth, closed it, then said slowly:

"To the best of my knowledge they are perfectly sound."

"Would you know it if—there was a question in that respect?"

"Yes. All my money is in the company. Naturally I'm rather keen to watch things. But Morse could tell you more of that. Or Frawley——" He checked himself, as if he had forgotten for the moment that Frawley was dead. "Why do you ask?"

O'Leary shrugged.

"Oh, I have no information to the contrary," he said. "It's only that all of you are somehow involved in the same business and—there's always the question of motives in a case like this." O'Leary was rolling the little red pencil back and forth between his slender fingers. "By the way, Killian, it's queer you didn't hear any voices in Frawley's room when Miss Keate, here, heard them. You're quite sure you heard nothing?"

"Quite sure," returned Killian smoothly, although his dark eyes were inscrutable and—yes, a little wary.

"It seems as if you could have heard the sound of voices through that wall, if Miss Keate could hear it through the door."

"It does seem so," agreed Killian easily, turning his unfathomable gaze toward me. "Exactly. *If* Miss Keate heard voices, it seems as though I should have heard them also."

I could feel my face growing warm.

"You probably did hear voices," I flashed. "You couldn't have helped it. And I'd like to know why you refuse to admit it now. Unless—perhaps you were in Mr. Frawley's room, yourself!"

His dark eyes met mine. They were defiant and guarded at the same time.

"Perhaps I was," he said easily. "If so, that lets me out of your calculations, O'Leary, if you're looking for a criminal, because I was definitely and completely barred out of Frawley's room at the moment when he was shot."

"What is that you are saying, Lal?"

It was Matil's voice, low and grave, with that fascinating little catch in it. She had approached without my being aware of her presence, although O'Leary was standing before she spoke.

"Here's a chair, Matil," said Killian. "I was only saying that I, myself, may have been visiting with Frawley when our nurse, here, heard those convenient voices in his room just a few moments before he was shot."

Matil paused with her hand on the back of the chair. Her eyes met Killian's for a long, significant moment, although I could not guess what the meaning of that look was. Her young face was very pale and troubled, blue shadows lay delicately under her long black eyelashes, her soft lips were set rather desperately, but her chin was still up, and her slender shoulders erect.

"I don't understand you, Lal," she said finally.

He moved his shoulders restlessly, thrust his hands into the pockets of his soft tweed coat, and his dark eyes held her gaze.

"If so, however, that lets me out of calculations," he

reminded her. "Because, you see, it is quite evident that I was barred out of Frawley's room when he was actually shot."

Certainly something was going on behind those harmless sentences that was hidden from me. I looked from one to the other, traced a few silly little marks with my pencil, and wondered what that hidden meaning could be.

All at once Killian laughed. It was a bitter laugh, anything but mirthful, and on the heels of it he turned abruptly away.

"It's a stock situation, of course," he said rather unpleasantly to Matil. "But—so it goes, anyhow. One does revert."

"Why—why, Lal," said Matil, faltering a little, but he did not hear her, or did not choose to hear her, for he was halfway across the room. Presently he took a hand at bridge, in which he appeared to find a deep, if somewhat over-fervent, interest.

Matil's blue eyes followed him, looking perplexed and darkly troubled.

"Miss Matil," said O'Leary gently, "why were you in Frawley's room? Oh, I know you were there," he went on quietly, as her troubled eyes leaped to meet his and one hand went suddenly to her slim white throat. "I know you were there. You came through the snow, so great was your wish to speak to him without others seeing or hearing your conversation. He must have helped you through the window. I think you did not talk long and you went back to your room the way you had come, through the snow, which soaked the slippers you hadn't taken time to change for shoes fitter to withstand the snow. And when you got back to your room you were extremely agitated. You did not close the shutters; you only partially lowered the window. And—I think you must have gone to his room very impulsively, for you even forgot to remove your fan before going and it was hanging to your wrist. And—" the girl was staring at him with wide, dark blue eyes, her lips parted a little, her face as white as the snow outside—"and a feather on your fan was broken somehow. A tip of it fluttered to the floor and you did not see it. Don't look so, Miss Matil. Tell me and—" he smiled; his whole face warmed—"try to trust me."

She made several trials before she could speak. Her slim fingers began to twist.

"I don't know how you knew that," she said finally in a husky voice. "But it's quite true. That is exactly what I did. I was in his room, probably five minutes. I had to see him. It—it was most important. I had to beg him to——" She stopped abruptly, her breath catching and a look of dismay stirring back of that helpless white terror in her face.

"To what, Miss Matil?" urged O'Leary gently.

"To—to do something for me. But I didn't shoot him." A sob forced its way into her throat. She choked it back, set her soft lips firmly.

"I know that," said O'Leary. "I know you didn't shoot him."

I think she retained a semblance of composure only by the greatest effort. She was conscious, too, as we always were during those days at Hunting's End, of the continual observance of others, of ears that were straining to hear, of quick, sharp eyes; she glanced swiftly toward the bridge table as if to be sure no one had witnessed her agitation. Then she leaned a little toward O'Leary.

"Who shot him?" she said in a tense whisper. "I must know, Mr. O'Leary. Oh, I must know!" It was almost a wail of terror and fear and some harrowing anxiety.

He shook his head slowly.

"I'm sorry. I don't know, yet. But I know you did not. Whoever shot him had to escape by the door into the main room, and you couldn't have come out that door and got to your room, whence several people saw you emerge after the shot, without Miss Keate, here, and Paggi having seen you."

She sat down then, wearily, as if she could not stand.

"This is all my fault, Mr. O'Leary. I should have let things remain as they were. I ought never to have stirred up old ghosts." She shuddered. "How I wish I had the last four days over again. I would never, never come to Hunting's End." Her haunted eyes went to the door of Gerald Frawley's room as if drawn by a magnet. "His death is my fault," she said in a slow voice that made me shiver.

"Nonsense! Your engagement to him had nothing to do with his death."

"My engagement to him! How did you know that?"

"He left a note to you. I think he had likely written it just after you left him that night. It mentioned your engagement, insisted that you permit him to announce it." He stopped speaking and she nodded in a dazed fashion, her eyes upon O'Leary's as if she could not tear them away.

"It struck me," went on O'Leary very quietly, "that he urged in a somewhat peremptory style. However that may be, the note through a—misadventure—has vanished." He paused and I scribbled furiously on the pad of paper. "I must ask you, Miss Matil, how your fiancé appeared when you left him—was he worried, troubled? Do you think he had any notion of what was so soon to befall him?"

"No," she said. "No, I don't think so."

"Do you remember," said O'Leary slowly, scrutinizing the end of the shabby stub of pencil with much interest—"do you remember, for instance, whether he—was wearing his toupee or not, when you left him?"

The girl's eyes widened after a moment and a faint little flush crept into her white cheeks, though her blue eyes did not falter.

"He was wearing it," she said. "I did not know he wore a toupee until we saw him there—dead. He—I think he was reading when I knocked at the window and he opened it for me and helped me over the sill. It was very cold. He still wore his dinner coat and was smoking a pipe. . . . That note, Mr. O'Leary, where is it? Why was it not given to me?"

It was just at that moment, I recall, and much to my relief, that I heard Aunt Lucy's cane give a premonitory clatter on the floor. I rose abruptly as O'Leary, a spark glinting under the soberness of his clear gray eyes, began to explain in guarded terms about the note. Aunt Lucy's black cane was as often a blessing as it was a curse.

She kept me at her side most of the afternoon, reading to her out of the Old Testament, massaging her, and bringing her reports of the storm. She grumbled considerably about the snow, I remember, and sent me once to the kitchen to see how the dog was getting on. Upon my report that he had so far recovered as to lap a little of Annette's soup, she muttered something indistinguishable to the effect that if that didn't kill him nothing would, and lapsed once more into one of her fits of brooding silence. I picked up my knitting, but found I had lost one of the needles and dropped a number of stitches into the bargain, so I stared out the window at the snow, shivered, thought I should stifle in the atmosphere engendered by the little heater, and longed for my nice little apartment in Barrington where there was no snow, no shut-in fear, no dead thing, cold and waiting and unrevenged.

Brunker brought tea trays to the room. The tea was very strong and the thin little biscuits were damp and not too plentiful. Aunt Lucy looked at her tray in scorn and demanded cheese, which, when it arrived, she ate voraciously, staring fixedly at the merciless snow behind the gradually darkening window pane, reaching automatically for tea which she downed in great gulps, and chewing as if each bite were the last she was likely to get. Which, to tell the truth, was rather more likely than it sounds, for more reasons than one. Food was scarce, and getting scarcer; the snow showed no signs of letting up, and I knew that, even when it stopped snowing, it might be some time before any of us could get to Nettleson. And while the poisoning of the dog was bound to blunt our appetites for the time being, still Nature does reassert herself and that very powerfully. I ate every last crumb of the biscuits Brunker had allowed me.

After tea Aunt Lucy dozed again, and I slipped out of her room to taste the fresher air of the main room.

Apparently everyone had gone to rest and dress for dinner for the long room was quite deserted, the fires burning a little low, a few lanterns shining here and there, and long shadows under the stairway and balcony and around the grand piano whose white birchbark finish loomed up ghostily.

A door toward the kitchen opened. Morse came out and without a glance in my direction knocked on Killian's door. It opened, Killian's tall figure stood for a moment silhouetted against the light, and then Morse entered and the door closed.

Evidently they had something to say to each other. And immediately it occurred to me to test the acoustic properties of that wall that was between Killian's room and the room where the dead man lay.

I acted on an impulse, that being a part of my unfortunate temperament. I had not more than pushed open that door into Frawley's room when I regretted my ill-considered act. The air struck me cold and dank and inexpressibly chilling. It was almost dark in the room; I could distinguish the cold bare outlines of furniture and the sheeted figure on the bed.

The sheeted figure on the bed.

My eyes were caught and held by that figure. It looked as it had when last I had seen it; surely it looked the same. And yet—there was a kind of lumpiness about it. An absence of those stiff, stark lines that suggested cold rigidity.

I don't know how I managed to approach the bed. Somehow I did and touched that sheet and took it in my fingers and pulled it slowly backward.

Two white pillows were stretched on the bed, pushed into semblance of human form and covered with the sheet. And at the top of the bed, something dark lay curled complacently.

It was the nondescript cat, sleeping. It raised its head and looked at me with great, shining, wicked eyes and opened its red mouth and yawned.

It lay exactly where Gerald Frawley's head had lain.

But the body was gone.

CHAPTER XI

DEAD MEN HAVE WALKED

I THINK I screamed. I'm sure I screamed and backed out of the room, leaving the door wide open, and was unable to pull my eyes from that spot on the bed where lay the pillows and the cat, and nothing else. That was the horror of it: nothing else was there.

At any rate others came, running, crying out, gasping questions as their eyes followed my outstretched hands. It was twenty minutes, I suppose, before O'Leary succeeded in getting a semblance of order restored. And though my memory of that twenty-minute period is uncertain and chaotic, I do recall that very suddenly and simultaneously a kind of blanket of silence descended upon us; I suppose that that sudden silence marked the end of incredulous amazement and horror, and the beginning of speculation. And that speculation brought with it a kind of pall of horror.

I remember crouching in one of the rustic settles by the fireplace, leaning forward to warm my shaking, ice-cold hands, trying to control the wild terror that had taken possession of me. I vaguely recall Matil's face, which looked exactly as if it had been carved of white marble, the blanket that Aunt Lucy had tossed around her, and how I noted dazedly that she had got out of her bed and into her wheel chair without help, and how her purple lips mumbled and muttered to herself, and something of the others' terror-struck, incredulous faces. And then I recall Lance O'Leary pushing the thin cat with his foot out of Frawley's room and into the main room, how reluctant the cat seemed to be to leave the warm bed it had made for itself, and how O'Leary closed the door and advanced toward us, Barre and Lal Killian trailing behind him and Morse getting up from a chair to follow. As O'Leary approached I caught a black flash in his usually serene eyes and noted the white fury in his face.

"There *is* a question of decency," he said in a low tone that somehow cut sharply through the miasma of horror. I sat up, pushed my cap off my right ear, and took a long shaking breath.

"Somehow I'd expected decency at least among you —a kind of sporting decency. I'd expected a grain or so of breeding. One of you is a murderer—you know that and all of us know it. I suppose a man or woman equal to murder is equal to anything—but I hadn't expected callous, deliberate brutality. You might have let that poor dead body lie in peace. You might have had some respect for the dead. One of you has done this, of course. I don't know why, now. But I'll find out. Up till now I've counted on a halfway coöperation from a few of you, a sense of fair play. I know, of course, that not one of you, unless it is Miss Matil, who asked me to come here, has been in the least willing to have the truth brought to light. But still I expected the—well, the fairness, the—the decency of the well bred. I see I've been mistaken. And I suppose there are no cowards like those who've been shielded. Well, from now on it's war, since you will have it so. That dead man didn't get up and take himself away. One of you——"

"How do you know that?—how do you know that?" cried Annette sharply. She was standing, a vast blue bulk on the edge of the little group. Her eyes were like two blue marbles sunk in yellow paste. One fat hand clutched a long and very shining carving knife with a curved blade. If she'd been drinking as usual, the thing had shocked her into sobriety. She went on with a shower of rapid French, to which we all listened in spite of ourselves, and wound up briskly with an English phrase or two which in contrast seemed peculiarly clear and impressive. "Dead men have walked again, before now! Me, I have seen it."

"O—o—o—o——" It was a convulsive, sobbing crescendo from Helene.

"Not when you are sober, Annette, my girl," said Paggi sharply, although his face was exactly the color of an over-ripe tomato. "Now, now, none of that!"

"Annette," said Matil quickly, "put down that knife."

Barre took a quick step forward, grasped Annette's flourishing arm, removed the carving knife from her threatening grasp, and stepped back, keeping the knife in his hand.

Rage left the cook's fat face; those glittering blue marbles sunk farther into the surrounding flesh as her eyelids drooped sullenly. She stepped backward.

"There is a devil," she said in a sullen monotone. "A

devil is in this house. A devil. A devil. And—hear me,
you cold-blooded Americans—murder is in the air.
Murder. Some of your cold blood will be spilt before
morning."

"Annette!" cried Matil again, but gaspingly. And
I could feel the hair back of my ears stir and crawl.

O'Leary was looking soberly at the cook. Some of
the white rage had left his face but he was far from
being his bland, imperturbable self.

"There's no use talking like that, you know," he
said calmly, addressing Annette. "No use at all. But
as a matter of fact—I think you are probably right."

His clear words fell into the shocked silence with
the effect of very sharp shining little stones falling into
a deeply brooding lake; I could almost see the circles
and circles of ever-widening comprehension and then
terror.

"Why—why—O'Leary——" stammered Morse incredulously.

"Murder! Murder!" mouthed Terice in a kind of
numb whisper, her wild eyes on O'Leary's face.

"You can't mean that, O'Leary," expostulated
Barre. "Why, if you mean that, we must—we must
guard ourselves. Guard each other. Guard——"

"Guard against *whom?*" inquired O'Leary, and—
well, it was a peculiar and an unspeakably chilling thing
to see, all at once, eyes going about that group, even as
mine went, lingering, speculating, fearing—at each
meeting pair of eyes. One of them—guard against one
of them. But whom?

"There's not much use looking for the body in the

lodge," went on O'Leary more coolly. "It may be hidden somewhere inside, of course, but I'm inclined to think it's outside, probably not far from the house—hidden in the snow. I shall search for it, however, and when the snow melts—I promise you I will find it."

I looked at Matil. But her dark blue eyes held only still horror. There was no shade of frustration, of the wildness of grief and pain and lost love.

"And as for dead bodies walking," continued O'Leary more briskly, "they don't. Do they, Miss Keate?"

"I—I'm sure I don't know," I said, taken by surprise.

"What!" said O'Leary.

I recalled myself.

"That is—certainly not. *Never.*"

My tone, even in my own ears, lacked conviction, and I saw Annette nod her head with a grisly hint of commendation.

"Well, they don't," said O'Leary. "I assure you it simply isn't done. At ten o'clock this morning I was in that room over there. Frawley's body was still there at that time. Some time since then and now someone has entered that room, disposed of Frawley's body, and left the room. I suppose that—er—cat slipped in unobserved and couldn't get out. I looked all about the room before I followed the rest of you out of it. It was all bolted as usual. The only means of entrance was through this main room. Now then, I think it very unlikely that there was any time during the hours between ten this morning and the present moment when this room was entirely deserted and all the bedroom doors closed so that——" He stopped abruptly. "There *was* a time. While we were working over the dog in the coal room. You were all, I believe, in and out. There might have been a few moments when this room was deserted. A very few moments, however. Well, I can weed out your comings and goings by rather exhaustive inquiry. It will simplify matters if——"

"I will tell you," said Terice suddenly. "I was in this room until a few moments ago. I sat in that chair by the window, reading. My own room is cold. A refrigerator. I couldn't bear to stay in it. And when you all went to look at the dog—I remained here." She moved her small, wiry shoulders impatiently. "I do not like sick dogs. And that is the only time the room was left almost alone. Look—I was in that chair—over there. And I tell you, Mr. O'Leary, no one went into that dead man's room. No one. No one." She leaned back in her chair, her glittering eyes fixed on O'Leary's, her mouth jerking in spite of the tight-set lips, stiff with panic.

There was something in her manner I could not understand. Was she daring O'Leary to suggest that she had moved the body? Was it triumph? Was it fear? What was she gambling for? Why were her eyes so eagerly defiant, her mouth so tight, her hard jaw so set?

I think O'Leary was perplexed, too, for his cool

gray eyes studied Terice for a long moment or two. She met his scrutiny undismayed, very convincingly. Finally she added:

"And I can and will swear to that—if it comes to the need of swearing."

"It can't come to that need without a—a body," murmured Julian Barre. He stopped to sneeze and then to cough, and moved closer to the fire. His fine eyes went to Paggi and then on to Morse and Killian. His words when they came slipped out quietly, his casual manner veiling their significance. "If the body is gone how can we prove there has been a murder?"

O'Leary whirled toward Barre.

"Just what do you mean by that?" he asked sharply. "I don't like the sound of it, Barre. You'd better explain yourself."

"I mean exactly what I said," said Julian Barre. "If there's no body how can we—how can *you* prove there has been a murder?"

O'Leary's eyes narrowed; his finely cut features seemed to sharpen a little.

"So—you are inclined to take the obvious advantage of the situation?" he asked unpleasantly.

Barre nodded his handsome head in a dignified way.

"I am," he said quietly. "You are a meddler here, O'Leary. While Matil's intentions in bringing you here were doubtless of the best—hear me out, please, my dear," he interpolated as Matil made a motion to speak—"still, I think she was—ill advised. Your presence has already brought about one murder. Who knows what will happen if we stir up this thing. We can't bring back Gerald Frawley. We can do—immeasurable damage to the lives that remain in this hunting lodge."

"I see," said O'Leary. "You will all simply keep silent about the matter. And what about my own statement?"

Barre's eyes looked directly into O'Leary's. "What had been done—can be done again," he suggested deliberately.

"I suppose you mean it's my word against—the combined statement of the rest of you?"

"Yes," said Barre quietly.

"And perhaps a nice gift—for me—if I agree with you?"

Barre took the extremely unpleasant note in O'Leary's deadly soft voice calmly.

"I am at your services in that respect, O'Leary," he said. "I admit—openly—that while I much regret Frawley's death—Frawley's murder"—he corrected himself as if at a concession to the quick gesture of O'Leary's hand—"while I regret it, I can see no possible benefit in dragging it, and of course Huber Kingery's death, into the courts."

O'Leary had become bland again; his gray eyes were enigmatic.

"What about the nurse?" he asked. "She is also an outsider. How can you keep her quiet?"

Barre glanced at me negligently.

"That could be arranged," he said easily.

"What——" I gasped, and checked myself, but with great difficulty, as I caught O'Leary's glance.

"And Frawley's clothes and bags—and the fact that probably half the office force knows that he came to Hunting's End with a party and exactly the personnel of that party?"

Barre made an easy gesture. Paggi was staring at him from shadowed olive eyes, Killian was giving all his attention to a cigarette lighter that refused to work, and Morse was drumming on the arm of his chair with thick nervous fingers and staring into the fire.

"Ah—but those of us at Hunting's End know that he wandered out into the snow and—was lost. Lost."

"So that's your little plan. You fixed the coroner once; you could again," said O'Leary after a moment. "Very nice indeed. You are an opportunist, Mr. Barre. Or—or did you make the opportunity?"

"What do you mean? Do you mean——"

"My meaning is quite clear," interrupted O'Leary. "Did you push that dead body through the window, venture a few steps from the house, dragging it, until you got to a snowdrift that looked like a good hiding place?"

"Oh——" cried Matil, and put both slim white hands to her eyes.

O'Leary glanced at her.

"Sorry, Miss Matil," he said.

Barre shook his head.

"No," he said quietly, "I didn't. But if I had, I wouldn't admit it. And since it has been done, I defy you, O'Leary, to prove a murder without the body. Against the combined words of—all of us."

"You have no respect for law, then, Barre?"

"I have as much respect as the next man," said Barre. "But I value—other things more. And I think everyone in this group feels as I do. We can't bring Huber or Gerald Frawley back. And—I saw a murder trial once. I know what it did to every life it touched. I know what it does to—one's soul. To say nothing of one's social position, one's financial security, one's reputation for business integrity. I frankly don't want to go through it. And—" his eyes went to Matil with a kind of lingering sadness—"and I don't want anyone I—love—to go through such—such beastly degradation." He added the last words bitterly, dropping for that second or two his mask of easy aloofness.

Killian stirred uneasily, opened his mouth as if to speak, thought better of it, and tossed his cigarette into the fire. It fell lighted end up and continued to smoke, like a small white volcano, trailing thin blue smoke above the red embers.

Morse rose.

"You convince me in spite of myself, Julian," he said dully. "It's a mess, any way you look at it."

"What about you, Paggi?" asked O'Leary in a curiously flat tone.

Paggi shrugged.

"I know nothing about law," he said. "But I—I want my bread and butter as much as anyone. And I lose it if I'm dragged through the courts. Besides"— he moved his thick shoulders restlessly—"they might say I did it."

"They might," agreed O'Leary dryly. "They might

say any of you did it. They might even discover that one who is guilty. Remember that."

"Oh, how can you?" cried Matil suddenly. She took a step or two forward past O'Leary and faced the others and stood slim and straight, her white hands clenched, her little chin lifted, her eyes blazing. "How can you? Are you all like this? Have you no decency? Are you all liars—all—all rottenly selfish? You've given me the unhappiest girlhood a woman ever had. You've thrust selfish, horrible secrets upon me. And now I'm a woman, you are trying to do the same thing. You are vile. I despise you. You think money can do anything. You think in terms of prices." She stopped to take a long shaking breath, and to steady her voice. "Listen to me. I promise you this. If you succeed in this scheme, I will go to the police, myself, and tell them the whole shameful story. You *can't* stop me. I don't care what you say, what you threaten. I will do it!"

"Sentimental fool," growled Lucy Kingery, stirring suddenly. Her long earrings flashed. "Just like your mother."

"Matil—Matil!" Barre was at her side. "My dear, my dear, I never dreamed you felt like this. We will do exactly as you say. It was your father—it is your right. I only spoke for what seemed to me the best way—the way that would bring the least distress, the least sorrow. Forgive me, Matil. I'll agree to anything you want. If you want us to take the whole thing through the round of police, of arrests, of trial, of ugly grilling testimony——" He stopped himself. "No,

I'll try to influence you no longer. I thought I was sparing you pain. I never once dreamed that the secrecy hurt you so. Believe me, Matil, I'll agree to anything you want."

It was then, I think, that she suddenly began to sob—long broken-hearted sobs that shook her whole young body. Barre put both arms around her, but she pulled away, failed to see Paggi suddenly at her side holding out his hands, turned and went swiftly to her room. No one spoke until the door closed. Then Aunt Lucy seemed to pull herself together.

"Dinner," she said. "Dinner. Ain't it time for dinner? What are you doing standing there, Annette? Get to work. You, too, Brunker. And wait, bring me some whisky, Brunker. I—I feel cold."

She had her whisky; from the color of the drink and the way she choked as it went down her scraggy throat, I think she took it straight. Brunker had not asked, seeming to know her likes. Paggi accompanied Brunker to the serving table, and returned with his olive eyes brighter, gleaming with that lambent flame, and his red lips redder. I think the others felt the need of stimulant, too, for, by the time I had got Aunt Lucy back to her room and into bed, earrings and all, and had myself returned to the main room, a little air of forced animation had laid itself over the still horror the room had held. Up till then, I remember, there had been practically no drinking, but I think the grisly uncertainty regarding that cold, dead body was the last straw. It seemed to rob them of every vestige of what we call morale; it pulled away the kindly little veils of conventionalities and left them stripped and raw and ugly.

Terice and Helene showed a growing tendency to bicker: Helene became sillily sentimental, insisting upon Jo's attention, and Terice became spiteful, rather insulting, huddling in a corner of the divan, her eyes glittering like those of a sulky cat about to flash swift claws. Paggi became sullen under Helene's demands, Barre fell into a guarded silence, and Morse stared in a troubled, anxious way at the burning logs. Brunker, his face cold and dispassionate as always, came and went, and in the silence I could hear Annette's tuneless little song from the kitchen. O'Leary, I think, had spent some time in Frawley's room and had searched the whole lodge before Brunker announced dinner. He looked very tired as he came downstairs at the mellow tinkle of the gong—a tinkle which sounded strangely melodious and lonely amid that thick, brooding silence.

And the dinner itself was a horrible affair. No one dressed for it; I believe no one wanted to enter one of those cold, lonely bedrooms, just then. Matil joined us, dry-eyed now and cold and white, disdaining them all, but still maintaining somehow the relation of hostess to her guests. The meal was terrible, and none of us cared to eat. The food consisted mainly of creamed vegetables, fish patties, and for dessert a mixture of canned fruits which had been frozen, and coffee. There was no bread at all, and Helene did not trouble to conceal her dislike for what food there was.

And I cannot forget the evening which followed.

O'Leary got Terice into a corner off by the piano, where she fingered a bright Turkish tapestry and looked like a cornered rat, and talked to her a long time; I tried to find my missing knitting needle and, failing that, stared at the shining black windows and the fire and the rushes and gray water and ducks in the panels between the doors, and the rest just sat in ugly silence, saying nothing and looking covertly over their shoulders and at each other. Aunt Lucy refused to stay in her own room—and I did not blame her, for the oil had run out of the little heater and there was no more than barely enough for the lanterns, so that the room was icy cold—and came out wrapped in a huge gray wool shawl that had floating fringes, to sit bolt upright in her cobweb, moisten her wide mouth every now and then hungrily, and stare at all of us in a most disquieting fashion.

I remember that once Killian in his aimless, restless strolling about the room stopped at a radio that stood on a table under one of the black windows. It was an old set, with a battery and a cone speaker. He tinkered over it for some time. Paggi joined him presently and they seemed to be trying to get the thing connected. For my part, I hoped they would fail; the thought of hearing voices and music and all the ordinary familiar details of a radio program floating gayly through the air to penetrate the anxious, waiting, frantic silence of that room would only emphasize our enforced isolation, our desperate need for contact with the world. If only we could send our own voices across the air; establish communication with that dear world of familiar things that seemed so far away, so inconceivably remote! But of course we couldn't. We had to remain there waiting—waiting—for the snow to stop and release us from that bondage of horror. I think Matil shared my thoughts for she stirred suddenly, moved her foot under the collie's head who lay huddled at her feet, and said suddenly:

"I can't bear it. *I can't!* We must *do* something. I can't bear it!" She stopped herself as abruptly as she had spoken. It had the effect of a frenzied appeal for help, but under my very eyes she became stern and white again, and I found it hard to believe she had spoken save for the fact that her slim hands were twisting and twisting against the blue wool frock she wore and her eyes were black with pain.

Morse stirred restlessly.

"There's nothing we can do, Matil," he said. His voice sounded ragged; his eyes wore that strained, troubled look that had become habitual with him.

"I can't do anything with it," said Killian suddenly, turning from the radio. "Here, Julian, you are our radio expert. Come here and get this thing into working order."

But Barre must have felt much as I felt, for he gave a shrug of distaste, and did not even trouble to reply to Killian.

Paggi lingered at the radio for some time; I could see his broad, thick shoulders bending over it. It always struck me as being strange that Paggi, short, thick, dark-faced, could yet exert such a magnetic physical appeal. He was lightly graceful, buoyant, vibrant with life, extraordinarily vital—was that why the hidden flame in his dark eyes was so insistent, his red mouth so demanding? But when that dark gaze returned always to Matil's whiteness, lingered on her neck where the soft white silk frill met the softer whiteness of her throat, followed the slim lines of her ankles and legs and softly curved young body as if they could see through the silk and tailored wool, I felt little chills run up from the small of my back. And they were no Freudian chills, either; I may be an old maid, but I am not a simpleton. Rather I found myself harking back to Greek mythology and, for no reason at all, kept thinking of Persephone.

Helene, I think, made the first move to go to bed, and then flatly refused to do so and had to be helped up the narrow stairs, with Jo Paggi on one side, dark and inscrutable then, and Morse on the other, and Killian, his eyes mocking, watching them. And the way we separated and went to our rooms was the most perplexing and strangely terrifying thing in the world. You see, we all realized quite perfectly that there was no murderer hidden in any room for—were we not all there together? Had we not seen Brunker going up the stairs and into his own room on the gallery? Did we not know that Annette was bolted securely, probably with a bottle, into her own room off the kitchen? And the rest of us—were all together. The murderer, whoever it was, was there in plain sight all the time, was one of us. I marvel yet that we could go along, eat a little, sleep a little, carry on somehow, never knowing when our hands were touching hands that were red, when our eyes were meeting eyes that held blood-guilt.

Yes, so long as we were together, we did not fear so much. It was when we separated that terror clutched us. It was Terice, I think, who murmured sullenly that she thought we all ought to stay together in the main room that night, upon which someone else, Aunt Lucy, I believe, said grimly that in that case we wouldn't dare close an eye. So we separated almost in silence. I slipped the bolt on my door as soon as I entered the room and have no doubt the others did likewise. I looked to the bolts on the window, too. And after Aunt Lucy had relinquished her tray—and whatever supplies were running short they did not include cheese for the slabs were thicker than ever, as if to make up for the lack of meat, and I can still see her smacking grimly over the little greenish veins in the slices of Roquefort—as I say, after she had given up her tray and I had got her into her gray flannel and into bed, I—well, I bolted the door from my room into the bathroom. It was the first time in all my life that I deliberately made myself inaccessible to a patient, but I must admit that O'Leary's words had shaken my belief in my present patient's helplessness. And I did not just like the appearance of her great, bony dark hands, which were singularly strong-looking.

Though I had an impression of a wakeful night during which the dark hours dragged, the snow and wind surged wildly against the sides of the lodge, and menace lay in every rustle and creak, I believe I actually slept quite a little. And I am sure I heard no sound, save for, once, a muffled, far-away howl from Jericho, which broke off abruptly and sounded as if it came from Matil's room.

But I have often speculated on the thing that night held. In my mind's eye I can see a door opening stealthily, a figure bulking largely for a moment against the still red ashes of the southern fireplace, O'Leary's head lifting cautiously from above the back of the divan to watch, his silent getting to his feet, his cautious slow approach toward that bulking figure; then another door opening, an inch at a time, silently, stealthily, with infinite caution, a third figure creeping, creeping upon O'Leary with—what?—in its hand; then rapidly the quick blow, the swinging door, the panting struggle—and all at once darkness and silence again and the wind sighing down the chimney, blowing on the red ashes until they lit a little and showed a crumpled figure on the hearthrug: a figure from which, perhaps, came a moan or two.

When Brunker knocked frantically on my door in the cold gray light of morning, he awakened me from a sound sleep. I remember his words, repeated over and over:

"Nurse, he's dead. Nurse, Nurse—he's dead! Mr. O'Leary's been killed."

CHAPTER XII

SNOWSHOES

WELL, he wasn't dead, though I'd a rather dreadful moment or two before I found a fluttering pulse and got a stimulant poured between his blue lips, while Brunker and Killian lifted him onto the divan and the others stood around offering breathless suggestions. Fortunately O'Leary has a thick skull which, public opinion to the contrary, is an excellent thing in a detective; a blow that might have killed him proved to be only a bruise, ugly and bloody and painful-looking, but not of necessity dangerous. I got out my instrument bag and cleaned the wound and took a few stitches in it, managing somehow to control my fingers, which had a tendency to shake. And I did not feel easy until the color began to creep back to his lips and he finally opened his eyes, said something unintelligible about snowshoes, looked more clearly at me, and tried to sit up. I pushed him backward.

"Stay right where you are, and keep your mouth shut," I said brusquely; the suddenness of my release from anxiety turned me to a kind of anger.

"Go lie down yourself," he retorted hazily, closing his eyes again. "You're as white as a sheet." Then he seemed to remember something. "The snowshoes!" he cried more clearly. His eyes opened again and darted around the circle of faces—faces which had been a moment ago so apprehensive. Now, it seemed to me, one or two of them at least looked just a trifle disappointed. And it was true that with O'Leary out of the picture certain rather pressing problems would be solved. There they all were, however—no, wait! *Was everybody there?*

Killian seemed to be struck with the same thought for his eyes, quick, now, and sharp, were going swiftly about the group, and he stepped hurriedly toward Newell Morse's door.

Newell Morse, of course! His was the face I missed in that circle.

"Newell! Newell!" Killian was calling through the door. He knocked a time or two, then swung the door open. From where I stood I could see the room, the empty bed. Killian entered the room, picked up a paper that lay on the dressing table, and returned slowly to us.

"Here's the note. It's addressed to you, Matil." He looked at her hesitatingly, and then placed the note in her hand. She opened it, read it through, then read aloud:

"I can't stand this. There's murder in the air. I'm going to chance it to town. I'll take the snowshoes—the drifts are pretty solid. I believe I can make it and get help. I've got to get to Frawley's safety-deposit box and find out who killed him and why. I can't stand it any longer. I'm going. Frawley had it fixed so that the only means of access to his box is by number and in case I don't make it you'd better have the——"

Matil stopped suddenly as if she had read a word or two more than she had intended to read, went swiftly to the fireplace, and flung the note on the log where it blazed up cheerily.

Then she faced us.

No one spoke. So Morse had left, was trying to get to town, to bring us help and to find—to find who had killed Gerald Frawley.

And he had got away.

My eyes went to the southern fireplace. The crossed snowshoes were gone. Morse even now was skirting drifts with them. Would the snow be frozen sufficiently to hold up his weight? Could he resist the bitterness of the cold, the stinging ice in the wind, the blinding snow? Could he find his way along those trackless, snow-covered hills?

"Did you know he was leaving, O'Leary?" asked Paggi suddenly. "Did you try to prevent him? Is that how you got knocked out?"

A thoughtful look came into O'Leary's gray eyes before he closed them weakly—so weakly, indeed, that I regarded him with suspicion—and said in a die-away voice:

"Yes, he got me. I decided to spend the night here on the divan—thought I'd better stay awake." He paused as if for breath. "Morse came out of his room. I followed him—saw what he was doing—he heard me." He paused again, very, very weakly, and I knew he was lying quite shamelessly. "Anyhow, he got me. Whew—this hurts like the blazes, Miss Keate. Can't you do something for it?"

Upon which he sat up and promptly and in good earnest toppled neatly over on the divan.

Killian brought more brandy and Matil cold compresses and presently O'Leary opened his eyes again, sensed what had happened, and looked very much ashamed.

"You'll stay quietly in bed to-day," I said sternly. "If you get to running around and sitting up and fainting all over the place you'll get yourself in a fever and be sick. You've just escaped death."

"In other words, don't crowd your luck, O'Leary," said Killian, adding: "It looks like the matter is out of your—our hands now, anyhow. Morse evidently figures he can fix the guilt if he once gets to town, so all we need do is sit tight and wait."

"Do you think he'll make it, Lal?" asked Matil in a low voice.

Killian shrugged.

"Possibly." His unfathomable eyes went to the white shrouding veils beyond the window panes. "Yes, I think he will. He's pretty good at skiing, you know. Won the Efftstone tournament six years ago; he's quite at home on snowshoes. Yes, I think he has a chance. And he'll manage to get us help."

"Unless——" Helene's green eyes narrowed and she lowered her voice to a shrill whisper. "Unless— he's—*escaped.*"

Helene was not subtle as a rule. I think her use of the word "escaped" with its implication shocked me almost as much as the suggestion itself. Escaped! Was Newell Morse the murderer then? And had he decided to risk everything on a last desperate gamble with the snow and storm?

Things crowded into my mind to corroborate the suggestion: his uneasiness, the note Frawley had left him, the fact that he had been the last to hold any particular conversation with Frawley—that is, the last whose identity we knew—the fact that he alone held access to Frawley's safety-deposit box and that his own arrival at Barrington would now precede ours by a large margin, large enough to let him destroy or manipulate any papers left by Frawley to suit his own needs, and above all the memory of his healthy pink hands shaking—always shaking. Escape! Well, it might be.

"Oh, no," cried Matil, sharply. "It couldn't have been Newell. Not Newell!"

Paggi shrugged.

"My dear Matil, it must be Newell or—one of us standing here. Which other one would you choose?"

Matil said nothing, of course, at that, although it seemed to me her dark blue eyes went to Helene and then Terice in a somewhat suggestive manner.

"Newell . . ." Barre was saying speculatively. "No—I can't believe it. I can't. And yet—he told no one of his plan. He tried to get away without anyone knowing it. It seems to me he would have spoken—to Matil, at least. Or to me or Killian, his business associates." He interrupted himself sharply. "I can't believe that Newell Morse killed Frawley."

Killian shrugged again.

"Well, Julian, would you prefer one of us?" His

graceful gesture included Annette's shrewdly listening bulk and Brunker's still white face.

Another silence fell. There was nothing that could be said.

It has often occurred to me as being a continually perplexing quality of this life that things so seldom turn out the way you think they will. Now, if such a case had been presented hypothetically to me I would have assumed that the strain of anxiety, of fear and horror would be worse than ever after Morse's disappearance. That we would, one and all, dread the revelations that would follow Morse's arrival in town, or would fear, with about equal fervor, his failure to arrive and the eventual falling of that safety-deposit box, and whatever records the thing held, into the hands of the police.

And it seemed to me, too, that there would have been some natural anxiety and alarm for Newell Morse, himself, battling the terrors of the miles of ice and snow and bitter, bitter wind—the treacherous drifts, the shrouding veils of snow, the winding road, lost and buried now in snow, that lay between him and Nettleson.

But instead of all this there was evident, almost at once, the most peculiar air of respite; there was a kind of relaxing of taut nerves, a letting down of strained reserves. Relief was almost a tangible thing. It was in their eyes, meeting one another's more easily, more freely; it was in the insouciance of Lal Killian's whistled little air, "Take off your skin and dance around in your bones," as he went to the front door, pulled it

open, shivered in the sweep of wind and snow, and
with difficulty closed it again. But not before we had
all seen the cold, impenetrable drifts that banked up
against the door itself and sent crisp showers of snow
into the room.

"Sweep up that snow, Brunker," directed Matil
absently. It seemed to me that her voice was faintly
smoother, easier, freed a little from the horror that
had kept it frozen for two days. "Then serve breakfast, please. And Annette, bring some coffee for Mr.
O'Leary at once, please. You'd feel the better for it,
wouldn't you?"

"So Morse has gone," murmured Paggi, as if to
himself. "Look here, Julian. Don't you think that
looks—well, I hate to say it, but it does seem to me
that maybe he—thought things were getting pretty
warm for him."

"In that case," said Terice sharply, "we can all
breathe more easily. There's one thing certain," she
went on, at the prompting, I suppose, of her hard
stratum of common sense. "Either he'll get us help and
bring this horrible waiting to an end or—he's the murderer himself and we don't need to dread every
shadow on the wall." She ended with a little burst of
candor which I think she had not intended and a
shiver.

Helene dropped into a chair. She sighed. Her face
relaxed itself.

"Well," she said sighing. "It's a relief. I feel that
I may be able to eat some breakfast after all." Her

eyes found me. "Are we waiting for Miss Keate to get dressed?" she asked idly.

Conscious for the first time of my dishevelment, my hastily donned dressing gown and slippers, and my frousy hair, I directed Brunker and Killian to carry O'Leary up to his room—overriding O'Leary's objections with a decision born of more years of nursing recalcitrant patients than I care to mention, and went to my own room. After a shower and the donning of a fresh uniform I felt distinctly better. I found the others at the breakfast table when I returned to the main room, and saw Brunker disappearing up the stairway with a tray for O'Leary balanced gingerly in his wide hands.

Aunt Lucy had got one of her talking devils that morning and kept us engaged, if not entertained, with a lengthy account of some duck hunting Huber Kingery had enjoyed on his last trip to Hunting's End. She turned to Matil frequently for corroboration, so frequently that Matil said at last, with a weary little sigh, that she'd a diary of that trip somewhere which Aunt Lucy might have if she wanted it. Since Aunt Lucy patently did not care to wade through the diary, she said so at once, adding somewhat sharply that she should think Matil would remember exactly what the bag was.

"There were teal, I remember," said Aunt Lucy, crunching some dry cereal, which she ate without adding any canned milk. "But we threw the teal away. Nothing but breast anyway on teal. They taste all right

early in the season but you get pretty tired of them.
It's when the northern ducks come down that you get
good hunting. Canvasback is my favorite. Surely you
can remember, Matil, how many canvasback there were
in that last bag. The last time Huber went hunting. I
should think you could remember that, Matil. Don't
you know, we all went with him. Helene, how many
canvasback did he have? It was a record. Don't you
remember how we talked of it that night? That same
night Huber—was killed."

Helene shuddered.

"Really, Matil," she said pettishly, "I was just beginning to feel a little more comfortable. Can't your
aunt talk of something else? I don't see why she has
to drag us back all the time to—to such unpleasant
topics!"

"Did you ever have snow like this?" asked Killian
hurriedly, as Aunt Lucy's spoon suspended itself over
the bowl of cereal and her dark face grew darker, her
hollowed eyes fixed themselves vindictively on Helene,
and her long earrings winked maliciously.

"Ain't she finicky?" said Aunt Lucy, not to be de-
flected, and speaking with all the delicacy of a steel-
riveting machine. "Ain't she fastidious? You listen to
me, Helene Paggi. It may be an unpleasant topic, but
it's more unpleasant to number a murderer—" she
paused a little to sweep the circle with her eyes before
they returned meaningly to Helene—"to number a
murderer among your guests."

Swift red blotches rose to Helene's face; she struggled to her feet.

"What do you mean by that?" she cried shrilly. "If you mean me, I could tell you a few things. How about yourself? How about——"

"Oh, sit down, sit down, Helene." Barre was thrusting her somewhat unceremoniously into her chair. "For heaven's sake let's have a little peace."

"Oh, so Helene has her ideas," murmured Terice silkily, leaning forward. "Go on, Helene, you interest me."

Paggi thrust his chair violently backward. His face, always liverish-looking in the morning, was dark with rage.

"Can't we have one decent meal?" he burst out furiously. "I need food—I'm hungry. My temperament can't stand this constant bickering. I am an artist; I ought to be protected from such things. My whole nervous system is ragged. I——"

"Oh, *Lord!*" cried Lal Killian in exasperation. "*Everybody's* nervous system is ragged. Shut up, Paggi. You make me feel sick!"

"You're a brute, Killian. You've got no more nerves than a donkey. But you can't help that. You're just a puppy; that's what you are. Just a puppy——"

"Gentlemen—Lal——"

"It strikes me you are a trifle mixed," I broke in sharply, thinking that so long as we were calling names I might as well have a hand in it. "Brutes and donkeys and puppies—you're acting like a baby yourself, Mr. Paggi." He winced at the "mister" so I repeated it. "That's what I think, Mr. Paggi. Now do be still, both of you, and eat your breakfast and keep these mutual compliments for a more suitable time. . . . Now what's the matter with you?"

Killian was standing very straight and quite white beside his plate.

"I believe Signor Paggi is about to apologize," he said, as stiffly as any boy in his teens.

Paggi's green eyes glinted.

"Jo apologize!" cried Helene. "I'd like to know what for. He knows what is becoming a gen——"

"Helene, *will* you keep quiet?" asked Paggi, his swarthy face like a thundercloud. "Certainly, Killian —one speaks before one takes time to think. Possibly, we are all a little nervous, a little overstrained."

"If that's an apology, I accept it," said Killian, still stiffly. "But—we have a hostess, you know."

"Matil!" Paggi was on his feet, buoyant, vibrant, entirely at ease. "I beg you to forgive me. I—I am emotional. I admit it. I am carried away by my feelings. I am an artist. Things affect me more deeply than those who are—cold-blooded and thick-skinned. Forgive me." He took her hand in both his and pressed it, and Terice smiled nastily at Helene and Helene's eyes had spiteful little lines around them.

"Sorry, Matil," said Killian shortly. He slipped into his chair again, took up his napkin, and looked at me. "We *are* acting rather like babies," he admitted, but his smile did not reach his eyes.

Matil withdrew her hands.

"Finish your breakfast then," she said coldly. "It seems rather terrible to me that we should be quarreling when poor Newell may be——" She stopped abruptly.

"Now, Matil," said Barre kindly, "don't worry about him. If Newell was driven for some reason into murder—isn't it better that he should go this way, of his own accord?"

He meant to comfort Matil, of course, but it struck me as dubious comfort.

"Oh, I don't know," said Lal Killian coolly. "Newell has a good chance of getting through."

"Then we've seen the last of him," said Terice callously; her metallic curls were bent over her plate and her face a mask of paint. "He will have got what money he needs and got clear away out of the country before this snow stops. Well——" She shrugged. The rings flashed on her hard little hands and she looked speculatively at the windows. "I'm glad he's gone."

"Why are you so sure he—he is the murderer?" asked Helene.

Terice moved her wiry little shoulders again impatiently.

"Why, Helene—don't you see? What other motive would be strong enough for him to risk what he risks in going out in that blizzard? It's his only chance to escape, that's what I think."

"It seems to me, madame, that you are rather anxious to shift the blame to Newell's shoulders," commented Paggi, his olive eyes lifting from his coffee and then returning so swiftly that I caught only a glimpse of the shifting whites.

"Just what do you mean by that?" flared Terice. Her eyes glittered, her heavily painted lips pulled back a little from small teeth. "If you mean, did I do it?— think again, big boy." Matil made a gesture with her hand but Terice continued: "Whoever shot Gerald Frawley hid his body—and that lets me out. I'm too little." She giggled very unpleasantly and looked at Helene's arms. "Helene, now, might be able to do it."

Matil stood.

"There's no use in being vulgar, Terice," she said quite clearly.

"Oh, you've always despised me, Matil," said Terice easily. "I can't say I've liked you, either. And as for vulgarity," she concluded cheerfully, "I know I'm vulgar—but a little vulgarity is good for anybody."

Aunt Lucy snorted painfully.

"You *are* a common little———"

"*Aunt Lucy!*" cried Matil, covering the ugly word that trembled on the old woman's purple lips.

"More coffee, please, Brunker," said Killian. He laughed mirthlessly, his dark eyes on Matil. "Do sit down, like a good girl, Matil," he begged. "I so dislike eating my breakfast in a standing position. That's better," as she slipped into her chair again. "It strikes me that our relief at having poor Newell to make a villain of has gone to our heads a little. I'd like to suggest that we try to rest as much as possible to-day. It might be good for all our nerves, especially those extremely sensitive ones belonging to Signor Paggi." His voice was solicitous; it was only the mocking light in his eyes that made Paggi bridle resentfully. "Besides, the snow will surely stop to-day and we may be able to get away."

"Can you get along without me for a little to-day, Miss Kingery?" I asked. "I think Mr. O'Leary needs some attention."

"Certainly, certainly," said Aunt Lucy brusquely. Her gaunt hand shot out and gripped my wrist; it felt hot and feverish. "Do you think he's going to die?"

"*No!*" I said forcefully.

No one spoke as I mounted the little stairway. Once on the gallery, I glanced over the rail. Julian Barre was lighting a cigar which he had managed to treasure; his cold was worse that morning and he looked as if he hadn't slept. Helene was playing with the silver at her plate and Paggi was placing his cup carefully in the saucer.

"It seems to me," he said in a low voice, not knowing that I have extraordinarily acute hearing, "that our red-headed nurse cherishes a rather strong—er—interest in this O'Leary. Friends, are they?"

No one replied for a moment. Then Terice laughed.

"Jo, you've a biological mind," she said. "I'd like you to be psyched."

"They are acquaintances, I believe," said Matil coldly. "Mr. O'Leary said she was his nurse during a recent illness—appendicitis, I think he said."

"H'mm," said Paggi. Then he sneezed, sneezed again, and cast a bitter look at the fire. "I've got a rotten cold," he said. "Oh, I'm not blaming you, Matil. Still, it is rather unfortunate, you know. Does anyone mind if I do a few exercises this morning?" he added, and as Killian said, "Oh, Lord," Helene nodded vigorously.

"I'll accompany you, Jo," she offered at once. "But don't sing too much with that cold."

"We've all got colds," said Julian Barre, coughing. "My throat feels like the devil. By the way, Jo, I don't want to be too critical but it does seem to me that there's a little vibrato effect that's getting into your voice that sounds frightfully affected——'"

I closed O'Leary's door.

A breakfast tray depleted of coffee stood on the table and O'Leary's eyes were brighter and more natural-looking.

"Now then," I said sternly. "What actually happened last night?"

"A grenadier," he murmured. "A very grenadier of a woman." Then his face sobered, looked suddenly bleak. "I don't know, Miss Keate," he said wearily. "I only wish I did. . . . I'll tell you this," he added after a moment of silence. "You find me at my lowest and at the same time, I know—I *know,* I tell you— that there's something, something quite simple, that——" He broke off momentarily. "How far have you trained your subconscious, Miss Keate? Can you make it sit up and say 'Uncle'? Mine's in a bad way, I'm afraid. But still—it's trying to tell me something. Something so simple that I didn't even see it." He was frowning. "Now—that radio: that's a peculiar business. Why don't some of them fix the thing up so it will function? That would be the natural thing for them to do. All that's the matter with it is that some of the wire is off the rheostat. I looked at the thing. I could fix it myself. Anybody could who's got any knowledge of radios."

"What's that got to do with the murder?"

"Nothing," said O'Leary flatly. "Nothing. It's just —unnatural. It's the abnormal that one's subconscious picks up——"

"But about last night," I prodded, having more interest in the outside of his head than the inside. "What about this bump? Do you know how close you came to——" I shivered. The room was very cold.

"You are awfully staunch, Miss Keate," said O'Leary, reaching out toward my hand. "I'd rather have you back of me, than—an army with banners."

"Nonsense," I said brusquely, and found myself sniffing. "I'm getting a cold," I said. "Have you— where's a handkerchief?"

"In that bag," said O'Leary, and watched me while I dug into the bag which I couldn't see very plainly, got out a very white linen handkerchief, blew my nose, cleared my throat, straightened my cap, and returned to the bedside, feeling brisker.

"Who hit you?" I asked.

"So definite, so delightfully succinct," murmured O'Leary. "She is herself again. Well, I don't know who hit me. Or what. You see, it was this way," he went on as I made an impatient motion. "I spent the night out there on the divan. The nights in this lodge have been altogether too lively and I decided that I preferred to be a first-hand witness to anything that might go on last night. To say nothing of feeling a kind of responsibility."

"Nonsense," I interrupted. "You are no policeman. I wish to goodness you'd marry some nice young girl who wouldn't let you take chances."

"And who'd give you a godchild every year?" he asked, his gray eyes dancing. "You've got to have somebody to worry over, Miss Keate. You might as well worry over me. Besides, what nice young girl wants a detective for a husband?"

"Well," I said doubtfully, "there's Matil Kingery."

He laughed then, so vigorously that it alarmed me, and I felt the bandages on his head anxiously and ordered him to stop.

"You are priceless, Miss Keate," he said, gasping. "There's nobody like you. I hope to the Lord you don't find a suitable girl for you'll have me walking up the aisle in a frock coat and a cold perspiration before I know it." The smile left his face and he leaned forward anxiously, looking at me in earnest apprehension. "Now understand me, Miss Keate, don't you dare marry me off. I won't marry. I don't want to. And if you take it into your head to find me a wife I'm as good as gone."

"It's for your own good," I said dubiously. "And here's Matil Kingery——"

He interrupted me very rudely and definitely.

"Matil Kingery's furiously in love with another man. Have you no eyes?" And as I stared at him in some perplexity, he continued artfully: "Don't you want to know what happened last night?"

"Yes, of course. Go on," I said, forgetting Matil for the moment.

"Well, as I say, I was spending the night on the divan in front of the north fireplace. I was completely in the shadow there, and couldn't possibly be seen behind the enormous back of the thing. But there was a faint glow from the red ashes, and my eyes being adjusted to the darkness, I could see fairly well. Anyhow, along about four o'clock in the morning—I suppose he wanted to wait until nearly daylight for he would have had still less a chance in the dark of night—Morse came quietly out of his room. I was watching, of course, anxious to know just what he was doing. I got up and, keeping to the darker shadows of the furniture, moved very cautiously toward him, intent on seeing what on earth he was trying to do over there by the south fireplace. And, just as I saw he was reaching for snowshoes, something struck my head, and—that's all I know. I'm not sure I know that—I only know I went out, and the snowshoes and Morse reaching for them are the last things I remember."

"And you don't know who struck you?"

"No—no, I don't know."

"Then—it sounds as if you were guessing at it, anyway."

"Guesses are dangerous; it might have been anyone. As I say, I was intent upon what Morse was doing. Stupidly careless of everything else. Depended too much on my sixth sense and it failed to function."

"Very unaccommodating of it," I said dryly.

"Very," agreed O'Leary.

"Of course," I suggested meditatively, "Morse might have taken someone into his confidence and that someone might have struck you."

"Because Morse got away you assume that someone was in cahoots with him? Helping him? Disposing of me, because I would certainly have stopped Morse? Yes—that's possible."

"That would limit it to Barre and Killian," I resumed thoughtfully. "I can't see Paggi risking his skin for someone else."

"Why don't you include the women, Miss Keate? Lucy Kingery looks as if she could fell an ox—from her wheel chair, too, if she wished to do so. And Helene Paggi has arms like a coal heaver's—to be brutally plain. And that little Baroness——" He paused and shook his head, wincing a little as the bandage rubbed against the pillow. "No, she's the stiletto type. If she wanted to dispose of anybody she'd do it more neatly—and very thoroughly."

"Why did you pretend it was Morse who struck you?"

"Not much reason. It's just a good rule to let people remain unsuspected and I knew, of course, that whoever struck me was there—probably within a hand's reach of me."

"Mr. O'Leary, who killed Gerald Frawley?"

He made a weary gesture.

"I wish I knew. Paggi has an unshakeable alibi—but, so far as I can see, any one of the others might have shot Frawley. You see, the motive is likely, as I have said, entangled with the death of Huber Kingery. And they are all silent on the subject of Huber Kingery's death. And as to the psychology of it—I mean only the capacity for crime—any one of them might be capable of it. Even your Miss Matil has the —er—determination, if nothing else. My head hurts like the very devil, Miss Keate. Can't you do something for it? I'm not going to stay in bed. That's absurd!"

"Yes, you are. You try to get up and I'll take your clothes downstairs, out of your reach."

"Oh, Miss Keate," he protested, shocked. "You wouldn't do that! Why, I've got to get up."

"I can do it and I will." I eyed him severely and added: "I've kept many a typhoid patient in bed that way."

He looked at me in horror.

"I'd trusted you," he murmured in a stunned way. "And now you reveal black depths of iniquity." He looked speculatively at the clothes hanging in the wardrobe and at his dressing gown. "A woman who would do that would do *anything*."

"I mean it," I said firmly. "You needn't look like that. Do you think I want to have you ill on my hands, up here in this outlandish place, with tons of snow between me and a doctor?" The thought of snow sobered me. "When will this snow stop! It's kept it up like this for two days and three nights, and here it is, the third day and it's still snowing. Can't it ever, ever stop!"

"Oh, it will stop," said O'Leary. "It will stop. And when it does—heaven help us! For no human can."

A chill crept up from the small of my back and tingled around my ears.

"Why—why, what do you mean?"

"Surely you know. With the melting of the snow, Frawley's body's got to be disposed of; there's got to be a race to Barrington to get that damn safety-deposit box; there's got to be a hiding of clues—a prompt snuffing out of every scrap of knowledge." He looked at me gravely. "And I greatly fear, Miss Keate, that that last may entail—another murder. If it hasn't already occurred."

I was standing, every nerve aquiver.

"If it hasn't already occurred. Do you mean——" The words stuck.

He nodded.

"I doubt very much, Miss Keate, if Newell Morse was permitted to leave this lodge."

CHAPTER XIII

IN THE PANTRY

I COULD not speak and O'Leary did not. The snow swept steadily against the window pane. Someone downstairs ran a few light scales on the piano and then very lightly tinkled a few measures from Grainger's "Country Gardens," which sounded extraordinarily bright and gay and tender, almost unendurably so, coming on the heels of what O'Leary had just told me.

"They are gayer downstairs this morning," commented O'Leary.

"Yes. There's a general impression that Newell Morse is the murderer. That and the body out of the house have relieved them very much," I said absently, and then aroused to a fuller comprehension of what he had told me. "Do you think Newell Morse was—was murdered, too?"

"I think it likely," he said, calmly enough. Then suddenly he let a flash of bitter impatience overcome him. "If I could only get out of here—get to Barrington— I could do something. Could find out what I want to know. Could stop this wholesale slaughter. But I'm bound to this house—all of us are—penned in with murder at large!" He broke off abruptly and smiled wearily. "I'm not often melodramatic, am I, Miss Keate?"

"If you could get to Barrington could you discover who murdered Frawley?"

"I think I could. Of course, the solution lies right here, in this hunting lodge, but if I could once get my hands on that safety-deposit box Frawley was so smug about, I could work faster." He frowned. "There's something—something so simple I've overlooked it. I've a feeling I'm going to have the key—I'm going to have it——" He seemed to be talking to himself more than to me. Not having much patience with premonitions, possibly because I myself have more common sense than intuition, I broke into his groping thoughts.

"But if Newell Morse did not shoot Gerald Frawley, who did?" I shivered, took one of O'Leary's coats and put it around my shoulders. Newell Morse, thick, ruddy-faced, boyish, yet terribly hunted by some secret—could he have been murdered, too? Would the melting snow reveal his thick body bereft of life? "If Morse is all right—and surely there's a chance that he is—" I paused inquiringly and O'Leary nodded, though reluctantly—"when will he get to Nettleson? When can we count on help?"

"Assuming that Newell Morse has escaped the double menace of murder and of death in the storm, we might begin to expect help by—by to-morrow sometime, I suppose. But I don't think there's a ghost of a chance."

There was a long silence. O'Leary's gray eyes were

fastened on the shifting white veils beyond the window pane and I was staring at the soft blue blankets on the bed, thinking, thinking, going around and around in a vicious circle.

"Look here, Mr. O'Leary, do you mind answering some questions for me?" I began presently, and as he made a gesture of agreement I began: "First, was Helene Paggi on the balcony the night Frawley was shot? Did she explain that scrap of lace? Did she shoot him?"

"She was on the balcony, though she insisted that she had only torn her dress sometime in passing," said O'Leary. "Terice von Turcum saw her. Signora Paggi tiptoed out of her room, past Terice's door, and stopped on the balcony. Terice thought she was watching Jo Paggi—suspected him, I suppose, of some flirtation with another woman. But Terice was inclined to hedge when I questioned her as to whether Helene actually shot Frawley. However, it doesn't matter. You see, before the body disappeared I—well, I examined it closely. And, no matter what you think, Miss Keate, that shot came from very close to the body. It was not fired from the balcony."

"But Mr. O'Leary, that—that simply can't be. I'm as sure that no one came out of the room as that I'm sitting here."

"Can't help it. That's what happened."

"I can't believe it," I said stubbornly. "And anyway, if Terice was telling you the truth, that gives her and Helene each an alibi, too. And if Morse didn't shoot Frawley, as you seem to believe——"

"I didn't say so, did I?" asked O'Leary.

"Why—not in so many words, perhaps, but that's what you lead me to think."

"Go on," he said, closing his eyes.

"Well, if Morse didn't shoot Frawley, and Paggi didn't, and Helene didn't, and Terice didn't—" I was checking on my fingers—"and I know Matil didn't, and Aunt Lucy is out of the question—I should have seen her go through the main room—why—why, that leaves only Julian Barre and Lal Killian, and I don't think Killian did it. And I don't think Barre did it."

O'Leary smiled.

"You'll admit Frawley was killed, however."

"I'll admit nothing!" I snapped.

"Why are you so sure neither Barre nor Killian did it?" asked O'Leary.

"Because—well, Killian seems like a rather nice young fellow."

"He's madly in love with Matil. Why shouldn't he dispose of her fiancé?"

"Oh, no!" I cried. "Not like that. He is no—no——"

"Passion's a dangerous thing," said O'Leary. "And there's a volcano smoldering away, down below Lal Killian's lazy eyes. And—it's been done, Miss Keate."

"Not this time," I said firmly. "And not among the sophisticate—if the word means anything. It would be so utterly silly. So—so futile. He is too intelligent a type for anything so absurdly stupid."

"Go on, Miss Keate. Why do you defend Julian Barre?"

"Well," I admitted weakly, "I rather like him, too. Not as I do young Killian, but still, he is much the same type, well-poised, contented with life, not anxious to risk his own skin for anything. And then— well, somehow I can't imagine a murderer going about his dreadful business without his teeth. And Julian Barre was not only in his night clothes and in his own room, but he'd not got his false teeth in his mouth when he came out, directly after the shot aroused everybody. I can imagine the murderer getting into pajamas and tousling up his hair and pretending to have been asleep. But whoever shot Gerald Frawley had very little time, remember, to stage any kind of appearance. And if I had false teeth, and was so emotionally aroused that I started out to shoot somebody, I certainly wouldn't take out my false teeth first! Especially if I was as careful about my appearance as is Julian Barre."

O'Leary smiled.

"Are you basing a man's innocence on whether or not his false teeth are in his mouth at the moment of the crime?" he asked.

"Not entirely," I said with some asperity. "You said, yourself, that the bolts from the door of Frawley's room into the bathroom and thence into Barre's room simply could not be worked from the wrong side. And since the window was barred and I can swear that no one came out of Frawley's door and across to Barre's door, which, remember, was entirely within my view—well, how could Barre have done it?"

O'Leary's gray eyes had clouded suddenly.

"And there's Annette, Miss Keate," he said softly. "She hasn't the ghost of an alibi, and moreover had been drinking. And drinking seems to affect her more actively than many people. If she'd a grudge against Huber Kingery for any reason—and she might well have had (she's been in his household since she was a young woman, and remember Huber Kingery's somewhat purple reputation where women are concerned)— and heard what Frawley said at dinner, which certainly hinted that he held rather significant knowledge of some kind—well, does it sound possible?"

"In theory, perhaps. But I feel so sure that no one came out of that door."

"Oh, come now, Miss Keate. Can you swear that no shadow slipped quietly through that door in the first instant of your surprise and shock, while you and Paggi got to your feet and stared at each other? There must have been an instant or two of which your memory is rather vague. Couldn't someone have slipped out the door of Frawley's room and hidden—perhaps in the main room, there under the shadow of the balcony, or behind the grand piano—or even have got to the kitchen door, later to join the others? I don't trust anyone's memory at a time like that."

I groped absently in my lap for my knitting, looked about, remembered I had not brought it upstairs, and tried to get a firmer grip on myself.

"You are confusing me. I believe you are doing it on purpose. I was so sure. I wish I had my knitting; I've lost the needle somewhere. No, no, I am positive

that no one came out that door. I won't let you change
my mind."

"And then, there's Brunker. Don't overlook anyone, Miss Keate. Let's not be snobbish or exclusive
about this."

"But Brunker—he's just—just Brunker."

O'Leary moved impatiently.

"Well, Miss Keate, as I said before, *somebody* certainly shot Frawley. You are sitting there placidly
proving that nobody could have done it."

"If only we could prove it suicide," I said longingly.

"That would help, wouldn't it? Any other questions? You sounded like you had a number of them."

"Oh, I have. Whose hand was at the window that
night—that night I shot at it? And why? And who
took that toupee? And why? And who left it in the
chair where I found it? And whose hand was under my
pillow? And *who* returned the toupee to Frawley's
room and had the—the——"

"Guts?" suggested O'Leary blandly.

"—the courage," I said hurriedly, "to replace it on
his head and even take time to tie that towel again?
And why was the dog poisoned and who did it and
when? And——"

"Wait a minute, wait a minute, Miss Keate. One
subject at a time. I don't know who took that toupee
in the first place. But I think whoever took it knew
that I had searched the body and the room, wanted
very much to know the numbers of the famous safety-
deposit box and thought that as a last hope Frawley
might have hidden the numbers in the toupee. It was a

last resort, a slim chance, but if only a slim chance, it was worth trying, for the person who wants that is desperate. I'm not inclined to give the matter of the toupee much importance. Especially its disappearance from under your pillow. I feel sure that your patient helped herself to it and probably quite simply and directly decided it was better on the head of the dead man where it belonged and put it there. She's quite capable of it for she doesn't lack—" he paused here and said "courage" in a mincing way which made me long to shake him for his impudence. "Look here, Miss Keate—test her. See if she is actually going about anywhere she pleases. I don't trust that old lady for a minute."

"Test her? How?"

"Oh, I don't know. You've a fertile brain. Figure it out and tell me what happens. And don't ask me why I think that hand under your pillow was hers. Who else would be so overcome with fatigue—as she must be after doing so much sitting in wheel chairs for the last five years—as to have her hand drenched with perspiration? That's why it was so hot and sticky and wet."

"Oh!" said I in a small voice, adding at once more briskly: "Yes. Yes, of course. That's exactly what I thought." (I never lie, never; still one does have a professional pride.)

"That covers the toupee problem—so far as I can, anyway. Now as to the dog: that was likely done an hour or so after we had our little conference by the kitchen fireplace. Remember the dog was left in the

main room that night? Whoever did it likely figured it
was a good time to get him out of the way. A dog
that is apt to bark or growl or raise any kind of commotion is not the nicest thing to have around—speaking from the viewpoint of the guilty person. It's possible that the dog prevented something once—I don't
know what but I've an idea that it was an attempt to
remove the body. Probably the dog foiled one such
attempt and so was poisoned. And it's impossible to
discover who took the poison from the pantry shelf.
People were all about everywhere that first day we
were here. Anything else?"

"Good gracious, yes. All kinds of——"

"Sh-sh!" S-s!" O'Leary held up one hand and listened a moment, his eyes intent on the log door leading, I surmised, to the bathroom between his room
and Paggi's room. And in the little moment of silence
I was sure that door moved—almost imperceptibly, but
still moved. At his gesture I crossed the room lightly,
laid hold on the bolt, and swung it open. The bathroom was empty but the door into Paggi's room was
just settling silently into place.

O'Leary was sitting up in bed and saw what I saw.

I returned to his room, closing the door firmly behind me.

He lifted his eyebrows.

"Signor Paggi is curious," he said lightly. "I wonder if——"

A knock at the door leading to the gallery interrupted him. I opened the door. It was Brunker in his

starched white coat with fresh sheets and towels over one arm.

"Are you through with your tray, sir?" he said impassively.

"Yes," said O'Leary, more curtly than was his custom when speaking to a servant. "I don't suppose you were in Signor Paggi's room a moment ago?"

"Oh, no, sir. I came directly up the stairs. Shall I change the linen, sir? You might sit in this easy chair while I put on fresh sheets."

"Indeed you won't," I said tartly. "You lie down again. You're as white as a—look out!"

I caught him by the shoulders as he toppled dizzily forward and eased him gently back on the pillows. My little instrument bag was standing on the table where Brunker, I suppose, had placed it after he and Killian had carried O'Leary upstairs, and I dug out a bottle of ammonia salts and held it under O'Leary's nose. He thrust me away somewhat peevishly, protesting that he was no woman and saying very black things about smelling salts, and Brunker stood by, his bald-looking eyes roving over the room in a way that seemed to me impertinent, although I could not have told why.

"Here, Brunker," I said as O'Leary began to look more like himself. "You can help me and we'll have the sheets changed in a jiffy without disturbing Mr. O'Leary in the least."

"Certainly, miss," said Brunker.

Disregarding O'Leary's resentment, that is what I proceeded to do. O'Leary muttered several bitter com-

ments regarding nurses but was too weak to rebel
openly.

"Do you like Hunting's End?" he said finally to
Brunker.

Brunker reached for the side of the sheet opposite
me and shook his head slowly. His flat features were
stolid, his light, lashless eyes expressionless.

"No, sir, I can't say I do."

"Why not?"

"Oh, one thing and another, sir. One thing and another. Shall I tuck this under, miss?"

"Such as——?" prompted O'Leary as I nodded.

"Well, it isn't a pleasant place, sir."

"Have you and Annette always accompanied the
family here?"

"Yes, sir."

"I think you told me the other day that you had
been with the Kingery family for some time. Fifteen
years, was it?"

"About that, sir."

"How did you happen to go to work for the late
Huber Kingery?"

"Mr. Kingery had advertised for a houseman. I applied for the position and he liked me and took me
on. And I've been in the Kingery household ever since.
And that's the truth, sir."

"Was Mr. Kingery a good master?"

"Yes, sir. Certainly."

"Pay you well?"

"Yes, sir."

"You ought to have a little laid by for a rainy day,

by this time. Here, go easy with that pillow, Brunker. My head hurts like hell."

"I'll arrange it. Give it to me," I said.

"I say, you must have a nice little savings account by this time, Brunker," repeated O'Leary.

"I ought to have, sir," said Brunker rather bitterly. Then his face resumed its impassive look. "Anything else, sir?"

"Not at present, no." With a nod O'Leary dismissed the man, and as the heavy log door into the gallery swung gently but tightly into place he smiled faintly.

"That man can hold his tongue if he can do nothing else. It took me more time yesterday to drag from him a few facts about the hunting party here at the time Huber Kingery was shot than it did from any of the others, and then he told me nothing I didn't know already. He had seen nothing, heard nothing, he knew nothing of any of the party. And if he and Annette don't know more about this outfit than they themselves know I'll eat my—best new shirt."

He ended on a sigh that was almost a groan and I did something that I'm willing now to admit I shouldn't have done. Though as to that, I don't see that, in the long run, it made any difference; still if I hadn't he would have refused to stay in bed and would have been up and downstairs all that long day. I went to my little bag, reached for a rather heavy bromide, told him it was aspirin, and made him swallow the little white pills before he had time to note their clear,

bluish-white color. I was quite justified in doing so;
I feared that the wound on his head was more serious
than he guessed and I knew the only thing to do was
to keep him in bed and quiet for a few hours. I knew,
too, that I never would succeed in doing so unless I
resorted to some such thing, and before I left the
room I had the satisfaction of seeing him drifting off
to sleep in spite of himself.

It was then only that I adjusted the window so he'd
have fresh air without freezing to death in the process, bolted his door into the bathroom, wished I could
lock the door to the gallery but of course could not,
and finally left him. I found the others scattered about
the main room. Paggi and Helene were at the piano,
Helene running various exercises very lightly and
smoothly over the keys and Paggi humming in an
oddly nasal way, very soft, and yet delicately precise.
It was singular that the only time Helene and José
Paggi seemed truly married was when they were at the
piano together; Helene was a superb accompanist and
Jo seemed to rely on her with, for those fleeting moments, the fine faith and involuntary confidence that
one occasionally sees in marriage. They were actually
a unity when he sang and she accompanied him. I wondered then, and have wondered since, whether or not
Jo Paggi really would have left Helene for another
woman. I doubt it very much; at least, if he had done
so, I'm sure he would have come back to her to sing,
and after all that was his life. The rest of it, pro-
foundly though he was affected thereby, was really

only superficial with him, though I think he never did
realize that. Strange how little one actually knows
about one's self! And it is often too late when one
makes these discoveries.

Well, Helene and Paggi were at the piano, Lal Killian was scowling at the snow with a remarkably savage look on his face, Matil and Annette were having
a low-voiced conference near the kitchen door, Aunt
Lucy was in her wheel chair by the north fireplace,
staring from her nest of gray into the flames, and Terice and Julian Barre were playing poker, I think. At
least they seemed to be drawing for cards somehow,
and then looking anxiously at the hands they held, and
there was a steadily growing little heap of coins on the
table between them. Terice had her usual feverish look
when cards were brought out and the blue smoke from
her perpetual cigarette made a little cloud around
them.

Matil turned away from Annette as I came down
the stairway, and Annette, looking sulky, vanished into
the kitchen.

"Heaven only knows what we'll have for lunch,"
said Matil to me with a helpless little laugh. "It's
rather—difficult. We may have to resort to oatmeal
and water before this snow stops."

"We'd better be glad for the water," I said. "How
is it we are so well supplied?"

"There's a tank on top of the butte. It's a great
help. Father always used to say man could do without
everything but soap and water." Her face clouded a little as she mentioned her father, but she added:

"There's plenty of soap, too, but I'm afraid it wouldn't have a very pleasant taste. I wish—I wish there was as plentiful a supply of—" her voice dropped and she glanced quickly toward the others as if to be sure they could not hear—"of logs. For the fire."

My heart, which was heavy enough already, sank lower still. It was bad enough the way it was. Suppose the storm kept up—no, that was impossible; but suppose it stayed cold, suppose the snow did not melt. Suppose it was days before we could get to town.

"I've told Brunker to be as sparing as possible. Helene has already complained but I didn't tell her the reason. It is chilly in here right now, but—but there's so little left."

"Don't worry," I said, with more courage than I felt. "This snow can't last forever. It must stop to-night or by morning. It simply can't continue like this. And in November the snow will melt. It won't stay on long. We'll soon be able to get to town. Besides, Mr. Morse may have reached there by now. Perhaps help is already on the way."

She shook her black head definitely.

"That is not possible." Her soft lips tightened convulsively. "That is not possible, Miss Keate," she repeated more steadily.

"Have you no hope of his getting through?"

"None," she said rather coldly. I noted the pinched blue look around her straight little nose, the faint purple lines under her blue eyes, the heaviness of her satin eyelids—heavy with much weeping, I thought. Yet she was not the type of woman who sheds tears easily.

Terice laughed rather shrilly, Paggi shot a black look across at her, and Barre rose, pushing the little stack of coins toward Terice. As he approached us it seemed to me he looked older in the cruelly clear light of morning. He was immaculate as always, impeccably groomed, his faintly gray hair brushed in that smooth crisp wave back from his forehead, but his eyes were lined, too; his face had a kind of spent look, as if the strain of the last few days had told on him physically, and now and then something at the corner of his lean jaw twitched a little. I think it bothered him for he put a hand to his cheek and looked at me as if a little embarrassed. He'd managed to get a heavy cold, too; his voice was hoarse and he coughed frequently.

"Matil," he said, "ten minutes with your Aunt Lucy nearly floored me and Terice has all but finished the job. I wish you'd talk to me awhile and smooth out the wrinkles in my disposition. What's the matter with Terice? Is she as hard up for cash as she seems to be?" He took out a monogrammed handkerchief and passed it lightly across his forehead and firm lips. "Whew! It's rather terrible. Can't you—can't some of us lend her some money? Why, she acts as if she needs every cent—and needs it rather desperately. And after all Terice——" He stopped abruptly, with the manner of one who stops on the very verge of a rather dreadful social misstep.

"You mean she's my responsibility?" asked Matil directly.

"No," said Julian Barre sharply. "Don't be silly, Matil. I meant nothing of the kind. I suppose every one of us has lent her money before now, but she does have her pride, you know. She'd rather gamble for money than to come out and ask for it." He glanced at me. "Funny sort of pride, but that's what it is," he said to Matil, with an air of closing a subject he had better not have begun.

Killian strolled up just then, the savage look gone and his face as lazy and enigmatic as ever, and I left them.

Annette, in the kitchen, was poking at the fire when I entered.

She looked up blackly.

"Oh, it's you, is it?" she said. "I don't know what's the matter with people to-day. Everybody out here in the kitchen, under foot. I don't have a moment to myself. Why don't you all stay in the other rooms where you belong? It's my kitchen not yours—and I wish you'd tell the rest of them that."

I did not trouble to reply, got a drink of fresh cold water and left.

And I did not return to the kitchen until about five o'clock that night. The intervening hours had passed very slowly and uneventfully. We'd a terrible lunch, mostly of canned asparagus which, for no reason at all, I have always distrusted. O'Leary had slept heavily with only a degree or so of fever, which relieved me very much, and the others had spent the day huddling for the most part around the rather sparse fire and—waiting. That was the agony of those days at Hunting's End: the terrible inactivity that was thrust upon us.

As dusk began to gather under the balcony and in the corners of the room, the little spirit of—not gayety, but of relief and even hope—that had characterized the morning quite suddenly and completely left us. Our circle had vacancies that seemed definitely significant there in the twilight and chill. Frawley was dead, his poor body somewhere in the snow. Morse— where was he? And upstairs lay O'Leary who'd barely escaped with his life. No, it was not possible to ignore those things, really to escape their intrusion into the room. During those first few hours of the morning, it might have been momentarily possible to put them a little aside, to hope for relief, but now we knew that it had been an illusion only. The cold draft along the floors, the steady sweep of snow outside, the moans of the wind as it swept under the eaves and poured its icy breath through every crack of the windows, the sighing of the sparse fire, and the curious hush, a waiting hush that oddly enough held fear and a kind of dread, within the lodge—all proved it had been only an illusion of release. That murder still bound us, exactly as it had bound us all along.

And I remember groping absently among the cushions of the chair in which I sat for my lost knitting needle, thinking that I must have dropped it somewhere about there and failing to find it, and thinking at the same moment with the other part of my mind that it felt as if Gerald Frawley's body were still in that cold room so near us. There was a definite feeling of death—of something ugly and unexplainable and threatening hanging over us.

The feeling of proximity to death was so clear and so compelling that, I recall, a bizarre idea entered my head that perhaps that body had returned to its resting place in that quiet room, and I actually got up, walked to the door of Frawley's room, swung it open, and peered within. The body was not there, of course, and I returned to my place acutely conscious of the startled gaze of those others around the fire, though when I looked directly at them every head save Matil's was instantly averted.

I dislike being idle, particularly when I am disturbed or uneasy. Aunt Lucy had scarcely spoken since morning and had needed no attention; she'd got one of her moodily silent spells and simply sat bolt upright in her chair, staring savagely at the ducks on the wall panels all those long hours. The tension was growing unbearable; everyone seemed to be waiting for something, heaven only—or more likely the powers of darkness —knew what. I was hungry, too; and tea had been omitted—an omission which drew a sharp word from Helene, a sharper word from Paggi, and precipitated one of those ugly little quarrels to which I had grown so accustomed that I listened wearily, with only half an ear.

However, as we began to hear Annette stirring around in the kitchen I rose. I happened to have one gift: I can and do make nice baking-powder biscuits; really nice ones, white and flaky inside and brown and crisp on the outside. Annette apparently balked at any kind of hot breads, and besides I was beginning to long for something the chastity of the ingredients of which

I myself could vouch for; that rat poison had not yet turned up and the episode of the dog, who still looked gaunt and weak, had proved that it was rather efficacious.

Once in the kitchen, however, Annette warmly disapproved of the idea, intimating that I had no business there. And as I went to the pantry door she became openly belligerent.

"You'll not get into my pantry!" With a quick motion, astonishing in one of such bulk, she moved between me and the pantry door, standing defiantly before it, her feet wide apart, her fat hands on her great hips. The shining blue marbles that were her eyes retreated till they became glassy blue slits, her face was flushed, her breath reeked of wine. "Pig," she cried, and wagged her head.

I looked at her in disgust. The firelight glinted rosily on her white apron.

At one side of the pantry was another door leading to a store closet; I was as likely to find flour there as in the pantry. I turned swiftly toward that door. She darted toward me, grasped my wrist, but as I gave her a sudden push toppled a little against the wall. I had my hand on the latch of the closet door. Even as she lunged forward again and I felt her hot breath, I pulled upon the door.

Snowshoes came out first, clattering past me. Then something heavy sagged against me, slipping inertly, heavily to the floor.

Annette shrieked. The light above the table wavered.

It was Newell Morse. He'd fallen so the light fell on his congested dead face. His coats were thrust back. The knobbed end of my long steel knitting needle shone from a dark, still wet patch on his shirt and caught a highlight from the red fire.

CHAPTER XIV

A LOG OF WOOD

As MUCH as I have thought of Newell Morse's death and of the moments that followed that grisly discovery, I can never recall exactly what happened. I have tried to recall what I did, what I said, how the others found us. But I can't; it's as if my memory had gone numb for those few moments. It seems to me that Annette shrieked and babbled and shrieked and I could not understand anything she was trying to say. There is a kind of confusion of voices and lights in my memory, and sometimes I can see myself standing as if frozen in my white uniform with the body pushing against my starched skirt. And I do have a rather definite impression of O'Leary in his gray and scarlet dressing gown seeming to waver in the doorway.

But the first thing I really recall is sitting on the wooden settle by the fireplace, hearing voices go on and on and on, and all at once beginning to comprehend what the voices were saying. They were all talking at once, Terice and Helene and Paggi and Barre and Killian, with even Brunker putting in a word every little while and Annette, with her white apron over her head, standing in the background still babbling. Matil was sitting straight and stiff, with her face like a white mask and her hands twisting and twisting, and Aunt Lucy was mumbling disconnectedly, while her great eyes never wavered from that door along the west wall—the door that had led first to Huber Kingery's dead body and then to Gerald Frawley's and now—all at once I remembered that Brunker and Lal Killian had carried Newell Morse's body into that quiet, cold, deserted room and placed it on the bed. And that all of us had trailed stupidly along after them and somehow had found our way to the only warm spot in the whole hunting lodge.

And just as Lal Killian said, not very brilliantly and in a curiously hoarse, strained voice, "Someone did it last night, as Newell was ready to leave," Lance O'Leary drifted, a slight gray shadow in his dressing gown, with the white bandage crooked around his head, through the kitchen door into the main room and approached us. He looked quite as white as the bandage but did not hear my expostulatory exclamation. He sat down weakly in a chair, leaned his elbows on his knees and his head on his hand. In the firelight his face was very white and drawn, with taut, haggard lines around his mouth and eyes.

The rest of them stopped talking suddenly, but Aunt Lucy kept right on.

". . . in Huber's room," she was muttering hoarsely. "In Huber's room. That is the third. The third dead man in Huber's room. First Huber and then Gerald Frawley and now Newell Morse."

One of Matil's hands went out toward her aunt beseechingly, but Aunt Lucy did not appear to note the slight pathetic gesture. Julian Barre, standing beside Matil, was looking unbelievably old and spent; one hand gripped the top of Matil's chair stiffly, the tiny muscle at the corner of his jaw twitched and twitched. Jo Paggi was plunged into a deep chair, his hands in his pockets, his olive face darkly flushed, his glance darting so quickly here and there that I caught only the quick flash of the whites of his eyes. Helene, bulky and awkward on the arm of his chair, was drawing long breaths through her sagging mouth—breaths that were convulsive and jerky like sobs; her eyes, too, were wary, and her supple, strong fingers were pulling in shreds a little colored chiffon handkerchief. This one was green, the shade of Helene's eyes, and I watched a shred of it flutter to the floor before I realized that Aunt Lucy had begun again. Behind the wheel chair stood Lal Killian, white and silent, and beyond him Brunker, his icy face showing neither fear nor horror, and his lashless eyelids lowered.

". . . in the same room. That's where I found him," Aunt Lucy was mumbling. "Just the same way, in his pajamas, barefooted, just ready for bed. He was there on the floor, exactly the same place——"

"*Aunt Lucy, please stop!*" It was nearly a sob from Matil.

Lucy Kingery's great hollowed eyes did not waver. Apparently she did not hear the girl's cry. Julian Barre took a step in her direction but Matil laid her hand on his wrist and he stopped.

"In exactly the same place—in his pajamas, barefooted, ready to go to bed. There's a shot and we find him dying—shot through the heart. Shot through the heart——"

O'Leary stood up suddenly. All at once the tired, haggard look was gone. He glanced at me; his eyes were very clear and shining.

"Can you help me a moment, Miss Keate?" he said. "I wish to—a nurse can help me better than——" He did not try to mend his incoherence. The others made a little lane for us. As I passed Annette I was conscious that she was peering at me with reddened eyes from behind her white apron.

O'Leary closed the door of that ill-omened room. Once again a sheet covered something that lay stiffy on the bed. But he did not approach the sheet.

"Sit down," he said to me. "Sit down. No, not on a chair. On the floor."

His face was not at all flushed, his eyes were quite clear; I hesitated on the verge of taking his temperature. Something in those gray eyes was compelling. I sat down on the floor, my starched white skirts crumpled around me. The floor was very cold; an icy draft swept along it.

"What on earth——" I began, as O'Leary walked to the door, got down on his knees, and groped along the logs.

"Hush!" He looked extraordinarily grotesque in the gray and scarlet dressing gown, his slippered feet trailing behind him, his bandage slipped rakishly to one side. Suddenly he sat back on his feet, frowning.

"What are you doing?" I demanded.

"*Will* you be still!" he whispered viciously. He

rubbed his hand over his eyes. "Listen. A man was shot in this room. He was shot at close range so the shot did not come from the balcony. But no one came out of this room. There was no one here at the instant he was shot. *Still* he was shot in this room. Miss Keate, what's the last thing one does before getting into bed—adjust the window, turn out the light——"

"Lock the door?"

"Lock the door. In this case, bolt it." He looked at the log door. It appeared very simple and innocent, just a thing of logs and nails and rough crosspieces. "Let's see, the body was lying just there. Heads down, Miss Keate." He moved to one side of the door, put his hands on the wooden bolt and lifted it very cautiously, a fraction of an inch at a time.

Up—up—— I was holding my breath, staring at the thing. Even so, I did not see the curious rough hole in the log that the lifting of the wide bolt disclosed until O'Leary whispered:

"Look! There it is! A revolver is hidden in this door. If I lift this bolt far enough to slip it into the latch it will—— Wait a minute!" He leaned over, holding the bolt with marvelous steadiness and taking care to stay out of range of that small, roughly hewn hole in the log. The hole was about half an inch in diameter, so cunningly contrived in the crack of the log that no one, lifting that bolt rapidly to place it in the hook, would ever see the thing or dream of its deadly significance until it was everlastingly too late.

I realized that later; at the moment I could only stare at O'Leary and that log door and wide wooden

bolt. I felt exactly as if I were dreaming. I had no wish
to move, to inquire, to question; I simply waited.

"The wire off the rheostat," whispered O'Leary.
There was a hint of triumph in his whispered words.
"That's what was wanted with it. It's fine enough and
still strong enough. It must be fastened to the trigger—when the bolt is lifted far enough, it pulls it."
He looked at the thing thoughtfully for a long moment or two. Then slowly he let the bolt fall downward again.

"Do you mean," I began, getting back my breath
and my voice simultaneously, "that there's a revolver
there?"

"Yes."

"In that door?"

"Yes."

I looked from O'Leary's face back to the logs in
the door.

"In the logs?"

"Yes."

I swallowed with some difficulty.

"Under—under that bolt?"

"Certainly. What's the matter with you, Miss
Keate? What—where are you going?"

"I'm getting out of this room," I said, with as much
dignity as is possible to one who is crawling on her
hands and knees.

"Well, wait a minute. You can't go crawling out of
the room like that. They'll think you are crazy."

"Maybe I am," I said dazedly. "Something's
wrong. And I notice you are on your knees."

"I don't mind standing up." He got to his feet—not without a rather apprehensive look at the log door. "The only thing to do is stay out of range."

I sat back.

"How do you know which way the thing is pointed? Maybe it has slipped sidewise."

"I'm not going to bolt the door. That is the only danger." He looked at the innocent-appearing log door meditatively. "Perhaps I had better take it apart—remove that revolver before somebody else is shot. No—I'm going to leave it there. It may be useful. I think I'll leave it there."

"But—how can you be so sure? How could anyone get a revolver into that door? There's only about a half-inch-wide hole; you couldn't get a loaded revolver through that and——"

"Where are your eyes, Miss Keate? Here, I'll show you——"

"No, no!" I interrupted sharply. "Leave that bolt where it is!"

"Nonsense! I'll be careful not to lift it too far. Look, Miss Keate. See how this little segment of wood has been removed and then replaced and puttied together. You'd never dream it had been touched. These logs offer a splendid protection for it. Wait—my knife's in my pocket upstairs." He glanced about. "Look in that bag of Frawley's; maybe there are some manicure scissors."

There were, and after rummaging a moment I handed them to O'Leary. I hated to touch the things in that bag; there were brushes and a straight-edge razor, handkerchiefs, toothpaste—and the man who'd packed them, who'd expected to use them—— I shuddered away from the thought, and crouching well out of the way, watched O'Leary digging delicately at the putty around an almost imperceptible crack.

"I'll just take the wire off the bolt here—see, Miss Keate, how carefully it's fastened to the under side—and then the bolt off. Where's something to use as a screw driver? Oh." As I handed him the razor, he gave me, even at that moment, a look of wounded masculinity but took it. "Now, we are quite safe. I'll have to lift the bolt off in order to get this segment of log out. . . . Ah—look, Miss Keate."

I looked. There was a small hollowed-out place in the log, barely large enough to hold a small revolver; it shone darkly blue, it was pointed directly outward. I leaned closer. A small wire was wrapped securely around the trigger, the end of it dangled free from the bolt.

"Clever! Oh, clever!" O'Leary was whispering. "And if it hadn't been for the radio not working and Aunt Lucy's harping on the peculiarly similar circumstances of the two murders—— Well, anyway, that's that. I'll just get this back into place again." He paused, looking thoughtfully at the revolver, then slowly and very carefully he removed it.

"Look here, Miss Keate, the initials 'H. K.' are on it. It was Huber Kingery's own revolver. H'mm—wanted it to look like suicide. . . . No, that's not the answer. In case it was ever discovered the revolver could be traced only to Huber Kingery—not to the

murderer. So that is why it was left undisturbed for
five years. The murderer ran more risk in returning to
the lodge and removing this revolver than in just leaving it here. And look—this is why the door was open:
it is very lightly balanced and hung. Frawley's hand
was on the bolt and likely pulled it toward him as he
fell, which, with the jar of the revolver shot, gave the
door impetus to swing open as it did. Yes, I'm sure
that is what happened."

He looked into the part of the revolver which, I believe, is called the magazine—anyway, it's in that back
part from which bullets are ejected. "Four more
shells," he said, still whispering. He hesitated a moment, then turned the little slender shells, which
looked to me like rather large capsules, out onto his
palm, reached absently for his pocket, said with a horrified look, "Good Lord, I've not got any clothes on!"
and slipped them into a pocket of his dressing gown.
Then he replaced the revolver, working very carefully
but swiftly, attached the fine wire to the bolt again (a
small nail had been driven into the under side and was
permitted to extend barely enough to provide anchor-
age for the wire), replaced the piece of log, wedging
in the putty neatly and picking up every crumb that
had dropped to the floor, and finally replaced the bolt.
Then very carefully he looked over the thing, wetting
his fingers and touching spots here and there, though,
to my eyes, there was no trace of what he had done.

Then he turned to me.

"Simple—so simple," he said, speaking in a very low

voice. "And effective. And something one wouldn't dream of in this ordinary, unimaginative world."

"Well, then," I said rather brusquely, "if it's so simple, who put it there?"

"I don't know who put it there," he said slowly. "But I know when it was done. It was done the last day of Huber Kingery's life."

"How do you know that?" I asked skeptically.

"It wasn't arranged since we have been here. It wasn't done during the five years the lodge has been idle, for what purpose would there have been? Whoever arranged that couldn't have known the Matil Kingery was going to bring the self-same party to the lodge that had been here that other tragic time, and that Gerald Frawley with his dangerous knowledge was going to use Huber Kingery's old room with— with death in the door. And I say it was done the last day of Huber Kingery's life because—why, simply because the thing worked at its first opportunity. The first time Huber Kingery bolted his door—he was shot. Whoever put it there must have had uninterrupted time that last day; he was entirely alone at the lodge for some time. If I could find out——"

"Matil has a diary."

"*What!*"

I nodded.

"She has a diary of that hunting party."

"A diary. She's a jewel. If only—— Look here, Miss Keate. Did she say that publicly?"

I nodded again.

"At the breakfast table."

His face sobered and he said very gravely: "I'm sorry to hear that. She—we must watch her, Miss Keate. I'm afraid she is in danger. Does she have the diary here?" he added with eagerness.

"I don't know. She just said, 'I've a diary of that trip somewhere,' as if she herself didn't know exactly where it was."

"If she's only got it with her," whispered O'Leary. "If the thing is in Barrington it won't help us in the least. Ask her to come in here a moment, will you, Miss Keate? Tell her I'd like to speak to her—anything, but get her in here."

She came willingly enough. I was conscious of a common look of mingled curiosity and suspicion from that silent group around the fireplace as we walked down the main room and entered the death-dealing door.

O'Leary went to his subject without preamble, and with such earnestness that Matil's blue gaze did not linger on the sheeted figure on the bed but met O'Leary's gaze at once.

"Miss Keate says you kept a diary of your last trip to Hunting's End; that you mentioned that diary this morning at the breakfast table." As the girl nodded O'Leary went on in a rather tense whisper: "Do you have that diary with you, here at Hunting's End?"

I held my breath for her reply. I think O'Leary did, too.

"Yes," said Matil at once. "It's just a child's diary, one event after the other. But I brought it along because it was connected in my mind with our last hunting trip here—with Father's last days. Do you want it?"

"Yes." O'Leary paused. "Wait a minute. I don't want anyone to see you give it to me. Is it a large book?"

"No. It's just a small brown notebook—about so big." She measured with her hands. "I was at the diary-keeping age. But as I said, it's just a record of events—'Helene and Signor Paggi sang until bedtime, Father and the Baroness went for a walk, we all rose at four to get down to the blind before sunrise'— that kind of thing."

"That's exactly what I want," said O'Leary, his gray eyes gleaming, his bandage more rakish than ever. "Can you get it for me at once? But hide it. Don't let anyone see you bring it. You see, they all know you have the thing—and while I have the only revolver in this lodge, still—" he glanced at the still body on the bed—"still there are other ways."

"Do you mean I am in danger?" asked Matil directly, her little chin lifting, her blue eyes dark and steady.

"I'm afraid you are. I'd say give it to me publicly so everyone could see it was out of your hands and into mine, but there are two rather urgent arguments against that. One is that I don't want the one who is guilty to get any hint of the fact that I've discovered—" his eyes wandered to the bolt of the door and he said merely—"what I've discovered. And the second one is that so long as you do not seem to be aware, in any way, of the fact that that diary has any significance, you are perfectly safe. So—yes, hand it to me secretly. Hide it about your dress somewhere. You are sure you have it?"

"It's in a pocket of my dressing bag; I slipped it under the mirror. I'll be right back."

He held open the door for her—a gesture which was somewhat marred by his extraordinary appearance —closed it as she walked away, and turned to me.

"Since you are gallivanting about in it rather continually, it's lucky you brought such a handsome dressing gown along," I remarked waspishly. "I'm glad it is nice-looking."

"It's your own fault," he said briskly. "You made me stay in bed this morning and I took such a long, strangely deep sleep that I rather suspect you of having a hand in that, too." He eyed me suspiciously, and as I began to bristle a little he held up one hand. "Never mind, never mind. The thing that matters is, maybe, when Matil gets back, we'll know who killed Gerald Frawley and Huber Kingery."

"Maybe," I assented grudgingly, though my heart was thudding with excitement. "But what about——" I gestured toward the bed.

O'Leary's eager eyes sobered at once.

"Poor Newell Morse. He prepared his own death —by loyalty to Frawley's last request. Someone, who knew Morse had a chance of getting through to Nettleson and then to Barrington with his dangerous knowledge of how to claim that safety-deposit box, did not dare let Morse get away. He knew, too, that he was in danger as long as Morse lived. He watched, saw Morse take down the snowshoes, got me out of the way with, probably, an andiron, took your steel knitting needle, which made as good a dagger as he needed, and killed Morse, who must have been taken by surprise. Yes, that's the way it must have happened."

"Why didn't he kill you, too, while he was at it?"

"Probably thought he had! Although I believe he wouldn't deliberately do so unless he—had to."

"You say 'he' always, Mr. O'Leary. Do you mean that you are sure it is one of the men?"

"No. No. I'm not sure about anything——— Ah!"

It was Matil. Her cheeks were flaring scarlet, her breath coming in little gasps through crimson lips.

Her hands were empty.

"Someone got there first," said O'Leary, without waiting for Matil to catch her breath and speak. He spoke so quietly that I think she did not sense his bitter disappointment.

She nodded.

"Yes. And—I know who it was. It was Helene Paggi."

Lance O'Leary's eyes below that white bandage became slate-colored.

"Helene Paggi? How do you know that?"

She flung out her hands palm upward. Her voice with that fascinating little break in it was low and uneven.

"You see, we have all spent most of the day around the fire in the main room. It is the only warm place in the house, so we had to stay there. And we could see everyone who came and went. The architecture is very simple. Anyway, Helene wanted a magazine in my room, and without asking me went in to get it. She came out with a magazine right enough, so I didn't think of anything else."

"Helene Paggi," said O'Leary slowly, as if the fact had some significance, though I, for one, could not see that it had. "Helene Paggi. And you think she has the diary now?"

Matil nodded.

"I think so. of course."

"No one else has been in your room?"

"No. I'm quite sure because there have been people in the main room all day. And—well, it is only natural, I suppose, that we—watch each other so!" The last few words were in a rather dreadful little whisper.

"When did you last see your diary?"

"Oh, I'm sure it is Helene who took it, Mr. O'Leary. You see, after I had spoken of the thing this morning at the breakfast table, I went and looked to be sure I had brought it along. And there it was behind the mirror, just where I had slipped it the afternoon I packed to come to Hunting's End. I left it there, of course. I didn't dream that anyone would want it. And really, Mr. O'Leary, I don't want to disappoint you, but I'm sure there is nothing of any value to you or anyone else in it. It's just one of those childish things: as I said, a mere record of events, one thing after another. There were no impressions that could be of value; nothing. Some girls of seventeen may be gifted in that way and might have made a valuable record, but—I was not."

"Can you remember any of the things in your diary? Can you remember anything in particular about—your father's last day here at Hunting's End?"

"You mean, the day before he was—killed?"

"Yes."

"Why—we went hunting. I think——"

"Who?"—incisively.

"I—a party of us." She closed her eyes in effort to recall more exactly. "I'm sorry I can't remember precisely how many. I remember Father, of course, and the others——"

"Did anyone stay here in the lodge?"

"I—it seems to me someone did." She was speaking very slowly.

"Who?"

"Oh, I—I *can't* remember, Mr. O'Leary. I'll try to. I'll do my best. But it was all driven out of my head by what happened in the night."

"And only Helene Paggi was in your room this morning?" murmured O'Leary, as if turning some thought over and over in his mind, examining it from every angle.

"Only Helene Paggi," repeated Matil. "And Brunker, of course, with fresh linen. But what about —about Newell Morse, Mr. O'Leary? Can't something be done? Oh, I knew I was wrong in coming! I knew I was wrong. I should never, never have stirred up this dreadful thing. It is as if—as if murder was in the lodge—just waiting for us." She caught herself up as her voice shook and her hands began to tremble; I put my arm around her and she hid her face for just a moment on my white-clad shoulder. Then she straightened up, shoulders erect. "I—I think I'll go back to the fire. I'm cold." Resolutely she kept her eyes from the figure on the bed. "Is that enough, Mr. O'Leary?"

"Quite enough," said O'Leary. Somewhat to my surprise, there was a touch of jubilance in his voice again. "Thank you, Miss Matil."

"Poor Newell Morse," said O'Leary as the door closed firmly. "I warned him; if he had listened to me he might still have been alive. I tried to save him—well, poor fellow. Can you remember where you lost your knitting needle, Miss Keate?"

"I haven't the faintest idea." That long steel knitting needle! How often had I scratched my fingers or arms on it or its mate and vowed to get ivory needles, or tortoise-shell, and put away the old-fashioned steel pair. Well, I should have to do so now—providing I could ever bring myself to knit again.

"It doesn't matter anyway. It wouldn't mean anything, for anyone might have picked it up—any place. It was a rather neat stab, right into the—— What's the matter, Miss Keate?"

"Oh, *don't!*" I shuddered. "Don't you see it's *my* needle! That's what is the matter. I've helped operate too many times to be squeamish but this—this is different. I think—I think I'm going to have a chill!" I concluded in some astonishment as my teeth actually began to chatter.

"No, you're not. You're just cold; it's like a refrigerator in this room. We'll go back to the fire. But, Miss Keate——"

He paused and then said in a slow whisper: "Does it occur to you that now no one has an alibi? Not even you?"

And he opened the door and I walked past him.

Why, of course, no one now had an alibi. No one. Not even I.

CHAPTER XV

A SPIDER IS TRAPPED

THEY were still crouching around a rather sullen fire; Annette had taken her apron off her head and restored it to a more normal place for aprons and had stopped babbling French, and Julian Barre was standing at a window, his haggard eyes on the fast-gathering blackness outside, and Lal Killian was seated, but those were the only changes in the group. Terice was smoking feverishly, Brunker was still standing in the background exactly like a yellow-pink wax statue, with features that were unfinished in the matter of eyelashes and eyebrows, Helene had been crying, for her eyes and nose were red and her face blotchy, and still leaned heavily against Paggi, who, apparently, had not moved, and Aunt Lucy sat upright in her chair and stared from her cobwebs. It was rather horrible to see how the group had dwindled—the more horrible in that it limited our range of suspicion in so dreadful a fashion.

To tell the truth, I was a little surprised when O'Leary began to inquire into the circumstances of Newell Morse's death quite as precisely as he had inquired into Gerald Frawley's death, though with less result. It seemed to me very evident that Newell

Morse had met his death by the same hands and for the same reason that Gerald Frawley had died—and, more than likely, Huber Kingery—and this being true, the solution of one murder would bring with it the solution of the others. However, he questioned us all at some length, though I think that, all along, he knew much more about Newell Morse's death than any one of us knew—or, rather, than any of us but one knew. That was, as always during those days at Hunting's End, the rather ghastly consideration that was constantly before us. One of us, one of that little group, was guilty. And, that being true, none of us was safe. Yet we did not know whom to guard against.

I had not liked Annette's reluctance to let me open the doors of the pantry and store closet, and said so without mincing matters when O'Leary came to me. It was rather difficult to tell of those few horrible moments in that great shadowy kitchen, of the opening of that door, of the snowshoes, and of that inert weight that fell against me, but I did so. Annette kept up a little staccato murmur all the time I was talking, and when I had finished O'Leary turned to her sharply.

"Why did you refuse to let Miss Keate open the cupboard door?"

She gesticulated widely with her fat pink hands.

"I do not like her, that nurse. She had no business in my kitchen."

"When did you first know that Mr. Morse's dead body was in that cupboard?"

She spread her fingers wider, shrugged vastly, and

lifted her short eyebrows above those shrewd little blue eyes and their red pouches.

"I do not know it at all. *Jamais!* I only wish to keep that nurse *out!*"

"Are you trying to make me believe that you had not opened the door of that store closet during the whole day?"

"*Certainement.* Why would I open it? I have everything that there is. There is nothing in that closet but —oh, flour maybe, cans of caviar, oatmeal. One cannot make the meal of caviar, flour, and oatmeal." Her shrugs, her bright blue eyes, shrewd and quick, her large flourishing hands were things to see.

And she stuck to her denial, willy-nilly. She knew nothing of the dead man, she knew nothing of the body being in the store closet, she had heard no noises during the previous night, she was as innocent as a *bébé,* but she did think—this with a glance at me— that it was strange that a knitting needle had stabbed him. Who, she would say if she were O'Leary, had possessed that knitting needle!

And the others were equally innocent; the singular thing was, too, that as each denied any knowledge of the affair, and did so with every evidence of sincerity, I found myself credulous. And yet—someone had killed Newell Morse. And it seemed to me likely that it was the same person who had struck Lance O'Leary. It was about then, I believe, that O'Leary began to inquire into the circumstances under which he, himself, had been discovered that morning, and Brunker produced an andiron from one of the fireplaces, which he said had been found beside O'Leary. Julian Barre and Lal Killian both corroborated Brunker's statement at once, and O'Leary looked at the andiron with a curious expression before he directed Brunker to return it to the south fireplace from which it had come. Brunker had been the first to find him, it appeared upon the necessarily belated inquiry, and had immediately called Julian Barre, and then, at Barre's suggestion, the nurse. And by that time others were rising. Brunker had nothing further to tell.

"Look here, O'Leary," said Julian Barre at last. "Suppose we let Annette and Brunker get us something to eat—and build up this fire a little. We'll all feel better if we get something hot to drink. It's— well, it's been a strain. I think we all feel it."

"Right, Julian," said Aunt Lucy, with such suddenness and hoarseness that everyone started a little. "You are right as usual. Annette! Dinner!"

"Dinner!" said Annette explosively. "Madame! There is no dinner!"

"Now, now, Annette," said Matil wearily. "Cook what there is to cook. We shan't starve as long as there is—caviar and flour and oatmeal." She smiled wanly, but Helene bridled angrily.

"So like your headstrong ways, Matil," she said. "Force us to come away out here with you and then have nothing to eat. I'm—" her anger relaxed into a thin wail—"I'm hungry," she said, and sobbed.

"Helene, you're a fool," remarked Jo Paggi with the utmost composure. "Stop that. Hush!" And Terice smiled maliciously.

"You never had the strength of mind to diet, Helene," she said. "Here's your chance to acquire a figure again."

We waited almost in silence for the meal. O'Leary went to his room and reappeared after a few moments, clothed again in the gray worsted he affected for daytime wear and with the bandage on his head adjusted more securely.

It was quite natural, I suppose, that with Newell Morse's murder the little cloaks of conventionalities to which we had clung so desperately during the preceding days and nights should finally and completely escape our clutches and vanish. I have never before or since that time seen men and women in their primitive, selfish state, and I never wish to again, for it is singularly disillusioning. Our treasured little masks of customs and behavior were gone entirely, and the sight of what was left was not pretty.

The dinner, such as it was, was rather awful. In the first place, it was so cold over there near the gallery stairway that we women all wore wraps; I slipped my blue and scarlet nurse's cape over my shoulders, Aunt Lucy bundled up in a particularly ugly gray shawl, and Matil and Helene and Terice had put fur wraps over their shoulders—Helene's wrap was a flowing one of mink with enormous dolman sleeves, in which, at a distance, she looked rather more like a huge brown bear than was entirely comfortable. Terice's ermine and moleskin had once, I think, been an evening wrap and looked remarkably shabby. And besides the discomfort of the cold, which was beginning to penetrate our very bones, the meal as a meal was a complete failure, though we did manage to come away from it less hungry. There were great steaming bowls of oatmeal, a food which I happen to detest, at every plate, and dishes of the strangest variety were up and down the length of the table, mostly olives and pickled walnuts and a selection of cheese in little jars; it looked very much as if Annette had simply scraped the store cupboards. It was a disheartening meal, to say the least, and under its influence Aunt Lucy became so extraordinarily unpleasant that I rose under Matil's imploring eyes, grasped the wheel chair firmly, and guided it—and its occupant, of course—away from the table and toward the fire. Aunt Lucy muttered considerably in the process and her earrings flashed dangerously but she was reconciled when O'Leary followed us, bringing our coffee. She brightened up, took the coffee and smacked at it in a most ill-mannered way before she thanked O'Leary and asked him to be seated.

But if O'Leary had hoped to talk to Aunt Lucy while she was in a garrulous frame of mind he was disappointed, for the others trailed after us at once.

And there we sat in silence, a strangely aware silence, as if every breath drawn, every sigh, every foot shuffled, every change of position on the part of any in that little circle was of tremendous significance. It seemed to me, then, that we passed an eternity sitting around that fire, with the snow blowing relentlessly against the black window panes, the wind sighing in the chimney, the dog moving restlessly about—and the chilling words carved on the mantelpiece staring down inexorably at us: "The End of all Good Hunting is Nearer than you Dream."

O'Leary stared into the fire with thoughtful gray eyes. Paggi sat hunched in his chair, his shirt bosom thrusting itself up under his fattish chin, his buoyancy for once subdued, his olive eyes alert to every sound. I think it was at the third uneasy circle Jericho, still gaunt and weak from his experience with the rat poison, had made of the long room that Aunt Lucy turned abruptly to me and shot out the word "Soda!" with her customary vehemence. I rose and went to the kitchen. Annette and Brunker were in the kitchen, of course, though I did not hear any movements or clatter of dishes. At the pressure of my hand the swinging door pushed open silently, without a creak of its hinges. The kitchen was rather dimly lighted as usual by several lanterns; the fire glowed redly. Annette and Brunker were seated at the kitchen table, eating. I could see Brunker's stolid pinkish face and Annette's broad blue back and wispy gray hair.

She was mumbling something between bites which I could not understand but I heard Brunker's response distinctly.

"You made a mistake," he said in his expressionless way, "when you refused to let the nurse go into the pantry. If you had let her open that door, she probably would not have opened the door to the store closet at all. I'll take some more beans."

That was the smell that had been assailing my nostrils with such attractiveness since I had opened the door. I peered over Annette's shoulder. A dish of beans steaming in tomato sauce stood on the table; Annette had unearthed the plebeian food from somewhere and had kept it for her own and Brunker's delectation. Ordinarily I dislike beans, having had too much of them during certain dreary days of 1918, but now my mouth watered.

"Don't talk to me!" said Annette sharply. Her broad hand went out to a tall bottle. She poured a generous glassful of red liquid and set the bottle down on the table with an emphatic whack. "You have your own ax to grind. Don't think I'm blind either, Mr. Brunker. I know more than you think I know."

Brunker's lashless eyelids lifted and lowered with incredible rapidity.

"What do you know?" he said smoothly enough. He popped an enormous forkful of beans into his mouth and repeated in a muffled way: "Just what do you know?"

I could almost see Annette's little eyes narrow shrewdly and her loose mouth smile.

"More than you think I know," she said again. Then her blue fat shoulders leaned forward toward Brunker, whose lashless eyes watched her steadily. "I know, for instance, why you have remained in the Kingery service. Why you did not leave. Me, I know these things!"

The door behind me pushed open again, this time with a decided creaking of hinges. It was Jo Paggi at my elbow. Brunker got halfway to his feet, and Annette twisted her blue bulk to peer over one shoulder at us. I suppose they thought I had entered with Paggi, for neither of them looked in the least disturbed.

Paggi advanced to the table. His thick nose was sniffing eagerly, his olive eyes were glistening and were fastened on the dish of beans.

"I knew it," he said in a relishing way. "I knew I smelled beans and tomato sauce." He pulled up a chair to the table, Brunker stood up, and Paggi reached for a plate with one hand and a fork with the other. He seemed to find the things blindly, by instinct, for his eyes never left the beans. "Tomato sauce," he murmured softly. "Annette, I know you've got a little garlic somewhere about. Yes? Oh, excellent! Look, my girl, slice a little, dice it—so fine." He measured with his thick but rather sensitive-looking hands. "Fry it in butter. Hurry, my girl. I starve."

Annette was no more adamant to Paggi's magnetism than other women might be; she got out a small onion-like lump, sliced and diced it with a despatch that made the keen little knife in her broad hands flash and glimmer in the firelight, there was a smell of frying butter, and almost in less time than it takes to tell, she was stirring an odorous mixture into the tomato sauce. I found myself drawing closer to the table. The dish really looked very nice, indeed. I took another step.

"Come, Miss Keate," said Paggi, turning to laugh at me. His white teeth glimmered; he ladled out generous helpings with incredible rapidity. I found myself seated at the table between Brunker and Annette and opposite Paggi, eating my beans with the keenest relish.

I can only suppose that the food mesmerized me. Certainly that was the strangest, most nightmarish business in all those strange days at Hunting's End. I can still see myself seated at that kitchen table, with the cook, flushed and loose-mouthed and breaking now and then into her blithe little tune, on one side, Brunker, cold and silent but humanly intent on his own plate of beans, on the other side, and opposite me José Paggi, buoyant, gay, his eyes shining over his food.

The light glinted on my starched white uniform, on the cat curled up on the hearth, its tail twitching a little, on Paggi's smooth black hair, on Annette's wine glass, in the wide pupils of Brunker's still eyes which looked wider and darker under those lashless lids, and on the roughly finished door to the store room behind us.

It was not until the last bite on my plate was gone, and I saw with regret that there was no more in the dish, that I leaned back in my chair and a little silence fell upon us and I saw the incongruity of the thing. And it was at that moment, too, I think, that I suddenly remembered O'Leary's whispered words: "No one now has an alibi."

No one. Not Paggi, then, nor Brunker, nor Annette. Not even Aunt Lucy had an alibi—Aunt Lucy who was waiting for her soda.

Paggi leaned back in his chair with a sigh of gusto and repletion. Annette smiled at him and poured out more wine and Brunker rose and began to clear off the table.

"If Helene knew this she would kill me," remarked

Jo Paggi. He smiled at me, thanked Annette, and took the small glass in one broad, dark hand. *"A vous, madame,"* he said, smiling at Annette, who moved her vast shoulder with a coquettish little shrug and airily lifted one hand to tuck back various straying locks of stiff gray hair; oddly enough, she was not grotesque. A little look of understanding flashed between her and Paggi. He set down the empty glass, sighed with pleasure, and said again: "Yes, if Helene knew this she would kill me. She says she is starving to death. But how can I help it if her nose is not keen like mine!" He eyed the empty dish regretfully, scraped up a little sauce that remained on his plate, took it slowly on his tongue, and looked at me. "What's the matter, Miss Keate?"

"I was only wondering—why you lied about the footsteps on the gallery the night Gerald Frawley was killed," I said bluntly.

His face darkened in an instant.

"Lied! You accuse me of that! Me, José Paggi!" The anger left his face as quickly as it had come and he flung out his hands in a careless little gesture, lifted his eyebrows whimsically, and laughed. "Why, of course I lied. Miss Keate, you may thank kind heaven that you will never know what it is to have a jealous wife." He drank another small glass of Annette's red wine, his fat throat gurgled a little over it, and he placed the glass on the table again with a little click. "Helene is a cat!" he said, quite abruptly. "A fat, ugly cat." And he held out his glass again to Annette.

"But about the gallery?" I urged.

"Oh, yes. The gallery. Why, Helene was there, of course. Watching me. She's always watching me. Humiliating, is it not? Should I tell and embarrass myself? Never!"

Brunker, taking away Paggi's plate, gave him a cold look. Annette sang, "La, la, la, la—la, la," lightly and swayed her body from the hips in time with the funny little tune. Jo Paggi looked at her quickly.

"No, no!" he said. "You are wrong. It goes thus." He gestured with outstretched hand, and sang in his mellow tenor, lightly, the same strain, varying it a little and carrying it along a measure or two, when Annette joined him and I rose.

As they paused for breath I leaned over.

"But what were you doing in the main room that night?" I asked sharply.

His gayety did not diminish.

"Talking to you." He laughed and added: "And giving something for Helene to watch. Again, Annette."

"But why were you so uneasy, so nervous while you sat there before the fire?" I insisted, disregarding the mandates of good taste.

He shrugged, halting the tune to reply.

"Who wouldn't be nervous! You stared at me like a—cat with a mouse."

I left them singing.

I forgot the soda water for Aunt Lucy and had to turn at the door and go back for it. Brunker got the soda for me and watched me stir it into a cup full of water. The voices at the table went on, growing louder and more zestful.

"Annette!" The voice came sharply from the doorway. Matil was standing there, her blue eyes outraged.

Paggi whirled, his song broke off abruptly, he got to his feet and approached Matil.

"Matil, you've a wonderful cook. When we marry we will keep her forever and ever; paradise itself——"

"*Jo!*" Helene was pushing past Matil, her arms out, her supple fingers clawing at Jo Paggi. He retreated, and before she could reach him Killian appeared in the doorway, seized her and held her. She struggled for a moment, her eyes shooting green fire, then all at once she collapsed in Killian's arms and began sobbing gustily, hurling out half-stifled accusations to which her husband paid not the least attention. He was mopping his forehead with his handkerchief and looking anxiously at Matil and Annette, who retreated sullenly, picked up the thin cat, and began to stroke its back. It purred loudly, and Helene sobbed and Matil looked at Helene in Killian's arms, at Annette flushed and loose-mouthed, stroking the cat, and at Paggi, perspiring and apologetic. Then she turned swiftly and the door swung behind her. I followed. I think Killian made an attempt to follow too, but Helene clung to him and sobbed and I caught a somewhat bored smile in his eyes.

As I entered the main room Lance O'Leary was just coming down the gallery steps. He stopped me. Aunt Lucy seemed to have forgotten the soda water by that time, no great wonder, and was dozing in her chair at the other end of the long room, and no one was within hearing distance.

"I've been looking for the diary," he said in a low voice. "I've searched every bedroom on the gallery. If Helene actually has it she has hidden it somewhere, and when I taxed her with it a few moments ago she flatly denied having had it at all. She was frightened, though, when I mentioned it. She may have concealed it somewhere about her clothing—in that case, I may have to ask you to search her, Miss Keate. Look here, Miss Keate, just how far do you think she is under the domination of her husband?"

I set the cup of water and soda carefully on a little rustic table.

"She is quite mad about him," I said thoughtfully. "Absurdly jealous. He just now admitted that she was on the balcony the night Gerald Frawley was shot, watching him—Paggi, that is. He said she was a 'fat, jealous cat.' "

"Chivalrous," said O'Leary.

"I think she would do anything he told her to do," I went on gravely.

"Anything?" asked O'Leary softly.

I waited a moment before replying.

"She is desperately afraid of losing him," I said at last. "And Paggi—there's no use denying that he's extremely attractive to women."

O'Leary looked at me anxiously.

"My dear Sarah," he said. "I feel it my duty to warn you that if you are setting your heart on Paggi you will be doomed to disappointment. Paggi is already——"

"Paggi, nothing," I said warmly. "I only said he was attractive to women. I said nothing about myself! I hope I have reached an age of——" I caught the spark of delight in O'Leary's eyes and stopped abruptly. "It seems to me you have more important matters to engage your attention," I said curtly.

"You are right, Miss Keate. But you must admit that you and José Paggi are an irresistible combination." He smiled again and glanced quickly around the room. "Where is Matil?" he said sharply. "Is she—— Oh, there she is! She is all right, then. Well, I've got things to do." He stopped as if listening and looked at the black winking window panes. "If I'm not badly mistaken the snow is going to let up during the night or early morning and I've—got things to do before that happens."

"Things to do," I said stupidly.

"Things to do," he repeated very gravely. "When the snow stops, and there's a definite prospect of getting away, getting to town, getting help. As I said this morning, Miss Keate, only heaven can help us—unless I work fast now. So far, the snow has protected us— in a measure. First to find out from Terice who moved Gerald Frawley's body. Then——"

"Does she know? She said no one went into that room."

He looked at me in exasperation.

"Of course, she said that. She volunteered the information, too. Offered it freely and without being asked. Would she have done so if she had not known something? She is either in terror of telling what she knows, or—she is herself implicated. Then to find out from Matil why she permitted herself to promise to marry Gerald Frawley; there's something there beyond what meets the eye. And, Miss Keate, keep your eyes on Matil Kingery, will you? I've warned her as—as definitely as I could. She is—I'm afraid she is in rather grave danger, and I can't watch her every moment and she won't listen to me."

I looked swiftly toward Matil. She was standing beside Julian Barre's chair. Her hand rested lightly on his shoulder and she was looking down, smiling a little wistfully at something he was saying. As we watched he rose with the quick elastic movement of a younger man, drew a chair close to his own, and, at something the girl said, laid his arm lightly around her. Her dark hair pressed for a moment against his shoulder and he bent his own handsome head over her. The little picture was silhouetted for a moment against the red fire, then Terice laughed shrilly from behind the little cloud of smoke that surrounded her and said a few words we could not distinguish, a little commotion rose from the door into the kitchen, and Helene and Lal Killian entered, with Paggi following, and Matil sat down. A fit of coughing shook Julian Barre and at the sound Aunt Lucy stirred and blinked her great eyes and looked around rather dazedly.

As I took the cup of soda water, O'Leary whispered, "Remember, watch Matil," and I went to my patient.

I think she did not recall asking for soda, even when I offered it to her, though she drank it gulpingly, hiccoughed quite loudly, and demanded her bedtime sandwich.

"I'm going to bed," she said hoarsely. "The rest of you can sit up and tremble all night if you want to, but I'm an old woman and I need my rest. I'm going to bed, and I'll have the doors bolted, and there's no use in anybody trying to get in to murder me for you can't do it." She repeated her entire sentence slowly, staring from one to another of us with a wide inclusion that was not very flattering. Brunker, who had entered at the tinkle of the little hand bell which someone had touched, took Matil's request for Miss Lucy's sandwich with his usual impassivity, and Aunt Lucy began to draw her chair away from the fire. It was just then, I believe, that I caught O'Leary's gray eyes upon me in a kind of prompting look. Her bedtime sandwich, of course! What better bait could I have to induce the gaunt black spider out of her webs.

No respectful way to think of one's patient, I admonished myself, as I followed the smoothly rolling chair. It was rather grisly that, before entering the door which I opened, Aunt Lucy whirled her chair around a little, looked back at the group around the fire, and quite visibly counted, her lips moving as she did so.

"All there and accounted for," she said then with gruesome flippancy. "It's quite safe to enter my room, Miss Keate."

Her hoarse voice was purposely loud, I think, and

carried to those around the fire, for I saw Matil stiffen
and Terice darted a vicious look toward us. Then Aunt
Lucy's chair went smoothly through the door and I
followed and closed it. I looked into my own room
and the bathroom intervening and under both beds,
conscious of Lucy Kingery's scornfully amused regard
all the while. No one was there, of course, and the
shutters of both rooms were firmly bolted.

"There's no use doing that," remarked the old
woman, chuckling in a most disagreeable fashion.
"Matil and Julian and Paggi and Helene and Terice
and Killian are all out there in the main room, and
Brunker and Annette are in the kitchen. And Frawley
and young Newell Morse are dead. There's nobody
under the bed."

"Nevertheless I'm going to be sure," I snapped.
"I've had enough of this business."

"And you weren't here when Huber was killed,"
said Lucy Kingery. "Oh, if you'd been here then you
might have reason to be nervous. But he deserved to
die. He well deserved to die. Robbed everybody he
knew. Robbed me. And then made a will giving all he
had to Matil. Here, take my necklace—no, not my
earrings, just my necklace. Mind you wrap it up in
cotton before you put it in my jewel case. Once a stone
is scratched it is gone. Anything but a diamond does
scratch," she went on in a conversational tone. "And
I've not got diamonds. Not now." She stopped talking
as abruptly as she had begun. Just as I got her snugly
into bed, Brunker knocked discreetly at the door. I
took the tray, walked across the room and put it on

a table near the window. Somehow Annette had managed to save some cheese and biscuits and a bit of pudding which looked stale but filling. Aunt Lucy's eyes glistened from their dark pockets as she regarded the tray.

"Give it to me," she said hungrily. "Set it over here on the bed."

"I'll just fill your hot-water bottles first," I said smoothly. "That bed is like an icicle." I seized the two rubber hot-water bottles that hung in the bathroom and made my escape, closing the door firmly on her hoarsely remonstrating voice.

A straight rustic chair was just outside her door and I sat down, holding the two cold rubber bottles on my lap. Her black cane still stood against the fireplace, and though I could hear a hoarse murmur coming from the bedroom behind me I paid no attention to it.

No one looked at me. Killian stood at one of the windows gazing out into the blackness; Terice and O'Leary were bent over the radio, there behind the grand piano, with the light from a pewter lantern above them shining down on Terice's metallic blond curls and the white bandage on O'Leary's head; Paggi and Helene and Barre and Matil simply looked into the changing flames and said nothing. Helene was still red-eyed and took long sobbing breaths every so often and Jo Paggi brooded darkly, his boyish gayety still in abeyance. Yet, if one spoke to him how easily his red mouth would laugh, his white teeth would gleam, his olive eyes would become gay and magnetic.

Idly I watched O'Leary and Terice; their voices

were low, I could hear only the murmur breaking
through the heavy silence in the room, a silence that
was somehow alive and packed with feeling. I did not
think they were talking of the radio for once I saw
Terice's jewel-laden hand go to her throat and she
looked up at O'Leary and shook her head defiantly
and emphatically; as O'Leary apparently insisted, she
shrugged her shoulders impatiently, darted a swift
look about her, hesitated as if in indecision, and then,
while O'Leary waited, his gray eyes intent, seemed
suddenly to reiterate her negation to whatever he had
asked, for she drew her fur wrap more closely about
her, shook her head again, and turned away.

And once while I waited Matil moved suddenly,
rubbed one slim hand across her eyes, turned abruptly
as if looking for someone, saw O'Leary and Terice
under the lantern's light, half started out of her chair,
then, after watching them for a moment, relaxed again
and stared at the fire with a perplexed, troubled look.
The look, I thought to myself with my breath coming
a little faster, of one who is striving to recall something—and succeeding. Suppose she remembered that
last day! Suppose—— A sound in the room behind me
caught my ears. I glanced at my watch; it had been
twenty minutes since I had left Aunt Lucy alone with
her coveted tray.

I rose at once, laid my hot-water bottles on the chair,
and went to the door of her room. Opening it, I saw
my patient leaning back against her pillows, complacent, satisfied in her nest of gray flannel nightgown and
blankets. She licked out her tongue across her purple

lips and looked at me comfortably. Then she saw my eyes go to the tray.

It was still on the table by the window. But every scrap and crumb of food was gone from it.

"Matil came in and gave me my tray," she said with no visible compunction. "You ought not leave me abruptly like that, Miss Keate, when you know how helpless I am. Did you bring the hot-water bottles?"

"I'll bring them in a few moments," I replied. "Are you quite comfortable?"

"Very comfortable," she said. "Bolt my door, please, Miss Keate, and—you might keep an eye on your own door until you come to bed. I don't want anybody prowling in these two rooms. I'm just as scared about this affair as anybody." She looked at me with a touch of defiance. Her gray hair and dark face and scant gray beard wagged against the pillow. "I'm just as scared as anybody."

I bolted her door, went through the bathroom and my own room into the living room.

"Yes, you are!" I thought to myself. "And you are as likely to have done murder as anybody, too!"

CHAPTER XVI

THE SNOW HAS STOPPED

O'LEARY, whom I sought out at once with the confirmation of his suspicion, did not appear to be particularly interested. He had apparently finished his conversation with Terice and was sitting hunched over a card table, building little card houses and seeing, I had no doubt, every movement, every change of expression, every flicker of an eyelid among the silent group around the fire.

"I can't get a word out of Terice," he said in a low voice, watching Lal Killian light a cigarette, and carefully balancing one card against another. "She's scared. I'd like to know why." There was a little pause, while he placed another card against the trembling little structure. Killian got up again suddenly and walked toward the window. Every eye followed him.

O'Leary's hand lingered on the last card. A singular silence crept over the room. I believe no one breathed. Suddenly I was aware that the only sound I could hear was the subdued, faint hiss of the logs in the fireplace.

Killian had reached the window. He stared at it, then, rather slowly, drew the window upward, unbolted the shutters and pushed them back. I believe no one moved.

A gibbous moon was riding high. Its cold light made of the window a faint rectangle of pale light struggling half-heartedly against the light from the lanterns.

"It may interest you to know," said Lal Killian evenly, "that it has stopped snowing."

Still no one spoke and no one moved. Killian stared out of the window.

At last O'Leary's hand bore too heavily against the little house of cards. It collapsed with a soft whisper.

He rose, then, and walked toward the window, and I found myself following him. The air that struck our faces was still cold, but had lost some of its bitterness.

I could see the moon and the scudding clouds and the snow. It lay all about us, in great sweeping drifts and valleys. You could not tell what were hills covered with snow and what were drifts. It was a limitless confusion of whiteness, glittering in the moonlight, and dark, changing shadows. But the snow had stopped.

The snow had stopped.

"When the snow stops," O'Leary had said, "may heaven help us, for no human can."

It was singular that, much as the cessation of the snow meant to us all, and desperately as we had longed for it for three days, now that it had actually occurred no one talked of it. The faces around the fireplace were all turned in the direction of the window, and Brunker's flat face peered in for a second through the swinging door with Annette just behind him, but no one spoke. At the time, however, I did not see the strangeness of our silence upon a matter that concerned us so deeply; I merely accepted it as I had accepted other anomalies that characterized those dreadful days at Hunting's End.

Presently Brunker's cold face withdrew slowly behind the swinging door, Killian closed the shutters and the window, O'Leary fingered the bandage on his head thoughtfully, winced a little as he pressed the sore spot, and started across the room, and the others turned again toward the fire, their faces very still.

Matil rose and at once the men were standing.

"Good-night," she said briefly, and started toward her own room.

O'Leary whirled alertly at the sound of her voice and advanced hurriedly.

"Oh, Miss Matil," he said, "where's the dog? Here —take him along, won't you? Let him sleep in your room to-night."

She acquiesced lifelessly, as if it didn't matter, and O'Leary walked with her to the door of her room, the collie, still sad and dejected and unbelievably thin under his lovely gold and white coat, followed. I noted that before the girl entered the room O'Leary went in for a moment or two, then came out, they talked briefly in low voices, he nodded in a reassuring fashion to the girl, and waited, listening, while she entered the room and, I suppose, dropped the wooden bolt into place. But as he turned again toward us he did not look reassuring. There was a tight line around his mouth, his face was set into lines of something like anxiety. I think everyone had watched Matil's disappearance, but there was a queer shifting of eyes from O'Leary's grave face back to the fire. Funny how flames or red ashes

seem to draw one's gaze. I had never noted this so
definitely as I did at Hunting's End. We would stare
at the fires for hours at a time, it seemed to me, while
we waited—waited.

"Miss Keate," he said clearly, and as I walked toward him, my starched white skirt rattling a little under
my nurse's cape and breaking into the thick silence the
room contained, he added crisply, "May I talk to your
patient, please? I don't suppose she is asleep yet."

She wasn't asleep; I found her staring from her
great, hollowed eyes at the window.

"Open the shutters, Miss Keate," she said at once
as I entered the room and turned up the wick of the
lantern I had left burning over the dressing table.
"Open the shutters. The snow has stopped."

She was quite willing to see O'Leary; in fact, she
seemed to have one of her garrulous moods and to
welcome the outlet. As I unbolted her door, O'Leary
spoke to me in passing.

"There's a chair directly outside the door." He
lowered his voice to a whisper. "If you will sit there
you can hear everything we say—and at the same time
keep your eyes on Matil's door. And Miss Keate, if
anyone, mind I say *anyone,* approaches her door, for
even the most harmless-seeming purpose, call me at
once. Don't hesitate. Not an instant."

I went to the chair, of course. My heart was pounding a little as I glanced toward the fireplace, to see if
anyone had moved, and tucked up my nurse's cape
around me, and settled my cap firmly on my head. The
chair was one of the sins in rusticity that abounded in

the lodge and was none too comfortable. I wrapped my cape tightly around me and settled myself to listen, keeping my eyes firmly on the group around the fireplace and on Matil's door at one and the same time. This sounds out of all reason but was actually a simple matter under the circumstances.

It was a moment or two, I suppose, before I began to give the conversation going on in Aunt Lucy's room any attention. And when I did begin to listen she was already launched upon a rather bitter denunciation of Huber Kingery. Surely, I thought to myself, if anything would drag a spirit back from the nether world it might well be the virulence against it which Lucy Kingery expressed so freely. I am a literal-minded person, with not a scrap of imagination, but it did seem to me not an unlikely thing that Huber Kingery might come back to avenge himself.

And then I moved impatiently, searched with my eyes the blank log door leading to Matil's room, and wished I had not let my fancy run amuck.

". . . robbed everybody," the old woman was saying hoarsely. Her words came quite clearly to me but I think the group around the fireplace could not hear, for Terice's head was tipped a little as if she was straining her ears, and Helene wore a baffled look and kept watching as much of Aunt Lucy's room as the opening of the door had disclosed. "Robbed me, robbed the servants, robbed his friends. Yes, he was my brother. I kept his house. I devoted my life to him. I became an invalid through the shock of his death. But there's no getting around the fact that he was a scoundrel."

"Robbed everyone, you say, Miss Kingery? Even the servants? They had nothing, surely, that he wanted."

"Little you know of it," she said, and snorted. I could hear the bed springs creak a little as if she had shifted her gaunt, long body.

"The servants," said O'Leary musingly. "It isn't often you hear of a man in Huber Kingery's position robbing his servants."

"Little you know of it," she repeated.

"What did Brunker have that Huber Kingery wanted?"

"Ten years' savings," said the old woman promptly. "Ten years' savings. Ten years of his life. Huber got it, for shares in that damned trust company. Brunker has stayed on with us; hopes to get it back sometime. Money went into that trust company—but little ever came out. And as to Annette——" She paused and I could almost see her wide mouth leer and the knowing look in her hollowed eyes. "Annette was a young woman when she came to us. That was not long after Matil died—Huber's wife, you know, my niece's mother. Annette was a handsome young woman, too. Ah, there are many things people can be robbed of . . ."

She stopped without a period, lost apparently in some murky past.

"But—Annette—the cook—that doesn't sound like your brother," said O'Leary very mildly, as if not to break in upon her talkative mood.

"You didn't know Huber. You are wondering why I didn't put a stop to it—but why should I? It died a natural death. His pleasures were always brief. Besides—Annette was a good cook," she added practically. And after a moment of silence, she said in a musing way: "Those French women—they've got a way with men. Born in 'em. Why, would you believe there was a time when Huber would have married Annette! Think of it! Married his cook! I put a stop to that, myself. I wasn't to be supplanted by a cook I had hired. Not Lucy Kingery. Yes"—there was indescribable complacence in her voice—"I showed Huber how foolish he was to think of marriage. He never did again."

"Was Annette—bitter about it?"

"Annette!" Aunt Lucy was surprised. "Why, suppose she was, what difference did it make? She was a good cook. Excellent." She paused and muttered morosely: "Still is, but drinks too much."

I thought of Matil Kingery with her steady eyes, and wondered what kind of life her young mother had led between the brother and sister.

"But Terice and Helene, neither of them, had a ghost of a chance at Huber—that is, you understand me, so far as marriage. Huber'd got his lesson by that time."

It was just then that Terice rose, said something to Helene, and Helene rose, too. They stood for a moment near the fire, huddling under their furs. Helene said something to Paggi which I could not hear and he kissed her hand lightly and sat back again in his chair, and the two women—were they about to approach

Matil's door? No, they were walking toward the stairway, Terice ahead, her heels making little sharp sounds on the floor, and Helene more slowly, dragging a little, behind. They mounted the stairway, Terice hurrying a little, pausing to shake the ashes off her cigarette against the rustic railing, and Helene looking downward at Jo Paggi as if reluctant to leave him. I watched them trail along the gallery, their faces starkly white against the rough-hewn logs, dark and stained with smoke, that lined the east wall. Then presently I could hear them in their adjoining rooms, footsteps, a window lifting a little; and the bolts being dropped into the iron hooks made little dull periods.

"You see, I know that you do. You needn't try to deny it, Miss Kingery," O'Leary was saying very smoothly in the room behind me. "It is a great effort likely for you to walk, but not so great an effort, I believe, as it might be. Come now, Miss Kingery, tell me the truth. Haven't you been able to walk for some time?"

There was a long silence. Then Lucy Kingery laughed harshly.

"Well—yes. But mind, you're not to tell until I'm ready to have them know it. And then you must get some nerve doctor—psychoanalyst he'll call himself, or some such title—to say it was the shock of finding Gerald Frawley dead under the same circumstances as my brother Huber died that released me." I suppose O'Leary looked faintly astonished, for she chuckled again. "Oh, I read. I know about this stuff. And it happens to have suited me to sit in my chair and be waited on for five years. Why, man—I used to have to go out and find things to interest me; I joined in the struggle. And for five years everything has been brought to me. I know all the scandal, all the social activities, all the ambitions, all the disappointments. From my wheel chair I control Barrington society." The complacence in her hoarse voice was unbearable.

"But Barrington is not a large place as cities go," remarked O'Leary very softly.

"What do I care?" she said. "I'm a big toad in a little puddle." She paused again and added, something to my surprise, " 'I'd rather sit on a pumpkin and have it all to myself than ride to heaven in a golden chariot and be crowded.' Isn't that what he said? Quite right, too." She chuckled again in a very disagreeable manner. "Matil thinks I'm religious." Her voice changed suddenly, became heavy and brazenly defiant. "Well, I am."

"I don't doubt it," said O'Leary politely, and I could imagine her waiting sternly for his comment. "I don't doubt it, Miss Kingery. But—why did you want that toupee?"

Another silence. Was she going to reply to that? Lal Killian got up, his hands thrust into his pockets, walked restlessly the length of the room, glanced up at the gallery, and walked back to plunge himself into a chair again. Paggi did not stir and Julian Barre coughed rackingly and pulled his chair nearer the fire.

"I didn't want it. What I was after was that paper the nurse had. How did I know she'd got it? I have sharp eyes and good ears. Not much escapes me. When she handed you the note to Newell Morse that he burned, I saw the look on her face—she hadn't expected it to go to Morse, and human nature being what it is, I knew she had read the thing. Then her hand went to her pocket—something else was there. Likely another paper. Oh, I'm smart," she boasted. "Sitting in a chair for five years has made me sharp."

"But—why did you want that note? How did you know where she'd put it?"

"Women always put things under their pillows," said Aunt Lucy. Her strident voice was growing rough and weary. "And I—oh, I just wanted it. Curious. I like to know what's going on. So I got into her room, felt under the pillow and took everything that was there. I unbolted her door to the main room—naturally I didn't want her to know——" She left herself and her motives untouched and resumed: "I didn't like the toupee much. It belonged on Gerald Frawley's head and I put it there. Somebody was in the kitchen talking when I did it." She sighed raspingly. "It was hard work getting around like that. I'd walked some, of course, all this time—when no one was watching—but not very much at a time. This made me sweat——"

"You're tired now, aren't you, Miss Kingery?" said O'Leary quietly. "But just tell me, will you, what you know of Matil Kingery's promise to marry Gerald Frawley."

"Don't know anything about it," she said flatly, and then, sighing again, added: "Don't know anything about it, except that her father insisted upon it. Made her engage herself to him."

"Her father!" said O'Leary incredulously. "But he's —dead."

"I know, I know," rejoined Aunt Lucy impatiently. "But that was before he died. Matil was about seventeen or eighteen. It would take Gerald Frawley's sharp eyes to see what a woman she gave promise to be—she was at the gangly age then, long-legged, too thin. Yes, she'd been engaged to Frawley for five years." She chuckled in a grisly way that sent chills up my spine. "Joke on him, too. I don't think she let him touch her in all that time. I guess she was glad he was killed. I'm tired. I wish you'd go away. I'm tired of talking. What's the use of so much talk anyhow? Doesn't get us anywhere. And that's the way we go through life—talk, talk, talk about nothing." She sighed again. "Get out," she said with her customary gracelessness. "I want to sleep."

"I hope you sleep well—but I doubt very much if you do," said O'Leary in a rather startling moment of candor. "Thank you, Miss Kingery."

He closed the log door carefully behind him. His eyes went at once to Matil's door and then to the little group around the fireplace.

"Where are Madame Paggi and Terice?" he asked sharply.

"Gone to bed. So she did take the toupee!"

He nodded carelessly. His eyes were going rapidly here and there about the room.

"Look here, Miss Keate, this diary is somewhere in

this lodge. It has not been burned, I know that for a fact. It may have been tossed out into the snow but that would be too dangerous. There's the body in the snow to dispose of already as soon as the snow melts. No—I'm sure it is here in the lodge. I've searched the gallery bedrooms, every one of them, even my own. I don't expect you to find the thing but—watch out for it, will you? If only Matil could remember that last day! She told me, there at the door of her room, that all of them went on a hunting trip and the lodge was deserted all day. Somebody, of course, came back—but she can't remember. What's that?"

The three men around the fireplace all started a little, too, as a gallery door opened. Quick footsteps tapped along the bare floor. It was Terice, still wrapped in fur, her hard little face set. We all watched silently while she came down the steps. Then O'Leary walked over to meet her and I followed.

Once he whirled to shoot a quick look at the three men around the fire. Not one of them had stirred.

Terice von Turcum waited, clutching the rough log that served for a newel post with hard, taut fingers; the knuckles shone blue and the rings glittered. A pewter lantern hung directly above the first step and its light etched fine lines under the mask of paint on her little face. She was panting.

"*I'm afraid*," she whispered. Her hands left the newel post to clutch at O'Leary's gray coat, and then drew back. She cast one look at the men around the fire. We could see only the tops of their heads above the upholstery of the chairs; Julian Barre's hair was

crisp and shining and touched with gray, Paggi's dark
and oily-looking; his head was wide at the top and
easily distinguished from Lal Killian's well-shaped
head with its soft darkish hair. A little trail of blue
smoke crept upward, apparently from Killian's cigarette.

"*I'm afraid.* I—I can't stay up there alone. I simply can't do it."

I think she was quite sincere. Her little face was a
mask of terror. Her hard, ill-manicured hands shook
and clutched at the post frenziedly.

"What are you afraid of?" asked O'Leary.

I saw Paggi turn and peer around the side of his
chair. If he hoped to hear what we were saying he was
disappointed; the curiously thick silence and the size
of the room muffled our voices and made our words
indistinguishable.

Terice darted a hunted look toward the men around
the fireplace.

"I don't know," she gasped. The rouge stood out on
her cheek bones; her lips under the red paste looked
stiff and very cold.

From a window just beyond the stair railing came
a steady little sound. I seemed to have heard it for
some time before I comprehended what it was. *Drip—
drip—drip:* the snow was melting then, dripping down
from the eaves. It was warmer.

O'Leary twisted about deliberately so that he could
keep the three men at the fireplace and the door to
Matil's room in his range of vision. He did not look
at Terice at all, but kept his shining gray eyes on the

opposite end of the room. I turned to follow his gaze. My heart leaped as it seemed to me that I saw only two dark heads rising above the cushioned chair backs. I looked closer. No, the middle one was still there; Paggi had only sunk a little lower in his chair. And the door to Matil's room was bare and blank and untouched.

"Are you willing now to tell me what I want to know?" asked O'Leary directly. "You may be protecting yourself, you know, by doing so."

She hesitated.

"I'm afraid to," she mumbled. "I've been afraid to, all along."

O'Leary waited. She kept looking about the room, darting quick, furtive glances all around.

"I'm afraid to," she repeated. "How do you know that what I could tell you might protect me? What do you mean by that?"

"I mean that here, in this house, there is a murderer. Already two people have fallen victims to an ugly death. That person is in grave danger—he knows it, he knows he must act before we leave this lodge. Before help comes. He must act then—*to-night*. If you do not tell me what you know I may not be able to prevent—another murder."

She shrank back, her face distorted, her eyes frantic, and her teeth showing between tight lips.

"I—it may not help you," she whispered incoherently. "It may—the men who went into Frawley's room that day when you said his body disappeared may not have—may not be——" She paused, gasping for breath, huddling the fur coat closer about her as if it might give her a shadow of protection.

"Tell me," said O'Leary. "Hurry."

His eyes, fastened now on the little Baroness, were clear and compelling. She put a hand to her throat, pressing it against the painted, wrinkled flesh under her chin as if to relieve some obstacle to speech. Her hunted eyes clung to O'Leary's.

"Two men," she whispered. "It was two men. One went into his room. Another came out."

"What do you mean? Hurry."

"I was sitting in that chair." She gasped for breath but seemed finally determined to tell what she had to tell. "They didn't see me. No one else was in the room. Julian Barre—Julian Barre came out of Frawley's room. I saw him—I saw him, Mr. O'Leary, but he didn't see me; I was down in the chair, in the shadow. He thought everyone was in the kitchen seeing to the dog. But he did come out of that room. I saw him." She was eager now, gulping and panting in a way that was not nice to see.

"He came out of that room?" said O'Leary sternly. "What do you mean?"

"Another man went in. First. First, before Julian came out. It was——" She gulped again, painfully, leaned forward so her perfumes and the scent of her lip paste surged about us. "The other was Lal Killian. He went into Frawley's room. He came down the stairs and didn't see me and went—into that room. And he didn't come out. Julian Barre came out. I watched. Then several others drifted in from the kitchen." She was whispering so rapidly I could scarcely understand her. Something kept tugging at me to look around. Look at Matil's door. Look toward the other end of the room. But I could not tear my eyes from Terice. "Others came, and all at once there was Lal Killian again, going upstairs. But swear you won't tell him that I told you. Promise me. You must swear it. I'm afraid—I'm afraid—I——"

A scream tore through the long room. It was high-pitched, horribly sharp, sobbing starkly upward to the very rafters themselves. With it mingled the wild wolf howl of a terrified collie. It held us helpless in sheer terror—then it broke abruptly.

It was a woman's scream. It came from the end of the lodge. It came from Matil's room.

CHAPTER XVII
THE DIARY

LAL KILLIAN reached Matil's door first, although Paggi and Barre were close seconds. They were pushing at the door and calling to Matil when O'Leary and I reached them. Terice, I think, ran with us. At any rate she was there, panting, at my elbow.

"Why did you leave her alone?" snarled Killian as O'Leary came up.

"The door is bolted! Here, Jo——" Killian and Jo Paggi brought their shoulders heavily against the door. It was thickly made and did not waver.

"Hush!" Killian lifted his hand suddenly. His face was white, even his lips.

"Wait!" The voice was trembling, shaking, but Matil's. "Wait! I'll take the bolt off."

In the little strained hush I saw Killian wipe his forehead with the back of his hand. Jo Paggi's face was livid. Barre was biting his lips until they bled a little, his hands were clutching at the logs of the door as if he would pull them apart.

There was a little rustle inside the room, then the bolt moved and the door was open. Matil stood there, swaying, her white dressing gown ghostly in the semi-twilight.

"What is it? Where? What's happened?" Killian had her in his arms. "Are you hurt? Are you all right?" Then he and Paggi and O'Leary were at the window and Barre, supporting Matil who seemed weak and faint with fright, was looking anxiously over her head.

At the instant of entering the room I glanced about, saw no one besides Matil, and my eyes went to the window. Contrary, I think, to O'Leary's directions, she had unbolted and opened the shutters so that the moonlight reflected from the white snow and made a faint white radiance in the room, and as I glanced, a shadowy bulk loomed for an instant against the whiteness beyond and was gone.

I could not see for a moment past the crowding shoulders at the window, then I was aware that there was a commotion of voices, that someone was outside, that O'Leary and Killian were getting something bulky over the low sill and into the room.

We needed light. I turned swiftly, ran to the nearest lantern in the main room, snatched it from its hook, and darted back to Matil's bedroom. Helene was in the main room, fur coat clutched about her, her feet bare and her hair down her back and her eyes wild; she grasped at me, I eluded her clutch, and she followed me closely.

The flame in the lantern wavered but did not go out. I held it high.

Annette was standing between Killian and O'Leary. The snow on her skirts was melting and falling on the floor. Her shoes were sodden. Her face was flushed and full-looking, her mouth loose and mumbling, and her gray hair falling in wisps around her shoulders.

We could not understand what she was mumbling and O'Leary's sharp questions failed to awake a response.

"She's either dead drunk or mad," said Killian.

"She's drunk, I think, sir." It was Brunker's dull voice from the doorway. "She apt to get—wild when she's drunk," he said, rather apologetically. "Maybe I can help you, sir. I'm used to her."

"Annette!" Matil's voice was steadier. She drew away from Julian Barre's protecting arm and approached Annette. "Why were you out there at my window? Why did you—wave your arms, mouth at me —make such horrible gestures? Why did you do that?" She paused and said sharply: "Answer me!"

Annette was turning sullen. She eyed Matil with red blurry eyes that seemed to shrink from the lantern light.

"I beg your pardon, miss," said Brunker, "but you know how Annette is when she is like this. She—gets to thinking of—of what she considers her wrongs. I think she got to your window by mistake. It is Miss Lucy she has a grudge against."

"A grudge?" Matil was beginning questioningly when Aunt Lucy herself, in the wheel chair as usual, appeared at the doorway, swept Helene aside with one motion of her long gaunt arm, and glared at Annette.

"Annette, my girl, you get back to your room and sleep this off. You ought to be ashamed of yourself, at your age," Aunt Lucy's harsh voice rasped in our ears.

Annette regarded her sullenly. "Go on. Don't you hear me? Do you think I'm afraid of you? Go on to your own room. You know, my good woman, sometime I'm going to take you seriously. And you'll not have the home you've had for twenty years." Aunt Lucy leaned back wearily in her chair and spent her energy on a last, vicious order: "Get out. Go on. Do as I tell you."

Annette's bulk wavered uncertainly; Killian and O'Leary released her arms, she advanced, passed Matil without giving her a look, stopped before Aunt Lucy's chair and glared down at the old woman. With a clutch of her long hands Aunt Lucy whirled her chair back to give Annette passage.

"Get on," she snarled.

Brunker stirred.

"I'll get her safely to her room, madame," he said in a low voice to Aunt Lucy.

Aunt Lucy nodded grimly, watched the slow progress of the two down the main room for a moment, then looked at Matil with the first shade of softness I had ever seen her display toward the girl.

"Matil, my dear, I'm sorry you'd such a fright," she said. "Annette fancies she has a grievance against the Kingerys. But don't let it worry you." Then her great eyes swept the rest of us, fastened on Helene's bare feet, and she said abruptly: "I'd advise the rest of you to get back to bed."

There was a slight commotion, as everyone there seemed seized with a desire to leave the icy-cold room.

Killian, who'd been closing the shutters, pulled the window down with a bang, turned, gave Matil one long look, and picked up a fur coat that lay across a chair.

"Here, Matil, you're freezing to death," he said roughly. He wrapped the coat around her, then suddenly, as if his arms could not withdraw, he drew her closer to him and with a smothered little exclamation bent his face over her and pushed her soft hair back from her face and began to kiss her in a swift, broken way, as if he could not believe that her dear body was actually in his arms or her precious face lifted to his.

"You're sure you're not hurt," he said at last, pulling back to look straight into her eyes. I don't know what he saw there but he buried his face against her dark hair with a sigh that was almost a sob.

"I can't stand it, Matil," he said. "Tell me what Frawley was to you. Oh, don't pull away like that. I knew you were there, talking to him just a few moments before he was killed. I don't care. I don't care if you shot him. It doesn't matter. Nothing matters so long as I have you. But you must tell me."

Someone was coming along the main room toward Matil's door. I reached and without a sound closed the log door; I wanted this thing settled without interruption.

"Why—why, Lal. How could I tell you!"

"Don't, Matil. Don't cry like that. I—I can't stand it."

"I was engaged to him, Lal, ever since before Father died. Ever since that last hunting party here. It was Father's wish; I had nothing to say about it. Then—you—I was begging him to release me, Lal; I

—I begged him——" Her faltering voice broke and was muffled against his cheek. "No, no, don't stop me. I must tell you. He said No, he would hold me to that promise, that I'd feel differently after we were once married." He held her very tightly there, and her next words were so muffled against him that I could not understand them for a moment. ". . . and I told him I—I loved you, Lal, that I'd never, never be happy with him or make him happy. Then—then he helped me over the sill and I came back through the snow. I hadn't realized how terrible the storm was. I could hardly get to my room. But I didn't want anyone to know—I had hoped he would release me and no one would ever know of our engagement. I tried to be honest with you, Lal; you know I tried to be. No— wait, I must finish. Then I—I was exhausted when I got back here, to my own room. The wind and the snow even for that short distance were terrible. I got in through the window and sat down to rest and get my breath, and think. I was desperate, Lal, I didn't know what next I could do."

"Don't shake like that, sweetheart. He couldn't have forced you to marry him."

"But Lal, there was my promise to Father. One can't break promises like that. Then—then I kicked off my wet slippers and started to close the window. And —and there came that shot. Just then. It was as if my—wish had come true, for—for Lal"—I could barely hear her frightened whisper—"Lal, I *knew* he'd been killed!"

"Nonsense, dear, you were overwrought."

"Before I went out there, I *knew* he'd been killed. And—I knew I must get out of my dress, look as if I'd been asleep. It was terrible, Lal. I acted as if I had thought the whole thing out. As if I'd shot him myself. And I didn't! I didn't! No, no, don't stop me. I wanted to tell you and you—you've been so cold, so——"

"Don't, Matil." It was almost a groan. His hands were touching her gently, pulling the fur closer around her, smoothing back her soft hair.

"And I—got into the dressing gown and somehow got to that room. And he was dead and—and I was *glad!* Oh, Lal, I was glad!" She was sobbing wildly, and at last collapsed. His arms went under the coat, holding her closer to him so the fur wrap fell around both, enclosing them in a world of magic.

O'Leary cleared his throat sharply. Killian looked up with a start, as if he'd entirely forgotten us, and indeed everything but Matil.

"How long did you sit there on the bed thinking, Miss Matil?" O'Leary asked. "Ten minutes—fifteen?"

"I don't know," she replied, twisting around toward us. "I suppose it could have been that long."

"Look here, Matil. You're going to take cold in this room. Go on in to the fire." Killian bent to kiss her mouth—it was a long kiss and looked to be very nice, indeed—and then almost pushed her away from him. "Go in to the fire and get good and warm. I want to speak to O'Leary a moment."

The girl obeyed. Killian came closer to O'Leary.

"See here," he said. "I—I guess I've had my lesson. If anything I've got to say can help you——" He stopped, got out his handkerchief, touched his forehead and lips, and put it away again. "When I heard Matil scream——" He stopped abruptly again. "How about this nurse? She's from your office, isn't she, O'Leary?"

O'Leary smiled and shook his head.

"No, she's a bona fide nurse. But—she's in my confidence, if that's what you want to know."

Killian regarded me doubtfully.

"I guess it's all right, if you say so. But what I have to say—well, if it got out it would wreck things for Matil. The Kingery Trust—all her money—everything. And mind, I'm not sure of what I say. It's all just suspicion."

O'Leary was looking at Killian steadily; I wished that I knew what lay behind those clear gray eyes.

"Can you stand there in the doorway, Miss Keate —or no, I will. I don't want to let Miss Matil out of my sight again," said O'Leary.

Killian's hands clenched and he took a quick step forward.

"Good God! Do you mean she's——" He gulped. "She's—still in danger?"

O'Leary nodded.

"Go on with your story—suspicion—whatever you want to call it. And be brief."

Killian looked at O'Leary, walked to a position in the doorway from where he could see Matil sitting in a chair drawn close to the fireplace, with Barre at her side, took a long breath, and said:

"It's only a suspicion, O'Leary. But I think something is going wrong with the trust company. And I think Frawley—was in on it. And Newell—Newell Morse, you know—I think he guessed it. Maybe ran onto something at the office. You see, a manipulation of funds and securities is rather simple if—if the right men get together on it. Men who are in the right positions. But—this is the way I've figured it out. I think Frawley got scared—had something on somebody that was dangerous knowledge. He may have tried to use it; knew he was in a dangerous position and—told Morse where Morse could find what records he had. Records that would implicate—somebody."

"You mean Julian Barre?" asked O'Leary quietly. Killian flushed.

"No, I don't," he flashed. "You think I'm jealous of him. Well, I'm not. I gave up Matil when I found she had been engaged to Frawley all along, but—never again. And Barre isn't the only man who's connected with the trust company. You probably don't know that Paggi was hand in glove with Huber Kingery."

"Then is it Huber Kingery whom you suspect of manipulating the funds?"

Killian flushed.

"Sounds rotten, doesn't it?—five years after he's dead. And, of course, he couldn't have come back to kill Frawley. . . . Oh, I don't suspect anybody, but I do think Morse had stumbled onto something. Maybe I'm all wrong about it. I don't know. But that's what

I think. Take it or leave it. I can see you don't believe me. Well, you don't have to. Only——"

"Exactly what is your own position in the Kingery Trust Company?" asked O'Leary, rather coldly.

"Me? Oh, I'm in the investment department. I'm a kind of errand boy, really. Buy and sell bonds for our clients and for the trust company. We hold quite a lot of property in escrow, you know. And have quite a number of estates to manage."

"Anything else to say?" asked O'Leary crisply.

Killian's face was a quick dark red.

"You haven't believed me. I can see that. Well——"

He broke off abruptly, flung himself out of the room.

"Wait," said O'Leary quickly. "Frawley's body ——" But Killian did not stop, and at that moment my eyes fell on Helene standing by the fire. Her fur wrap had fallen a little open and I could see that she was wearing her night dress, for pale mauve silk showed between the folds of fur and her feet were still bare and looked cold.

"Don't let Helene follow me," I whispered to O'Leary, forgetting all about Killian's incoherent tale and the unsettled problem of the disappearance of Gerald Frawley's poor dead body, and I walked quickly down the length of the room, up the gallery stairs, and along the east wall, conscious all the time of the combined and suspicious regard of those below me. I think Helene did not guess at my intention until I opened her door, and if she started to follow me O'Leary stopped her.

A lantern was lighted and hung over the dressing

table. My eyes sought hurriedly along the open boxes and jars and powder puffs and clothing that cluttered the table. But it was there! Half hidden under a silk chemise. A little brown book.

It took only a glance to see that it was truly Matil's diary. I thrust it under my nurse's cape into the pocket of my dress.

O'Leary met me at the foot of the rustic stairway. Those at the fireplace watched us suspiciously. I think my face told him I had found it, for his eyes were shining and he asked me no question.

Under cover of the flowing circular cape I wore, I slipped the little book into his palm and walked toward the fireplace. He followed, a little behind me. About midway of the room he sheered aside suddenly, walked over toward the blank door of the room that had been Huber Kingery's—toward the room where two men had lain dead and where a third now reposed on that cold bed. The door shut firmly behind him. At once heads were turned back toward the fire; eyes averted themselves as I sat down. I looked at Helene; she knew, of course, what I had found in her room. Had she tried to follow me? If so O'Leary's presence had stopped her—possibly it had been too late, and she realized it, before she recalled the diary and knew my purpose in her room. Paggi's face was a curious yellow, his olive eyes going here and there. He got up, started away from the fireplace, turned as abruptly and sat down again.

We could hear the melting snow dripping, dripping, dripping from the eaves about the nearest windows.

CHAPTER XVIII
"BOLT THE DOOR!"

WHEN O'Leary opened the bedroom door suddenly and stepped out a kind of sigh went over that huddled, silent little group. We all watched O'Leary go to the kitchen, whence he returned almost at once with Brunker at his heels.

"Miss Keate," said O'Leary, his hand at the latch of that fateful door once more and his voice so clear that it carried sharply the length of the room. "Can you help me a moment?"

I rose at once and walked toward him. My feet dragged and were like lead. I could feel those eyes behind me watching, watching.

He opened the door, motioned me across the threshold. His face was as white as the bandage on his head. He was looking at something in his pocket—his revolver, of course. Was he going to have need for it?

"I'm going to make a guess," he whispered. "And I've got to guess right the first time. If I make a mistake I've lost my proof. If I'm right . . . Stand over there, Miss Keate, by that window."

I did so. I felt rather as if I were sleep walking and was yet curiously alive to every impression. I remember how long the body on the bed looked, how curiously stiff and rigid. Poor Newell Morse!

Then all at once Brunker was in the room, and coming slowly and somehow reluctantly over the threshold were Paggi and Barre and Killian and—that was all.

"I want you men to help me a little," O'Leary said quietly. "But first, Barre, why did you and Killian remove Frawley's body? What did you hope to accomplish thereby? I know you did it. It doesn't matter much because the snow is melting and we'll soon have help and find the body. But why did you do it?"

Barre and Killian's eyes met. There was a moment of silence.

"Might as well tell him, Julian," said Killian, adding something that O'Leary and I understood without further explanation: "I was trying to save Matil and she—there was no need. I know that now. I was out of my head." He stopped abruptly.

Barre cleared his throat.

"Well, you probably know the answer. We hoped to buy you off, O'Leary, to be quite plain. Frawley's body would be found under the melting snow in some of these canyons in the spring." He shrugged his shoulders. "I admit it. We thought we'd share the risk. Killian came into this room when no one was in the main room and the coast was clear. I was in my own room beyond the bathroom. He unbolted this bathroom door. I came in." He paused, then went on rather lifelessly: "You may as well know it. We thought —no body, no murder. It meant something to each of us to keep out of a murder mess and we couldn't hurt Frawley. It was hard work getting him—it— through the window. And cold." He shivered and stopped speaking to cough painfully. "But we did it. Somebody had to take the risk of coming out of this room. I did that, and no one was in the main room. Killian, of course, went out through my room. I bolted the door on this side after him. Later, when others were in the main room, he managed to get out of my room, we thought, unobserved. I suppose somebody saw him. Well, as you say, it doesn't matter. You've been determined to expose the affair. I hope you are protecting yourself, Mr. O'Leary. You are mixing in a rather dangerous business."

"That was a foolish thing to do, you know," said O'Leary. "But at least you've admitted it openly." He paused. I could hear the drip, drip, drip of the snow again. A cold breath swept through the broken window on my shoulders.

"Now then, I want a little help," said O'Leary briskly. I think only I saw how his eyes gleamed. "Brunker, will you take that corner of this upper sheet? And Killian that one. Hold on, now, don't let go." He was at the bed that held so gruesome a burden. I stared at him in perplexity. I think the men in the room were equally perplexed but they moved stupidly at his sharp request. "I'll take this one myself, and Paggi, take that corner—I want you to see something. It's rather gruesome—don't let go, Killian, hold on—we'd better keep the women out. Bolt that door, will you, Barre? Hurry."

What did he mean? What was he—— Then the words became significant to me. *Bolt that door!*

The three men around the bed were looking stupidly

at O'Leary, wondering what was his purpose. O'Leary had stopped, as if waiting for something. I noted that, though one hand held the sheet, the other was in his pocket.

"Hurry up, Barre. Bolt the door," he repeated, as if in impatience.

Barre walked toward the door. I thought the pounding of my heart would suffocate me. He reached it, took the bolt in his hand uncertainly, then—then stepped to one side. O'Leary's eyes flashed.

He dropped the sheet, walked to the door.

"Here, don't you know how the thing works?" he said quickly. He gave Barre a little push so he stood directly before the bolt and at the same instant lifted the bolt.

And in a flash Julian Barre jumped to one side, and dropped to his knees.

It was an involuntary movement. I think he could not have controlled it.

Slowly O'Leary let the bolt drop again. His revolver was in his hand.

"Get up," he said. "You've convicted yourself."

The men at the bed stood as if frozen.

"Yes," said Julian Barre at last with inexpressible weariness. "Yes, that's what I've done. And it doesn't matter. Nothing matters any more. I'm so tired. I'm glad to have done with it." His voice was the voice of an old man, the nerve at the corner of his jaw twitched violently.

Lance O'Leary looked at the man standing there before us. One of the men—Killian, I think—dropped the sheet, took a quick step toward Barre, and stopped, his face working a little.

"I might have waited till we got to Barrington, but I didn't dare," said O'Leary. "It would have been a race between us to see who could get to Frawley's safety-deposit box first. And besides there was Matil —in the note Morse left her, he gave her the numbers, thus leaving her the only one who had access to the deposit box. She also had a diary of that trip to Hunting's End during which you—arranged this." He motioned to the door. The men around the bed looked blank. Paggi started to speak and stopped as O'Leary continued: "Matil knew too much; it was a question of her life or yours."

Barre's shoulders were sagging; he straightened them with an effort.

"If Huber Kingery's ghost is in this room——" he began bitterly, then he broke off and turned to Killian. The turn brought his worn face toward the light; it was spent and haunted and aged, but his eyes were like glass and his cheeks hot with fever. "Give me a cigarette, Lal. You may as well explain to these gentlemen, O'Leary."

"There's a thing or two," said O'Leary quietly. "You were at the window the night Miss Keate, here, saw your hand and shot at it?"

Barre nodded.

"I thought there was a chance of getting that toupee back into the room. I had taken the toupee because I wanted that number—I had to have access to Frawley's information. He was peculiar. I knew you had

searched everywhere else, but he just might have left
something in his toupee—oh, it was a slim chance, but
I dared not overlook anything. That's how I got this
cold—out in the snow." A fit of coughing shook him.
"I didn't know anyone was in the room. There was a
revolver shot that missed me and I got back through
my window into my room. Later I left the toupee in a
chair."

"And—you poisoned the dog, too?" said O'Leary
softly.

Barre nodded, between coughs.

"Had to. He never liked me. Interfered too much.
The poison is in the snow outside the kitchen door.
. . . I regret Morse, I regret it all, but I had to do it.
I took him by surprise with the only weapon I could
find that was sure. I had to knock you out first,
O'Leary."

Lal Killian strode forward.

"Can't we—leave this, O'Leary, until he—until
we——" His young face was drawn and white. Well,
it was not a nice business.

"About Morse," went on Barre in a voice weak
from coughing. "I—hated that. But I had to. There
was a good chance of his getting to Barrington and
getting Frawley's deposit box before I could. I didn't
dream of his leaving a note."

"He knew that you had murdered Huber Kingery?"
asked O'Leary.

"He knew that I had the best of reasons to murder
Huber Kingery," said Barre, the bitter note creeping
into the weariness of his voice. Then he made a tired

gesture. "You'll find out all you want to know when we get to Barrington. I'm—I'm desperately tired. Can't we—wait till then? I couldn't escape you if I tried," he concluded, with a curious smile. "As I say, nothing matters now."

That was our last night at Hunting's End. I don't remember much of it except that we huddled around the fireplace trying to keep warm. And no one wanted to sleep. About three or four o'clock Brunker made some coffee, which brought a little life into our haggard, white faces. I do remember that the men talked in low voices and smoked and smoked, that Matil sat like a frozen little statue, her eyes enormous and sad in her white face, that Helene cried most of the night, and that Terice and Aunt Lucy said nothing at all. Once I stirred and asked Helene, in a voice I scarcely recognized as my own, why she had taken the diary. She glanced at Paggi, out of hearing distance, stammered a little, and finally admitted that she was afraid Matil had said something in it—something, I gathered, of Helene's relations with Huber Kingery —that if it came to Paggi's knowledge might even now "cause trouble." The phrase was hers and she said no more; I guessed that she was afraid of giving Paggi a definite excuse to divorce her. I shivered a little. After all, there is much to be said for simple old-fashioned decency.

It was about six o'clock, I think, when chance gave me a few words with O'Leary. We met in the kitchen, whence I had gone to get more hot coffee for Lucy

Kingery. Through the log door leading to Annette's room we could hear long, raucous snores.

"How long did you suspect Julian Barre?" I asked abruptly. "And why? Was it solely on account of what you found in the diary?"

O'Leary glanced at his watch.

"I've suspected him vaguely since—before Frawley was killed. Since, in fact, I found that he took such a remarkably active hand in hushing up Huber Kingery's murder. But I had no way of proving Morse's murder; I could only hope he'd confess."

"Wait," I interrupted. "Why didn't he put Morse's body out in the snow, too?"

"He was in too great a hurry to get safely back to his room," said O'Leary laconically. "But—oh, there were many reasons why I suspected Barre. I may as well tell you now. In the first place, there was that little scrap of conversation you overheard and told me of between Barre and Frawley—remember? Barre offered to exchange rooms with Frawley and Frawley openly hinted that Barre knew something of Huber Kingery's death. My surmise was that Barre first intended to exchange rooms with Frawley and remove the revolver in the door, before someone else was killed. Then from Frawley's hint, and from what Frawley said at dinner regarding his records being in a safe place, Barre became convinced of something that he had likely guessed—that is that Frawley knew of his connection with the fraud that has been going on in the Kingery Trust Company. How do I know it's that? I

don't know, but I'm willing to bet that that was where
the trouble began between Huber Kingery and Julian
Barre."

(And I might say here that he was quite right, as it
later proved.)

"They were all in the trust company, of course, and
all possibly involved," went on O'Leary. "But Julian
Barre was closest to Huber Kingery—and remember
how Miss Lucy declared that her brother 'robbed
everybody'? Why not, then, cheat his closest friend?
Then, too, it struck me as peculiar that Frawley had
bolted his door against a possible intrusion of a man
who was, supposedly, his trusted business associate. He
must have had some reason to fear Barre. And—oh,
that business of Barre's leaving his false teeth out—
that was overacting a little. A man like Julian Barre
would grab his teeth first if the house was on fire; care
for his looks and appearance was a matter of habit
with him. That was overacting a little. Not conclusive
evidence, any of this, but enough to draw my attention
to Barre. But after I found the hidden revolver, things
began to shape up a bit. Barre was a radio enthusiast
—why did he let the radio so strictly alone? It would
have been natural to work with it, try to get it going.
And the radio wire that was used in arranging that revolver—who but someone used to the insides of a radio
would have thought of the fine but strong wire off the
rheostat? And no one seemed even to see that that wire
was gone or to know what was the matter with the
radio. But the conclusive evidence was Matil's diary, of
course—and Barre's dodging when he thought he was

in range of that hidden revolver as I was lifting the bolt."

He fumbled in his pocket and drew out the little brown book. He opened it and pointed. I read:

> . . . and got up at four o'clock to get to the blind. Brunker and Annette brought hampers and we stayed all day. Everybody went, but in the morning Uncle Julian got a sandburr in his foot and had to go back to the lodge. Father laughed at him but Uncle Julian limped, and did not come back all day. Father had good shooting especially at sunset. I do not like Helene; she is too nice to me. . . .

I looked up.

O'Leary was looking gravely into the kitchen fire. From the log door came a snore from Annette.

That is about all. When we got to Barrington and O'Leary and the chief of Barrington's detective bureau got into Frawley's safety-deposit box, we found that O'Leary's surmise had been correct. To put it as I was given to understand it later, matters stood this way: For years prior to Huber Kingery's murder, he and Julian Barre had been systematically robbing their own trust company, speculating with funds, juggling properties and estates and securities until they, only, knew how much they held illegally. Frawley suspected some such affair, discovered proof, and went to Huber Kingery with his knowledge and demanded his daughter and a share of the gains as a price for silence. In the meantime Julian Barre discovered—and, I think, the story of it was his only plea—that Huber Kingery had arranged things so as to make Julian Barre appear to be the only one involved; to quote Frawley's written statement, Kingery's purpose, Barre found, was to make a cleaning and get away, leaving Barre to bear the blame when the company failed. Unwisely, but characteristically, Huber Kingery admitted it when Barre taxed him with it, and dared Barre to publish the facts. This, of course, Barre could not do, and in desperation he killed Kingery, took over affairs in the trust company, and he and Frawley entered into a kind of half-hearted conspiracy, loyal on neither side, to complete the business of defrauding their clients which Huber Kingery had begun. I believe it took much time and energy to straighten out the entangled affairs of the Kingery Trust Company.

But to go back to those last hours at Hunting's End.

About noon two cars laden with supplies came struggling along through the half-melted drifts. I have only the vaguest memory of how eagerly we persuaded them to take us and our baggage to Nettleson. I remember Annette carrying the cat in her arms and how dolefully Jericho huddled at our feet, and how Aunt Lucy wrapped up her head in a gray shawl and sat beside the driver, staring at the snow, which vanishes in the sand-hills with such rapidity. It was all rather nightmarish, and is so in my memory, for I was exhausted, half asleep on my feet, weary to the bone, and I'm sure the others were in a like condition.

O'Leary stopped over a day or so at Nettleson to make certain arrangements.

Once in Barrington I stayed on with the Kingerys a few days and was there when O'Leary came to tell me of the contents in the safety-deposit box. He was very grave, especially when he said Barre had confessed completely. Well, it had been an ugly affair.

" 'The End of all Good Hunting is Nearer than you Dream,' " he said musingly as he was leaving. "You knew Barre has pneumonia, didn't you? He can't last long." He paused, lost in some grave thought. Then he lifted his shoulders as if trying to let a weight slip from them. "I'll see you again, Miss Keate."

Matil and Lal Killian were in the hall. Matil was still pale and a little sad, but the hunted look had left her eyes, and they were shining exactly like twin stars.

"Congratulations, Killian," said O'Leary. "And you, Miss Matil—accept my wishes for much happiness."

"You've given it to me," she said softly.

The three of us stood at the window and watched O'Leary's slight gray figure lose itself in the late November twilight.

THE END